Contents

This Is Memorial Device

David Keenan grew up in Airdrie in the late '70s and early 1980s. *This Is Memorial Device* is his debut novel. He is the author of *England's Hidden Reverse*.

Further praise for *This Is Memorial Device*:

'I've never read a book quite like this . . . A rich, fun, honest, tender and rare gift, everyone should read it.' Cosey Fanni Tutti

'Dream-shaped, intoxicating and brilliant.' John Niven

'I don't often recommend a novel after reading only a hundred pages, but I will make an exception for *This Is Memorial Device* by David Keenan . . . It captures the utter seriousness, the all-consuming belief, the sacrifice to art, the veneration of ideas that was as true for a shonky band in Airdrie in 1984 as it was for David Bowie in 1967, or Man Ray in 1915, or Gustav Mahler in 1884.' Kenny Farquharson, *The Times*

'The last chapter is stunning, a soaring, existentialist, cosmic crescendo . . . A meditation on memory and perspective, on the magical forces of language, on the absurdity of existence and the dreadful thoughts bubbling like toxic fluid below the fragile surface of every human brain . . . In these creatively risk-averse times, it's heroically bizarre.' Sylvia Patterson, *New Statesman*

'Entirely exhilarating, constantly threatening to spin free of its axis and yet always hauled back by its author's command of his tune.' *i newspaper*

By the same author

England's Hidden Reverse

This Is Memorial Device

An Hallucinated Oral History of the Post-Punk Scene
in Airdrie, Coatbridge and Environs 1978–1986

David Keenan

First published in 2017
by Faber & Faber Limited
Bloomsbury House
74–77 Great Russell Street
London WC1B 3DA
This paperback edition first published in 2018

Typeset by Faber & Faber Limited
Printed and bound by CPI Group (UK) Ltd, Croydon, CR0 4YY

A CIP record for this book
is available from the British Library

ISBN 978–0–571–33085–0

10 9 8 7 6 5 4 3 2 1

Introduction to Why I Did It

I did it to stand up for Airdrie. I did it because of Memorial Device. I
did it because later on everyone went off and became social workers
and did courses on how to teach English as a foreign language or got
a job in Greggs. Well, not everybody. Some people died or disappeared
or went into seclusion, more like. I did it – well, I was going to say I
did it because back then anything seemed possible, back then being
1983 and 1984 and 1985, what I call the glory years. The glory years
in Airdrie – what a joke, right? But really that would be untrue
because back then everything seemed impossible.

Me and Johnny McLaughlin, that was us back then. We thought it
was important, what was happening. We thought it was important to
document it. I got a few pieces in the *Airdrie & Coatbridge Advertiser*.
It's happening on your own doorstep, man, I told them. This isn't
Manchester or London or fucking Chingford. This is Airdrie. I wanted
to put a cassette out, a cassette with all the local bands, Memorial
Device, of course, and Glass Sarcophagus and Chinese Moon and
Steel Teeth, but not Fangboard, fuck Fangboard, anything but them,
and I wanted to call it *This is Airdrie*. But of course I didn't. I wanted
to write and publish a fanzine, and of course me and Johnny did
publish a fanzine that ran for all of one issue before I dumped the
copies we hadn't shifted behind some bushes in Rawyards Park and
urinated on them, which might have been my greatest contribution to
the scene. But most of all I wanted to write a book.

1983 and '84 and '85 were the years of Memorial Device. Previously
they had been in other bands, bands that some people cared about
and bands that some people thought were a joke, but when they

came together it was undeniable. They sounded like nothing else. They sounded like Airdrie, which is to say they sounded like a black fucking hole. Everyone loved them or hated them and the people who hated them loved them twice as much. We thought they would go the whole way, we thought they would vindicate Airdrie, valorise Coatbridge, memorialise Greengairs. The rumour was that when Sonic Youth played Splash One in Glasgow in 1986 they asked for Memorial Device as their support act. Who knew what could have happened? But it was all over by then. And what's left to show for it? I could never put it out my mind. Over the years I began tracking people down, writing letters, making sad international phone calls in the middle of the night. I had my interviews from the time, I had written some stuff back in the day. I talked Johnny into doing the same. It's not about the music any more, Johnny said. Well, what the fuck is it about? Like I said, I did it to stand up for Airdrie. I did it because of Memorial Device. I did it because, for a moment, even when everything seemed impossible, everybody was doing everything, reading, listening, writing, creating, sticking up posters, taking notes, passing out, throwing up, rehearsing, rehearsing, rehearsing in dark windowless rooms at 2 p.m. like the future was just up ahead and we better be ready for it. And now already it's the rotten past. That's why I did it, if you want to know the truth.

Ross Raymond, Airdrie, Lanarkshire, Scotland
April 2016

1. Hidden Occluded by Chemistry by Water: *Ross Raymond meets Big Patty and Lucas Black in 1981 and everything changes and I know I know I hate it when I hear people say things like oh that record changed my life that book changed my life Led Zeppelin changed my fucking life when you know that really their life just went on exactly the fucking same but meeting Patty and Lucas and starting to go to shows with Johnny McLaughlin and buying records and hearing this music really did change everything although it might be more accurate to say it deformed my life rather than just changed it if you know what I mean. And if you do you're in.*

At the time that I met him, Big Patty lived somewhere near the top of South Bridge Street in Airdrie, which today is the worst street in Airdrie, the most boarded-up street in Airdrie, the street that most effectively announces it is all over for Airdrie, but the weird thing is I've no idea how I first got to know him, perhaps I met him one night at The Staging Post across the road from Airdrie Library, perhaps I met him at the library itself, I was a teenage sci-fi, horror and existentialism nut and that was my haunt, if you know what I mean, my medieval castle, but really I have no idea, which is weird, but appropriate, perhaps, because it makes it seem more like an amnesiac alien abduction than the beginning of an awkward long-term friendship, which, looking back, is closer to what it actually felt like.

He was my first introduction to the music scene. I spent the New Year's Eve of 1981 hanging out at his flat, which to me was a paradise of no parents and endless opportunity, but as the bells rang he forced us out onto the street and we ended up standing round in a park in the dark near Airdrie Academy hoping the future would walk right up behind us and tap us on the shoulder. Back then Johnny McLaughlin and I were working on our fanzine. We called it *A Night Is a Morning That You Hasten to Light*. Johnny came up with the title. It came from the French – something like that. For the first issue we had interviewed Big Patty.

The night before the interview I couldn't sleep. I was always that way when it came to big moments. I worried that my questions would seem banal. At that time in my life I had a bed underneath a skylight in the loft of my parents' house, right next to a radiator, where my cat, who was named Cody after Neal Cassady's character in *Visions of Cody* and whose memory comes back to me now like a puzzled ghost with great owl-like eyes staring out of the past, would curl up in the crook of my legs, and at the foot of the bed I had a bookcase filled with random dread; I was educating myself in suffering, sleeping naked in the woods, I told myself, books by Philip K. Dick and Christopher Lasch and Albert Camus and H. P. Lovecraft. Sometime in the night my mum came upstairs and knocked on the door of my bedroom, which I always kept locked because parents stick their noses in everywhere. I was listening to *Y* by The Pop Group, which was one of my favourite records at the time – I played it to death, almost literally to death, to the point that it wouldn't play any more without sticking and jumping – and I was smoking a cigarette out of the window while staring at a cluster of trees silhouetted on the horizon that I always associated with the future or the mystery of all of my life that was yet to come. Hold on, I said. When I unlocked the door she asked me what I was doing. I'm preparing for an interview, I said. I think I might be up most of the night, I said. Do you have any ideas for questions? I asked her. She thought for a moment. Yes, she said. You should ask him if he always tells the truth in interviews.

4

I've never done an interview before in my life, Big Patty said. How the fuck would I know? I had underlined a sentence from a philosophical text, something about the nature of love. He looked embarrassed. I have no idea, he said. I typed up the interview until 4 a.m. Then I fell asleep.

I had a paper round at this point – everyone in Airdrie had a paper round, it was a rite of passage in Airdrie – and I had two or three cassettes that I would alternate on the Walkman but mostly *Fun House* by The Stooges. I was delivering in Whinhall, on the outskirts of Airdrie, which was a desperate situation. Then I got a summer job in a flower shop in Coatbridge, then as a kitchen orderly in Monklands Hospital in Coatdyke. That put me off carrots for life. But suddenly I had enough money to buy records. Every Saturday I would meet Johnny and we would travel into Glasgow and buy two LPs each: the first Ramones album, The Sonics' *Boom*, *Easter Everywhere* by The 13th Floor Elevators, which is still the greatest psychedelic record ever made, Can's *Tago Mago*, *Metal Box* by Public Image Ltd, the first Roxy album, This Heat, Nurse With Wound, *So Alone* by Johnny Thunders – in fact anything by Johnny Thunders, everyone in Airdrie was obsessed with Johnny Thunders.

We cottoned on early that there were certain bars that the musicians liked to hang out in and certain cafes too but most of them are long gone so it would be pointless to tell you about them and heartbreaking too, the booths with the torn leather seats, the shakers stopped up with damp clusters of salt, the chipped Formica tables, all vanquished in favour of faceless coffee shops full of idiot middle-class couples and pregnant mums. On Saturday evenings, after lying around in Johnny's living room playing our latest purchases

– *The Modern Dance* by Pere Ubu or *Like Flies on Sherbert* by Alex
Chilton, which still sounds perverse and macabre, like a suicide
note where you're not sure whether it's a joke or it's for real – we
would head out to one of the bars and mooch around and scope the
scene. Occasionally we would bump into Big Patty and we'd both
feign surprise, wow, what are you doing here, we hang out here all
the time, etc. It got to the point that we struck up a real friendship,
which at first was exciting. I'm in, I thought, bohemia here I come.

Back then Patty worked part-time at a barber's shop in Clarkston.
I started going there to get my hair cut but at first I didn't have
the nerve to ask for him specifically and sometimes I would make
excuses, feign a coughing fit or just disappear altogether if the queue
ran down and I ended up stuck with the owner, an emaciated Italian,
or even worse, his shrunken son who everyone said was bulimic,
which at the time I thought was the female version of anorexia, which
only inspired further confusion. Once I took in a picture of Antonin
Artaud that I had photocopied from the front of a City Lights book
and asked for the same haircut. You have completely different hair,
Patty said. It's not possible. Then he told me that his band, which at
that point was called Slave Demographics, had been played on Radio
Scotland's alternative programme. To me it was a fantasy world.

Sometimes in the evening I would borrow my parents' car. I had
just learned to drive and I would drive all the way to Caldercruix
and up past the reservoir and then back to my old school, more like
old prison camp, then down to the Safeway car park and round past
the train station and once I saw Patty and his girlfriend at the time,
I never met her, it was just before we began hanging out and they
split up shortly afterwards, but I remember thinking that's a real

romance, that's lying back in the grass and talking about Sylvia Plath right there. She had dark hair, cut in a short bob, eye make-up like an Egyptian goddess. He was smoking a cigarette, probably a joint, I thought, and wearing a battered top hat and a pair of shades. I watched them walk off into their own life and it felt like I was watching my future self, my dream avatar, heading back to a council house in Cairnhill that opened onto a parallel universe.

My first gig was at an upstairs venue somewhere off West George Street in Glasgow. It was on the third floor of a building that also had a Chinese restaurant and a singles bar. There were two mutually exclusive queues, the punks and the straights. When Johnny and I finally got to the top of the stairs someone started singing 'The Trail of the Lonesome Pine' by Laurel and Hardy at us. Next thing I know I'm in the venue and drinking beer out of a bottle for the first time. They played a song by The Gun Club and Johnny and I danced. I had my hands in my pockets, I looked like a goon, basically, but Johnny had his head down and his arms in the air, dancing like he was completely carried away. Then I saw some girls that I recognised from Airdrie, real posers, and Johnny said to me, let's pull a Thunders, which was code for let's overwhelm these girls with credentials, which is what we tried to do. We're the most psychedelic guys in here, Johnny said to them. Then he slapped one of the girls on the ass. I was amazed. He was clearly in his element. And she didn't protest. In fact she laughed. Later I saw her getting off with some guy who looked like he was in his thirties with a bald patch on top of his head. I'm not even bald, I thought. What's wrong with me? Eventually the band played. It was Patty's new band, Occult Theocracy. They sounded like a clap of thunder on the furthest horizon of my brain. The singer, who everyone called Street Hassle and who you would sometimes see in the winter, in the snow, walking in the gutter with nothing but a cut-off T-shirt and a can of beer in his hand, took the microphone and forced it into his mouth so that he sounded like a buzzing fly and then he said, mama, he said, mama, then he hyperventilated for a while and then he said, mama, yeah, it feels good. When I got back home I stood in front of the mirror and I messed up my hair. I knew I'd never comb it again.

I bought an acoustic guitar, it was all I could afford, and on days off work, in other words when I wasn't having a chug in the staff toilet while imagining the cleaners in their underwear, I would sit in the park and pretend to play although in reality I couldn't play a damn note. I would see people checking me out. I wore a huge pair of black wraparound shades and one day I caught sight of Big Patty with a couple of friends and they came over and sat down with me. Patty looked like a cadaver. I guessed that he was on drugs. This is Beano, he said, introducing the taller of the two, who had a swollen drinker's nose or a bad case of rosacea – either way it was rough justice. The other one they called The Doug. The Doug wore a biker's jacket with a quote from John Cage written on the back in Tipp-Ex, something about having nothing to say and saying it. I had picked up a copy of Cage's *Indeterminacy* set on a recent record-buying trip and I tried to impress them. I listen to *Indeterminacy* at work on the headphones when I'm cleaning pots and pans, I told them. You'd be better listening to the pots and pans, The Doug deadpanned.

Listen, Patty said. Could you do us a favour? Sure, I said. Name it. No, he said. Forget it. It's not worth it. Come on, I said. I'm happy to help. He took out a cigarette and tried to light it but the wind kept blowing out the match and after about the fifth attempt he crumpled the cigarette up in his hand and threw it to the ground. I need you to return something for me, he said. Actually a few things: a bunch of cassettes. I borrowed them from this guy in Craigneuk but things turned a bit, well, a bit crazy, actually, so I'd rather, you know, keep my distance. Also, he has a bunch of my LPs that I need to get back. Can you help me out? I wanted to ask him why he didn't get Beano or The Doug to help him but instead I just agreed. Can you do it now? he asked me. Then he gave me a bunch of cassettes, album dubs with track listings written in almost indecipherably small pen. One of them had a Chocolate Watchband compilation on one side and the first Suicide album on the other, both of which I went out and bought the next weekend. Wait a second, The Doug said as I was about to leave, could you go some Buckie? Then he handed me a half bottle of Buckfast. I had never tasted Buckfast in my life and the truth is it was rancid but as I choked it down all three of them began clapping and chanting Ross, Ross, Ross so I felt obliged to drain the bottle in one shot. They looked at me in amazement. I was in.

The address was in Howletnest Road. I put my Walkman on and listened to 'Dirt' on *Fun House* on the way over. Iggy was a genius. It never sounded better. My entire body was vibrating with the music and the Buckie and the sunshine. When I got there the place looked like a dumping ground. The garden was a mess, there was trash all over the front grass and there was a filthy caravan parked in the driveway. It was an immediate bringdown. I started to feel nauseous. I could hear someone inside the caravan and it was vibrating with the sound of this sick-making high-pitched drone. But I knocked on the front door of the house instead and as soon as I did the sound cut dead and all movement in the caravan stopped. A tiny middle-aged woman answered the door with a cigarette in her hand and long grey hair. Yes? she said. I'm looking for Fred, I said. You mean Lucas? she said. Is Lucas Fred? I asked her. That was his nickname at school, she said. I don't encourage it. His name's Lucas. Or Luke. Sometimes he gets called Luke. Or Luciani. Is Lucas in? I asked her. No, she said, I'm afraid Lucas isn't available right now. Can I take a message?

I explained that I needed to return some tapes to him and to pick up some records. By this point the noises in the caravan had resumed and I could make out a steady thump and what sounded like a drunk stumbling into furniture. I was starting to feel a panic coming over me. I looked back over my shoulder and I could make out a word picked out in the dirt of the caravan window. eugroM, it said. There was a buzzing in my ears. I felt like I was dissolving into the ground. Then I saw myself from above on the path and saw a thin trickle of blood run from my forehead and pool on the ground beside me and watched as a figure appeared from the caravan and lifted up my body and carried me back inside.

Lucas was building a volcano in the middle of his caravan. The volcano, he explained, was the equivalent of a wheelchair for a physically handicapped person. It's a means of transport, he said. It allows me to make connections. The volcano was constructed out of old shoeboxes, crumpled newspapers, folded greeting cards, balls of wrapping paper. Long feather boas – pink, blue and purple – took the place of flowing lava. He held a red notebook in his hand. What did you say your name was again? he asked me. Ross, I told him. Ross Raymond. He wrote it down in his notebook. Have I ever met you before?

No, I said, first time, and I dabbed the cut on the side of my head
with an old T-shirt he had given me. He had laid me on a dirty blue
velvet couch beneath the window. I have had seven brain operations,
he told me. I have struggled with mental illness for most of my life.
But the creative part, the creative part has been the most rewarding.
He spoke in a soft, slightly distant voice. A moonie, I thought to
myself, a gentle lunatic.

The issue was memory. He had none, or very little, or rather all of his
memories were hidden, occluded by chemistry, by water particularly
– water on the brain, they called it – so that every moment was swept
away, the specifics of his day-to-day existence like the splinters of a
ship in a storm. This is the logbook, he said, thumbing through his
notes, moments reconstructed in the wake of a disaster. Then he
pointed to the volcano. And this is where the memories live.

I realised I had been set up. He would have had no idea what the
cassettes were, if they were even his. Do you know Big Patty? I asked
him. Big Patty, he said, breathing all over his name so that I could
almost smell it. Hold on a second, he said, and then he picked up
a green phone book with a dial on the front that made it pop up at
certain letters. Big Patty, he said. Patty Whitaker? Patty Thomas?
Patricia Black? He's a musician, I said. Plays in Occult Theocracy?
Music, music, music, he said. Music is one of the things that humans
can be proudest of. Would you like to hear some music? He put
a cassette in the player. It was the same sound I had heard from
outside the caravan, a single barely fluctuating tone. I took a look
at the cassette cover and it had the same tiny handwriting as the
Suicide and Chocolate Watchband compilation. The track was by the
Swedish composer Folke Rabe, a piece called 'What??'. I had never

11

heard anything like it before. It seemed to fill all the space in the caravan.

Have you ever been to Jos? Lucas asked me. No, I said, but I knew it, funnily enough. It's a town in Nigeria, I told him. Then you know the centre of the world, he said. At first I wondered if it was a genuine memory or if he had picked it up from somewhere else. But then I thought about my own opinions and I shut the fuck up.

<u>2. This Is So Pointlessly Wrong</u>: *Ross Raymond interviews Big Patty*
from Memorial Device for the second issue of the legendary fanzine
that got dumped behind a hedge and that never saw the light of day
and somehow only manages to ask one rotten question the entire time
can you believe it.

So, eh, the first question is can you tell me a bit about what was the
whole idea behind, eh, Memorial Device?

I was feeling . . . not disconcerted, not unreconciled – what's the word
that's somewhere between the two?

?

Awkward and out of sync, is that the best way to put it?

?

But out of sync with what, you know?

?

It was more like I was out of orbit. Like I had been hit with a piece
of space debris and knocked for a loop. I had been writing songs or,
let's be fucking honest here why don't we, struggling to write songs.
Struggling to be a songwriter. I had a few chords that I had learned
from The Modern Lovers. You know the ones, D, E, A, that other
weird D one, the one Johnny Thunders used in 'You Can't Put Your
Arms Around a Memory' and 'Lonely Planet Boy'. The most beautiful
chord of all. And I was trying to write lyrics.

You don't mind if I spark one up, do you?

?

We would go to my girlfriend's parents' house . . . They had this
cottage in Greengairs, it was quiet and boring . . . but they grew
their own vegetables so you could make your own food for free . . .
It sort of became my base . . . Here I was trying to make these
sounds and trying to express something but it seemed like it was all
craft . . . like I was trying to learn how to copy or emulate . . . that it
was counterfeit somehow . . . I would write these songs and I would
realise that the feelings in them . . . if you could even call them
feelings . . . they were more like . . . I don't know . . . they weren't
my own and they weren't anyone else's either . . . They were shop-
soiled . . . cheap . . . It was like singing to a plant . . . You are green
and you grow . . . in the rain . . . for a time . . . then you go . . .
It was that level . . . Although it wasn't really that level . . . That's
plainly stated in a way that I was incapable of back then . . . you
know . . . the whole Lou Reed school of 'I walked to the chair/Then
I sat in it' . . . That's how Lester Bangs describes it . . . You into
Lester Bangs?

?

Cool . . .

I mean, I liked that. I always have. But there was a feeling in me
that didn't come across like a chord progression and a melody. You
have to understand I had a lot of anger. A lot of frustration. I still do.
But I was never bored. That's what I hated so much about punk. This

whole thing about complaining about being bored. What's that crap Situationist cartoon I can't stand?

?

The one where the two French chicks are bitching about how there is nothing they won't do to raise the standard of boredom.

?

I hated that. These people are punks and yet they're complaining about how someone else won't make an effort to entertain them?

?

Give me a break. Wasn't the whole point that you made your own entertainment?

?

Then I had this awful feeling. Like it was all a drug. Something for sleepwalkers. Dreaming their way from generation through generation. Whether it was Frank Sinatra and I fucking hate Frank Sinatra. Whether it was Johnny Rotten or Bob Dylan. All these tossers singing from the same hymn book. Fucking choirboys. Or Elvis Presley but with Elvis maybe there was something different.

Did you ever hear about Sinew Singer?

?

He was this guy who came from Airdrie in the 1950s. Airdrie's sole contribution to rock n roll as something that would actually expand your senses.

You know how he got his name?

?

Check it out: his friend had a scrapbook that he filled with pictures of rock stars and pop stars. Buddy Holly. The Everly Brothers. Fucking Dion and the Belmonts, I don't know. They were leafing through it one night and he turns to a page that has a picture of Elvis on it. Early Elvis. Young Elvis. Elvis where he looks like a flick knife. And just looking at him he feels like he has stuck his finger in a light bulb socket. He says he literally felt his hair rise up into a kind of electrified quiff. And you know what he means. That haircut was aerodynamic. It came from rushing headlong into the future. He asked his friend, who the fuck is this guy? And he says to him, it's the new singer. But he mishears it as It's Sinew Singer and his mind is even more blown apart. He mishears it as this guy whose every muscle, whose every vein, every fucking sinew of his body, is singing. You know? Fuck Iggy Pop! And then he realises his mistake though not really because in that moment he became Sinew Singer. He took on the mantle and it was down to him to live up to it. That's genius right there, if you ask me. In my opinion genius is accidental, is mistaken, is actually wrong at first. And I don't care what you say. But it's hard to be wrong in a housing estate in Airdrie. Even though really they're all wrong! But they want to be right at all costs. They want to have an ironing board, a cooker and a washing machine. A duvet instead of a sleeping bag. A fucking concrete house with four windows. Some shitty car. A hoover. A job like a fucking jail sentence. A big TV in the living room. To be woken at six in the morning while it's still dark. And on top of that they want respect. For being right. How is it possible to respect anyone for being right?

?

How fucking simple. How mind-numbingly fucking dull. Congratulations. You did the right thing. You know?

?

People ask me why I asked Remy to join Memorial Device. What was it that made me ask this guy from a supposedly naff synth-pop group to play bass with us. The point is when I first saw Relate play I just thought it was so wrong. Here were these two bozos . . . these two clowns, basically . . . though more macabre and sad and desperate than even that . . . Their make-up was badly applied so that their mouths were like two black half-moons, making them look like puffy cadavers . . . or a fucking inflatable nightmare . . . The music was awful, godawful . . . and here they were jumping up and down . . . I remember at one point Remy gave this sudden leap combined with a scissor kick . . . He was wearing hand-painted pyjamas, basically . . . and he smashed his head off the ceiling of the venue . . . Of course they were doing the whole deal where they poured blood over themselves but it looked like Remy really had split his head open and was bleeding badly . . . and there was no one in the audience . . . okay, maybe four or five people . . . but no one was paying them the slightest attention . . . except for me . . . and by this point I was hooked . . . fascinated . . . or maybe it's more correct to say that I was

17

under its spell . . . It was compulsive . . . These people are alive, I said to myself . . . They seemed completely unaware of the lack of response . . . Their faces were contorted so that now they looked like tortured eggs . . . This is so pointlessly wrong, I thought to myself . . . I love it.

It's the same with Lucas. I mean Lucas is always performing, in a way. Because of his condition. He is always feeling his way into a new role. Every minute of the day. And I don't mean that to sound exploitative. But every performance is like the first one. Every time he wakes it's like the first morning on earth. With Lucas there is no possibility of being rote. He is perpetually new. I know there is a lot of suffering that comes from that too. I can only imagine. But I think there is something fulfilling for Lucas and for all of us in being able to make ritual use of forgetting and remembering. And of course that's how I came up with the name Memorial Device. To me it was like Shakespeare.

Do you want a hit?

?

Cool. No worries. As I said . . . I had been through my own artistic crisis . . . I was into punk rock . . . for a bit . . . who wasn't . . . but it seemed like everyone was going to jail . . . serving pointless sentences . . . The guys from The Tunnel . . . one of the great Airdrie groups . . . heavy ritualists . . . they had been locked up for desecrating graves . . . They had dug up a bunch of plots in Clarkston Parish Church looking for thighbones to make trumpets out of . . . That I could respect . . . That seemed like something worth doing time for . . . There was something tragic and naive about it . . . that appealed to me . . . but everyone else was going down for shoplifting . . . assault and battery . . . house breaking . . . possession . . . repeated drunk and disorderly . . . It was pathetic . . . I'm drawn to madness . . . I admit it . . . but only if it energises you . . . or if it destroys you completely . . . Only if you blow up or go tearing off . . . into another life . . . and another life . . . and another life running after it . . . These guys were just bums . . . I never championed the underdog . . . I never forgot they were still dogs . . . For me the people I respected were winners . . . maybe not in the eyes of society . . . but for me they weren't victims . . . They came out on top . . . even if they were skint . . . and covered in rashes . . . and couldn't look you in the eye . . . and were half insane . . . But it ended up where I was going to these . . . clubs . . . these . . . bunkers . . . really these fallout shelters . . . because that's what it felt like . . . I'd be sitting in the dark watching this punk group . . . going through the motions . . . acting gobby . . . playing three chords . . . staggering through a bunch of songs that really they had rehearsed to death . . . There was no spontaneity to it . . . no reality . . . no life . . . and that's when I began to think . . . Christ . . . we've dug these complexes . . . deep into the ground . . . we've built walls . . . we've filled in all the windows . . . we've painted the toilets black . . . we've drunk ourselves to the point of oblivion . . . just to keep life outside . . . Art was supposed to open you up to life and here we were . . . we had narrowed it to the point of a fucking black box . . . with a bunch of dirty mirrors lining the walls . . .

Alright, mate? Yeah, amazing mate, cannae beat it. What you up to? I'm doing an interview, mate, what's it look like? An interview, mate. I'm not packing, mate. I've nothing on me. Naw, mate, naw. Try me later, mate, try me later. Sorry, man, just some dick that I know. You know The Whinhall Starvers?

?

That guy plays bass with them. You sure you don't want a hit?

?

So I heard about a block of flats that was being demolished in the
East End of Glasgow . . . On the Sunday of the explosion I made my
way out there on my own . . . There were helicopters hovering in
clouds of dust . . . the crackle of police walkie-talkies . . . I saw no one
from the music scene . . . except one guy . . . a bike courier . . . who
frankly I couldn't stand . . . though I was feeling in a good mood . . . I
had risen early and I hadn't been drinking the night before . . .
so I ended up standing next to him . . . him in his shorts and T-shirt
. . . and wearing some kind of baseball cap . . . forgive me . . . but it
was repellent to me . . . especially his nose . . . his red runny nose . . .
but anyway . . . I looked around and it was all locals . . . it was like an
event . . . The building had history . . . It had gone up in the 1960s . . .
I thought of all the people that had lived there . . . It was powerful
. . . and people were eating chocolate bars and drinking drinks . . .
and smoking cigarettes . . . and the rumour was they had diverted
the trains . . . and suddenly this sound rang out . . . this air-raid siren
. . . or warning call . . . and everyone gasped . . . someone next to me
screamed . . . and you could hear the blades of the helicopters whirling
round . . . and the charges went off . . . and the building crumpled . . .
collapsing forward . . . and folding into itself . . . like a sick old man
. . . falling to his knees on the subway . . . but there was something
unmistakably artistic about it . . . In the sound of the explosion I
heard the years of planning . . . the decades of construction . . . the
span . . . of people's lives . . . There were tower blocks all around and

it missed them by metres . . . I was blown away . . . There was so
much going on . . . I said to myself . . . okay . . . from now on music
has to sound like a building coming down or forget it.

Look, mate, I gotta split, is that enough, is that okay?

?

Alright, mate, alright, catch you later . . .

Fuck!

3. Daytime Hangovers That Can Only Be Remedied by a Session of Furious Masturbation: *Scott McKenzie becomes the first of many people to get obsessed by Mary Hanna (this is before she joined Memorial Device) but more than that he isn't giving away though I tried him with follow-up questions several times he just blanked me that was his style his only ambition was to do as little as possible even though I kind of admire it and all of Airdrie salutes him for it in a really kind of slack half-arsed mooching-about-town way.*

I would say that Mary was in about fifty per cent of the best groups to come out of Airdrie in the middle 1980s. She was certainly in demand. At first some people speculated that she was a lesbian. But it was more that she was just aloof. How did I meet her? Well, I am glad you asked that question because that is another story and in fact it has nothing to do with music. It was the first summer after I graduated from high school. I was seventeen years old. It was the kind of summer that we simply do not get any more. I swear to god that the tar was melting in the streets. People were swimming in rivers. These filthy rivers. These stinky summer rivers. But even so. I took a job at a cement factory in Coatdyke. I worked on the desk, which was no work at all, lucky me. You do not get a lot of drop-in customers looking for bags of cement. Although of course you do get a few. It was normally people that had just bought their council house and were looking to build an extension, or freelance labourers. We dealt a lot with the trade.

My boss was an idiot, there is no point in pretending otherwise. When I filled in my application form he took it and he held it up to his face because he was also short-sighted and he said, that is good you have very neat handwriting. He thought that was the right thing to say.

He thought that was how you evaluated potential employees. And my handwriting was not even neat. It was actually a mess. I could not even read it myself. I am going to have the run of the place here, I remember thinking to myself at the time. I'll have my feet up.

Besides the boss there was a pool of men who looked after the delivering of the cement and the loading of it on and off the lorries and there was also a secretary named Rachel who looked like a duck. Or was it more like an emu. She had a long neck and a tiny head and she wore dark eyeshadow with her black hair pulled back into a tight ponytail. So maybe it was an emu. She was a fan of music and her boyfriend was balding with a long ginger ponytail. He would pick her up after work and they would go to the Glasgow Tech on a Friday night and they would drink pints of snakebite and they would dance to music by The Cure or The Sisters of Mercy. Or worse. Then she got a disease where her hair started to fall out. I do not know what it was called. Then she took to wearing a bandana on her head so that she looked like a nun. She looked like a nun who was wearing John Lennon-style glasses. It was not attractive but the boys in the delivery sheds would make jokes about getting the habit and that kind of humour.

You would get to know the customers and of course we invented nicknames for them all. There was one called The Wee Oddity and two called Hansel & Gretel and one called Two Tub Man. Everyone who worked there was covered in a permanent layer of dust. It got everywhere so that we looked like a bunch of walking statues. Early on I heard about a customer who they called The Artist. Every few months she would call in to buy a bag of cement for herself. She was described as a tiny girl with big sunglasses. And with long hair down her back and wearing skinny jeans. And with scuffed training shoes and often wearing no socks. And with a torn suede jacket on. She would hoist the bag of cement onto her back and walk home with it almost bent double. This I must see, I said to myself. But for the first few months there was no sign of her.

Occasionally we would have a works night out and the boss would book us a function room at The Tudor Hotel. Everyone would get pissed up and try to hit on Rachel. The boss made a point of only employing Catholics, which made her twice as vulnerable. Sometimes her boyfriend would chaperone her but then there would be jokes about Status Quo and about Jaffa Cakes and about seedless oranges so that they would have to leave early and we would be left to make up stories about our sex lives, which back then for me numbered one in its entirety. Although some of the men were married to wives that looked like small ugly boys, they never talked about their wives. They only talked about the girls they had sex with when they were at school. They had sex with them under railway bridges while playing truant or in the summer on the edge of golf courses. There was an air of sadness to it all that I experienced.

Everything came to a head at the works Christmas do in 1983. I had been drinking beforehand. I had met up with some old school friends in Glasgow and I had got well and truly hammered in the afternoon. Then I had jumped on the train to Airdrie, where I had fallen asleep on my back in a park off Forrest Street. When I woke up it was already getting dark and I had one of those daytime hangovers that can only be remedied by a session of furious masturbation. I tossed off behind a tree with my trousers round my ankles in the open air, just the way I like it. Then I walked to The Tudor Hotel. I had a carefree feeling as I made my way into town.

The boss had hired a DJ and there were a lot of employees' wives and girlfriends attending. I asked a few of them to dance out of politeness and also because I was still drunk. Their looks weren't up to much but they certainly smelled great. Middle-aged women were always attractive to me. Rachel was there on her own. By this point her boyfriend had left. He had been scared off, in other words. I could tell that she was acting funny. I could tell there was something wrong at home. I had a spliff in my pocket from earlier that day so I asked her if she fancied a toot. Is it illicit? she said. In that case, yes please. Illicit, that was a good one. We walked outside and we took a detour into the bushes. We made our way along the overgrown path by the side of the railway. I could barely see in front of me but she took me by the arm and so I concentrated on taking one step after another while leading us into the blackness. We came to a small wooden bridge that was lit up by the glow of the street lights and I fired up the joint. When I passed her the joint it was almost as if I had to bend down. She was so small. But she sucked it in like a pro and then she exhaled this big cloud of smoke without so much as a cough. I am pregnant, she said. I probably should not be smoking. Then she said, fuck this, and she took another hit. Who is the father? I asked her. Obviously my boyfriend, she said. Who the fuck do you think is the father? I'm sorry, I said. It's okay, she said. I know everyone says that he is a Jaffa. I pretended I did not know what she meant. You know what I mean, she said, seedless. Oh right, I said, although I had been in on the ridicule from the start. I saw a video at school of a foetus crying in a bucket, she told me. I do not want it, she said. I do not want my baby. But I do not want it crying in a bucket either. By this point I was completely monged. I started imagining myself in a bucket with my legs and arms all splayed and disconnected. For a second I thought I was choking on my own fluids. I need to stop thinking about this, I told myself. Then she began snatching with her hand in front of her. It was like she was trying to grab something from out of the air. Did you see that? she said to me. There are fireflies! There are no fireflies in Airdrie, I went to say, and certainly not in the middle of the winter, but then I saw one and then I saw several buzzing all around us. Oh my god, she said to me, they are doing the constellations. There is the Southern Cross, there is the Centaur! That is the only names that I can remember. She said some more but I was never any good at astronomy. But I can say that the lights moved in formation and that it was possible to make out patterns so maybe crosses, dogs and Hercules all might have been in there. I think I see my star sign, I said to her and I lifted her up and she immediately wrapped her legs around my waist and I kissed her and we held our lips together for the longest time. I had never kissed a woman who was pregnant by another man but it is true that it tastes different. It is saltier for a start. What are we going to do with ourselves? she said to me.

Afterwards she got drunk and fell down and a friend of the boss's wife had to take her home in a taxi. I walked home. I had another hangover already but it felt great. That was when Mary made her appearance. I turned up late for work the next morning and just as I was dragging out the signage I heard the door go and the sound of footsteps in the hallway. I looked up. She was wearing a pair of big black sunglasses. I need a bag of cement, she said to me. To take away. What do you think this is, I said to her, a Chinese restaurant? I was trying to make a joke but she just stood there and said nothing. Okay, I said. One bag of cement, coming up.

4. The Next Thing I Knew Remy and Regina Were Dating (If You Can Believe That): *Johnny McLaughlin gets a doing in George Square a real pasting in George Square actually I wasn't there but when I heard about it of course I knew it was gonna be over a woman and of course it was and it was a sore spot so when I asked Johnny to write something for the book he said that first off he wanted to set the record straight about what happened and besides Remy Farr who at this point had just left this heinous synth-pop group Relate and was still a year or so away from joining Memorial Device was all tied up in it too so I said okay but cut the bullshit.*

Even though Remy Farr got called Big Remy he really wasn't that big (but he did have a blockhead). Another thing was he never had moods (he didn't seem to have the standard emotional range of normal people). You never saw him angry or depressed although sometimes he would be quieter than others (but even then it felt more like a tide coming in and out, a planetary concern, rather than actual human feelings). He always talked at you, never to you, and it all felt like material he had prepared earlier (like a routine, complete with punchlines and build-ups) as if he knew exactly the way the conversation was going to go and had prepared a series of puns and ripostes well in advance (like he had thought of everything, had figured out every angle, so that it was impossible for you to steer the conversation anywhere that he hadn't anticipated).

There were rumours that he was gay (no one had ever seen him with a partner). He had been a member of a fairly notorious Coatbridge synth-pop duo both of whom dressed up in caked white face paint (and with huge black painted lips) and poured blood over themselves (on stage). They claimed Leigh Bowery ripped them off.

Back in the day the *Airdrie & Coatbridge Advertiser* had written a piece about them where they called Bowery out while debating the merits of fake blood versus real blood. The other guy in the group (I can never remember his real name, but his nickname was Wee Be-Ro because he wore so much make-up it looked like he had coated his face with flour) had argued for fake blood. Somehow it looks more real (he said), plus it flows better. Big Remy argued for real blood. It does something to you psychologically (he said). It smells like blood (it tastes like blood). At one point it was actually keeping something alive. It operates on you. Blood operates on you? Wee Be-Ro asked him. That's right, Big Remy said: blood is the surgeon.

That's the story of how their 12" single came about. I bought it at the time (which would have been 1982). Me and Ross would pick up any independent single released in Scotland back then, mostly from a booth (upstairs) in the Savoy Centre in Sauchiehall Street in Glasgow, where this guy called Jim and his girlfriend Moira (who always wore thigh-high leather boots and had crimped hair) ran a stall that stocked stuff like the first Disabled Adults EP, the early Pastels singles, Subway Sect, Scrotum Poles and The Fire Engines (they even had copies of the legendary Dissipated 7" back in the day) alongside 'Blood is the Surgeon' by Relate (that's what they were called, it was an awful name). Plus they got no respect because when Imagination played this big show in Coatbridge (on the back of their appearance on *Top of the Pops*), Relate agreed to support them (they tried to make the case that they were some kind of Trojan horse, smuggling performance art into the context of a choreographed pop gig, but no one bought it). So Big Remy had a lot to live down.

I was introduced to him one night at The Griffin (in Glasgow) (an unforgettable night really), where me and Ross had been out drinking with this guy Damien Cook (an old school friend who had his own share of personality issues), and at one point Damien bit through a pint glass (and then said, dare me to eat it) and later he picked a slug up off the street and cooked it over a gas flame (and swallowed it whole) and then he slept out on the balcony naked in the snow (it was late November) (at which point I thought to myself, let him die and give us all peace) but of course he leaped up in the morning as if he had just had the best sleep of his life (the next thing I heard was that he had a nervous breakdown and was living in Australia). Inevitably Damien and Remy ended up butting heads, two fatherless voids in search of an audience (I'm saying that with what I know now, so perhaps it's not fair), but whereas Remy had his script prepared well in advance, Damien's was more like a desperate improvisation on the very edge of falling apart (which isn't to slight Remy but maybe Damien was the greater artist).

Anyway a month or so later with this other guy that I knew (he wouldn't mean anything to you if I told you his name but his name was Drew McPherson) (he had really bad buck teeth and his nickname was Tusky – Tusky McPherson) we had gone to Joy of a Toy, a regular Friday-night club off West George Street (in Glasgow), and afterwards (while hanging about in George Square waiting for a late-night bus) I spotted Big Remy. I could make out the sleeve of the second Suicide LP through his record bag and so I went up and said hello. At this point I was dating this gorgeous chick (from Caldercruix) named Regina Yarr. She had been drinking heavily and earlier that night there had been a scene where she had locked herself in the toilet (and threatened to kill herself). Now all her make-up was smeared and her tights were skewed and she was staggering around in her stocking soles holding her heels in her hand (in other words she was hot as hell). She grabbed at Big Remy's record bag. I need this, she said. 'Mr Ray' is my second-favourite song after 'All I Really Want to Do' by The Byrds (or it might have been 'Chance Meeting' by Josef K). Remy acted nonplussed. It's nowhere near as good as their first album, he said. Plus it's produced by Rick Ocasek of The Cars, give me a break (which was rich coming from him).

Bullshit, Regina screamed. That's bullshit. In that case you should give me that album right now because I love it more than you do. Then she dropped to her knees and began tearing at the bag (literally). I went to pull her off and without thinking caught hold of her hair and yanked her head back at which point she bit my hand and I slapped her around the head without thinking (just a reflex movement) but then I ended up knocking her to the ground by mistake. You hit women? Big Remy said (immediately rounding on me). Suddenly we were surrounded by onlookers. He punched her out, someone said, he fucked her up. (Grow some balls, I remember someone else shouted, which was unfortunate given what we would later learn about Remy's history but whatever). Leave him alone, someone else said, he's just a wee boy (that stung). It was like people were coming at me from all sides. I started flailing and striking out (punching the air). Someone caught my arms from behind and held me while Big Remy (quite calmly, this was the weird thing, what did I say about his emotions) took potshots at my face (but it was a vicious attack all the same). As soon as I got away another two guys in suits that had nothing to do with it whatsoever tried to have a go (like my bloody nose made me fair game). Tusky McPherson split the scene without even staying around to help (or even to see if I was alright) so that was the end of our friendship as far as I was concerned (he's working in a bank to this day, what a dick). After a while the police showed up and they interviewed me in a doorway but the only thing they seemed interested in was whether or not I was gay (which had fuck all to do with anything but that felt like some kind of extremely petty form of divine retribution). I took the last bus home on my own. The next thing I knew Remy and Regina were dating (if you can believe that).

5. Rimbaud Was Desperate or Iggy Lived It: *Ross Raymond recalls hanging out with Richard the drummer from Memorial Device as he bores everyone to tears (but not really not deep down that wasn't true at all as we all found out later when Richard burned the whole thing to the ground) in another excerpt from the epic book on Airdrie that one day Ross was gonna write himself but that of course he never finished and that never had a title but that at various times might have been called* The New Book of Airdrie *or* This is Airdrie *or* Airdrie Calling *or* An Alternative Airdrie *or* Inverted Airdrie *even, that was always in the back of his mind because of the Memorial Device album* Inverted Calder Cross *then there was* Negative Airdrie *that was another option and of course* No Airdrie *he always thought that could have been a good one but maybe that was too obvious you know like* No New York *and then there was* Subterranean Airdrie *he toyed with that one for a bit,* Airdrie Underground, *who knows,* Go Ahead and Drop the Bomb on Airdrie, *he could never decide and what does it matter now anyway when there's no underground in Airdrie to speak of whatsoever and everything is on the surface and ugly in plain sight and why he is talking about himself in the third person all of a sudden that's another thing that we will never know.*

Back then Richard Curtis seemed like the dullest of the lot or maybe the straightest of the lot, it's fair to say, maybe the most seemingly ordinary, is what I'm trying to say, in other words to an onlooker or a mere acquaintance or an audience member he may have come across as a square peg in a black hole, which wasn't actually true but which in a way made him the most eccentric of the lot, the most unusual of the lot, in a way, which also made him the drummer, inevitably.

I met him after I inveigled my way into a recording session
by Meschersmith, that was his first band, under the guise of
interviewing them for the second issue of our legendary fanzine that
never saw the light of day. When I walked into the studio, which
had been assembled in the guts of a spooky half-abandoned church
in Plains, Richard was putting the finishing touches to an Airfix
model of a 1970s Yamaha motorcycle. What the fuck is he doing
making an Airfix model in a studio, I said to myself. The next thing
I knew they had roped me into doing backing vocals on a Buzzcocks
cover. Back then the rest of Meschersmith were all communists and
council workers, all except for the guitarist, Jim, who worked for a
local butcher, so the conversation tended towards the trivial and the
politically mundane, the going rate for paying roadies, cuts of meat,
the politics of local government . . . I was so bored senseless that I
made my excuses and left early.

My friendship with Richard was easy and reassuring. Every
Friday night he would meet me at the bottom of the street next to
the Chinese restaurant and we would walk to The Staging Post
in Airdrie, where we had already acquired the status of minor
celebrities, Richard through a Meschersmith video that had been
shown on late-night TV, me through my occasional articles in the
local newspaper where I would talk about the new groups and
encourage people to drop out and go see the world, all the while living
at my mum's house in Airdrie.

There were always would-be scenesters hanging round the bar,
vacant tosspots like Colin Grant – maybe you never heard of him,
lucky you – sweating about future publishing royalties that he would
never see, a really bitter couple with a crap band name that came

from some American TV sitcom bitching about how no one wanted to be seen as being able to play their instruments any more, girls longing to be groupies, the usual hangers-on, every one of them fretting over a vision of the future that would see them crowned with all of the worries that fame and notoriety would bring. We would mostly drink on our own although sometimes we would join groups of other musicians but even then we kept to ourselves or what Richard would do is he would reduce it to the trivial, he would bring everyone down, which actually was a good strategy. For instance, one half of the bitter couple – let's call her Stacey Clark, I really don't want to give her any publicity at this stage of the game – was prone to these emotional outbursts, these great declarations of instability and poetic madness, none of which she was even living. I saw her flat one night, one Saturday night when we went back there after closing time and she barely had a book in the house and her bathroom was all chrome fittings and I had a look through her record collection, which is always the first thing I do when I visit someone for the first time, especially what's lying around the record player, and it was okay, you know, Wire, Television, our man Johnny Thunders in pride of place, this is Airdrie after all, but then there was stuff like Dire Straits and Queen and worse, and right at the top of the pile there was this compilation of soul songs that had appeared in adverts for jeans and I took it out of the sleeve and it was played to death. But anyway she would bring up all this stuff, like Rimbaud was desperate or Iggy lived it, pat comments. She said she had hung out with Lou Reed once and that he had thrown her in a swimming pool in a hotel. It was a lie, of course, she had never even met Lou but the fact that she would boast about being abused by him in a swimming pool made you think, get me out of here right now. Then she would bring up some random exhibition or art thing, like, oh did you see the Fluxus exhibition in Edinburgh or the gallery show of who knows the fuck what and Richard would instantly intervene. I hate art, he would say. I would never go to an art gallery in my life. She looked at him like he had just confessed to fucking corpses, which was more her style, really.

There were times on the way home, and this is the only time it has happened to me in my life, I'm not gay, I'm not bisexual, I like women, as a rule, that I wanted to suck Richard's cock, I can't believe I'm saying this, and one night I came close to asking him – even though I wasn't particularly attracted to him, he wasn't my idea of handsome – outside of the flats on the main street, where I pictured pushing him up against the wall and going down on him in the light of the bin sheds. Do I regret not sucking his cock then and there? Ask me in another ten years.

Or rather don't because I doubt that I'll be any closer to the truth of my feelings then. Looking back I feel as if I was never really there, that I was storing up all of these experiences, gathering material as opposed to living it, always the author and never the character in the book, which explains why I wanted to be a writer obviously. I remember Richard would make these tapes, solo recordings of really minimal droney keyboard work with primitive drum machines and we would take a drive in his car – his wife was a battleaxe who never allowed him to play his music at home – and we would drive aimlessly for hours, sometimes as far as Gourock, where we would pull up at secret viewpoints and he would play me his latest tapes, listen to this, he would say, it's the sound of the ocean or it's a tornado on the surface of Mars, and at the time I wouldn't even pay that much attention, it sounded to me like a guy who had taped down a few keys on a keyboard and then walked away and done something else for forty-five minutes but now my memory of it is more like weather systems on distant planets or storms come crackling out of the past.

Richard was a great reader and a book hoarder, even though Margot, his mean-spirited wife who looked like Siouxsie Sioux back in the day, had relegated the bulk of his collection to a series of cardboard boxes in the attic. Still, he lived with his favourite authors on a day-to-day basis. For instance he would talk about the critic Lester Bangs like he knew him personally, like Lester said this or I remember Lester didn't like that. Lester had died in April of that year and we built a shrine for him in the trees behind Katherine Park that we would sometimes go and drink next to. Margot would never have allowed it in the house. We argued about *Astral Weeks*. Richard and Lester swore by it. At home you would go through his collection in the loft and see well-thumbed copies of *The Dharma Bums* and *Moravagine* but still he was living this mundane existence, jamming with his friends at the weekend, commuting during the week, and I would start to wonder if any of the books he read penetrated deep enough to have an actual effect on his life. My own life has been so seriously damaged by books – I've never been able to enjoy a paperback without wanting to commit myself to it forever – that his library seemed more like a collection of firearms that had failed to go off. But like I said, his ordinariness was attractive. I now wonder if that had more to do with my own inherited feelings of ordinariness. Like he was my way in, like there was some kind of sense of permission to his ordinariness, a bring-him-home-to-your-parents kind of mundanity that was acceptable to a deeply conservative part of myself. But soon enough I realised that neither of us were ordinary. Which in a way is the whole point of the story.

36

6. Everyone Was Looking for That Mythical Ménage à Trois: *Andrea Anderson visits Memorial Device at their rehearsal room which was actually in one of the archways near the train station in Airdrie and goes down a forest path in her imagination and nearly has to get some vacuous bitch down by the hair but thankfully not although she does manage to have an affair with Mary Hanna who set her hair on fire one night while watching a horror movie.*

They had a rehearsal room in one of the archways near the train station. That's the way I seem to remember it. The archways are demolished now so I can't say for sure exactly where it was but every fifteen minutes a train would pass overhead, I remember that for sure. The whole room would shake with this industrial noise. You can hear it on the early recordings. They said it added to the ambience and I always remember they had this landscape painting on the wall that seemed incongruous. But when I would turn up at the rehearsal to hang out – there was always an impromptu audience, people skulking around and drinking and smoking while they played – I would sit and stare at it, this forest scene. I would imagine myself entering it. The music would make it seem as if it opened up, like it was alive, this is only me, probably, but I would go wandering in the trees and the bushes along this path. At least I would picture myself going along this path. It was always confused like it wasn't really happening but I wasn't imagining it either, it was like a portal, in a way. Does this sound crazy? Like a portal that the music would somehow open up. And I never asked them about it. I kept it secret because I felt I had discovered the real reason that they had hung it there: it wasn't out of poor taste or ill advice, it was there to get inside. I can still see that path in my head right now. Patty would play this one chord on the guitar and he would keep repeating it. Richard would be playing this mechanical rhythm on the drums. Remy would be alternating between these two notes on the bass and Lucas would step up to sing – he was so handsome back then, big lips, big Bambi eyes, a long fringe – and he would start to sing and his lyrics would be about one thing at a time like thinking something and then doing something and then seeing something. One thing would happen after the next. In an automatic voice like it was playing out without any kind of personal volition. Of course they had that song 'Adherence', that song that seemed to go on forever, and sometimes I would listen to it and think, oh my god, everything is fixed, I'm here because I'm supposed to be, the path through the forest is real, mad stuff like that.

I had affairs. Everyone did. One night I got drunk and asked Lucas for a kiss, just one, I said, right on the cheek. His girlfriend was there and she got mad. But he kissed me anyway. With those big lips he could have swallowed my face. I dated this guy called Patrick Remora for about six months in the autumn of 1983. That was our season. He was kind of a tragic poet. He would do readings at the space and sometimes Patty would accompany him on guitar. They thought they were Lenny Kaye and Patti Smith though not really, they would scorn that sort of stuff and talk about Artaud and Breton and Éluard instead. Of course threesomes were all the rage. Everyone was looking for that mythical ménage à trois. Patrick said he only dated bisexual women – that was me down to a T – because he wanted to be around as many women as possible so he encouraged me to have as many female partners as I liked, which was actually easier than you would think in Airdrie. For instance, I dated Mary Hanna for a few months. No one really knows that. When I say I dated her what I mean is that we slept together on and off every weekend or so. Mary was impossible to get to know. This was before she started playing bass with Memorial Device. I had started at Glasgow School of Art but was already feeling disillusioned, everyone banging on about the patriarchy and hegemony and stuff like that, the tutors loved it, that's what they gave points for, but I couldn't care less about social commentary. Social commentary is not art to me. It never will be. I was looking for something else, for me it was serious. I would be coming home depressed and of course even these kinds of issues were anathema to Mary, she was one of those people who would just create without a second thought. At this point I had a flat in town. A bedsit with a bed built up on legs and underneath it a workspace where I would paint and eat and I had a small black-and-white TV set up. Mary would never sleep. My best memories are of lying in bed after we had made love and of listening to her down below, painting or writing, she was always writing in her journal, and all the time she would have the TV on low, late-night monster movies like *Creature from the Black Lagoon* or *It Came from Outer Space*, and I could smell the smoke from her cigarettes rising up and soaking through the mattress combined with the smell of her hairspray. Once she even set her hair on fire. She was so engrossed in this painting she was working on that I woke up and smelled burning. When I put my head over the edge of the bed I could see that her hair had caught fire – it was probably because of the hairspray, that stuff was highly flammable – and it was smouldering away while she worked, leaning on one elbow with a cigarette between her fingers. Another time she nearly gassed us by leaving a ring on the stove going. It was Mary that encouraged me to start painting.

At first I was working with film, doing these pastiche advertisements, stuff for the Milk Board and the Department of Tourism, fake nonsense, and Mary saw them and went crazy. She flipped. This is nonsense, she said. Who got inside your head? It was a good point: at that time I had no idea who occupied my head, all I knew was it wasn't me. She taught me to mix paints. She set me up with some brushes. We began going to shows together. At first I think Patrick was cheesed off because for all his talk he was really looking to be the star attraction in the relationship and to have me as some kind of perpetually dazzled fan, but as Mary and I became closer it sort of frustrated his plans.

That was when I first started painting landscapes. I got the idea from the painting in the Memorial Device rehearsal room. I couldn't get over it. What is it that moves you? Mary asked me. Landscapes, I said, personal landscapes. Then paint those. So silly that I needed permission but I did all the same. First I just painted straightforward landscapes, overgrown environments with thick bushes and dense trees and flowers blooming like crazy, then I began to paint rooms with landscape paintings hanging on the walls. I had the idea of an exhibition that would combine landscape paintings with paintings of exhibitions of landscape paintings. I tried to capture that same feeling of a portal. The feeling of stepping into a painting and seeing a painting.

I got the nerve up to give one to Lucas. I went down to their rehearsal room on a Saturday morning, they tended to play all day on a Saturday, and this awful woman was hanging out, this really severe girlfriend that Lucas had, no one liked her though admittedly she was gorgeous. I probably felt a bit in awe of her. So there was a lot of resentment mixed in. She didn't have a clue about music – she's probably married to some miserable alcoholic in the sticks by now – but anyway it was awkward, as you might imagine. I had

40

wrapped the painting in an old issue of *International Times*. It was the April 1971 edition with the topless woman with the machine gun on the cover and the girlfriend made some too-cool-for-school comment about it. I handed it to Lucas, who for some reason I now remember was wearing a black-and-yellow-striped T-shirt. He tore the newspaper off and held the painting at arm's length for a moment before saying anything. He nodded a few times – it was as if he recognised the scenario or the impulse that had led me to create it – then he handed it back to me. Life is a series of internal disturbances, he said. That was all. At first I was taken aback. Then I regained my confidence. It's for you, I said, I painted it for you, I was inspired by the rehearsals, I told him, it's a landscape inside a landscape but really it's me looking in from the outside. I began to create all these justifications in my own head, I began to come up with all these reasons that had never been there in the first place. His bitchy girlfriend called me a geek, fuck off you geek, she said. I was cowed but I kept at it. I'm not a geek, I'll have you know, I said, I'm an artist, I'm responding to that painting on the wall, unlike you, I said to her, this shit actually means something to me. I don't know if I really swore but in my mind I did. What do you mean unlike me? she said. You're a *vacuous bitch*, I said. I couldn't contain myself any longer. By this point Lucas was smiling under his breath, he was clearly enjoying the situation. I thought to myself, I'm going to have to get this *vacuous bitch* down by the hair. It was awful. I think her name was Paprika, Paprika Jones, something ludicrous like that. But nothing happened. In the end I was left standing there with this painting in my hand as the two of them walked off. I threw it in a skip on the way home and then I started all over again.

7. Wisps of Blonde Sawdust (Blonde Stardust): *Johnny McLaughlin is growing up in Airdrie or is it Belfast.*

(This is my favourite joke.) Paddy from Ireland goes on *Mastermind.* His specialist subject is the history of the Irish Republican Army (his questions start now). When was the Provisional IRA formed? (Pass, he says.) In what year did the Easter Uprising take place? (Pass.) How many people were murdered by the British Army in the Bloody Sunday massacre? (Pass.) Who pulled the trigger on Michael Collins? (Pass.) What was Martin McGuinness convicted and sent to prison for in 1973? (Pass.) (At which point someone stands up in the audience.) That's right, Paddy (he shouts), tell them fucking nothing!

(This is my favourite fact.) There are three thousand different types of snake in this world. (Another favourite fact.) There are more living things under the sea than on dry land.

My family relocated from Belfast to the west of Scotland (in the 1970s) and we might as well have been snakes living under water. Our entire existence was based around secrecy and being hidden (and saying nothing). In our loft we had a secret room (an annexe, hidden behind a series of tall bookcases in a walk-in cupboard). Every so often we would be called on to shelter a brother or a cousin-in-law or a complete stranger (a commandant with instructions to lay low or a foot soldier out to escape the heat). Some nights my father would allow us to be locked in with them (for a few hours at a time) where they would teach us to smoke cigarettes and to play card games (and how to take a punch). Other times they would play music and sing for us (they were all crooners, they all sang in the old style and idolised Perry Como).

It was the summer holidays (it was the summer of 1979). I was seventeen years old (and I was in love with a girl from Salsburgh who played the violin). Her mother was a spinster (prematurely aged) with a perm so tight it looked like it had been set on fire and was still smouldering, the way it must have once, between her legs, when she was seventeen years old herself and gave birth to Samantha. She worked part-time in a cafe with a name like Joey's or Machiavelli's (something sneaky) and although Samantha was banned from seeing any boys (the fire between her daughter's legs a reminder of the price of her own freedom) we were able to coordinate home visits according to her work schedule, where I'd wait at the bus stop (in sight of the front door) and watch as her mother got into the car and drove off, and once inside (in the labyrinth of their home, with dark corridors leading to rooms with dazed relatives sealed inside) she would lead me to a messy bedroom at the back of the house (with the curtains closed) and we would make love (in the bed she shared with her mother) to the occasional accompaniment of coughs and shuffles and doors opening and closing in the corridor outside, which by this point was like my brain (my own family policing my libido at a distance) reminding me that the blood that now rushed towards my penis and danced around its head (caught tight between her red, perfectly made-up lips) was once theirs and that somehow they had afforded me this pleasure (and so owned it forever) and the sound of people going by in the street outside in that time (and the smell of warm towels drying on the radiators) in that one perfect time where we made love on the fly and against the wishes of everyone, it made me feel like I was in hock to the beginnings of time (like sex with Samantha in the back bedroom could somehow be tracked back to the first orgasm of creation) and here we were, the aftershock (the endless re-enactment), the

43

children of children of children of children of children (and as guilty as any one of them).

I was a stockings man back then (and I will be until the day I die, so help me god). I was precocious enough at seventeen that I already had a fantasy in place. I had a way of moving her limbs (of lifting her leg to the side), of guiding my penis inside her with my hand, into her newly shaved pussy (shaved on my request), her turquoise panties pulled to one side, though back then there were only a few hairs, really, her vulva like an egg (domed, smooth, freshly blown), the prickly hairs like wisps of blonde sawdust (blonde stardust, I nearly said) in the drawers of a collector, which back then was how I saw myself (to be sure), as a collector, a connoisseur, a gourmet, a pussy-eater (a body-gorger) (a piss-drinker, a shit-lapper), a woman-lover, a tit-biter, an auto-asphyxiator (an ass-lover, a panty-smotherer), a heel-worshipper (a hose-hugger). I would do to their bodies what they would never dare (taste them in ways that they had never tasted themselves) so that their smell was my own as I gave it back to them. Samantha would cut her fishnet tights down to stockings and borrow her mother's suspender belt (back then who had a lingerie budget?), black silk except for a little turquoise flower in the centre, which I would tongue and taste her mother's perfume and talcum powder and warm laundry and I would think of her mother (dressed for sex and masturbating in their windowless bathroom) as her daughter lay dressed for sex beneath me, tearing at her frayed stockings, biting my shoulder, scraping my arms (the delicate buckle on her patent heels running up and down my back and leaving lines beaded with blood that looked like a child's first attempt at writing, gasps of silence, secret signatures), and so I went through all of these mute girls in my youth, these silent types, and had them write on my back or bite their name into my forearm. I'm John the goddamn Revelator (I said to myself).

The rest of my time I spent alone (an intuitive heartbreaker right from the start). I was a precocious reader (a dedicated listener). From late-night radio I picked up on what was happening in New York and San Francisco and London (and LA and Manchester). But when I walked out on the streets I felt nothing. I read Céline and Cendrars (and Ginsberg and Borges) and looked out of my window towards Glasgow and I saw nothing but fucking street lights (snaking off).

Then Michael made his appearance. There's someone new in the loft, my mum told me when I arrived back from one of our secret assignations (I immediately pictured it as the muse, inspiration itself, climbing the ladder of the brain stem and secreting itself in some forbidden lobe, some taped-off back room or abandoned dungeon, set on dynamiting the whole thing to hell).

I couldn't give a fuck about the IRA, Michael said, and he shrugged his shoulders and swept his long hair behind his ear (and stubbed a cigarette out in my mum's flowerpot). He looked like a hunger striker, with a black beard, sunken cheeks, clay complexion, red eyes, yellow teeth, greasy hair, cigarettes (a Holger Meins, a Bobby Sands), a stretcher case, really, but here he was, propped up on a pillow like a painting (his pale skin like a cracked old master), and he was cursing the Pope, damning the Catholics, a pox on Southern Ireland, a plague on Italian superstitions. What are you fighting for? I asked him. Living room, he said. That's Hitler you're quoting, I told him. Picture a world run by Catholics, he said. Think about it (okay, I'm thinking about it) (it stinks). It's sex as procreation, Michael said, which is like saying pleasure as function, which is like saying love as duty (which is like saying feeling as obligation), which is like saying heartbeat as slavery (which is like saying liberty as prison), which is like saying acceptance as apology (which is like saying today as tomorrow), which is like saying life as death. Fuck that, I said. Okay, he said (now we're talking). But you're just a wee boy, he said (that stung). What do you know? I've eaten women out, I said. I've strapped them to my face and drank from them like cups. Like cups? he said. Like cups that were overflowing, I said. Like goblets, like chalices. But the Protestants are worse, he said, shaking his head. Despite my intellectual sympathies, they're worse. They're mean. They have no warmth. They hate life and the world. They have as little belief in heaven as they do in next door. They despise all consolation. They exist to suffer beyond any display of suffering. Really, I might just as well have joined the mujahideen.

What are you reading at the moment? he asked me. *Vanity of Duluoz* by Jack Kerouac, I said (I fluffed it). Bullshit, he said. Don't tell me, he said. Charles Bukowski. William fucking Burroughs. Patti fucking Smith. Jim fucking Thompson. Hermann fucking Hesse (Bullshit von fucking Bullshit). Try this on for size, he said (and he pulled out a copy of *Diary of a Madman* by Gogol from his rucksack). Read the Russians, he said. And forget satire, he said. And forget metaphor, the Russians have no truck with metaphor. And forget time, they have no truck with time, either. When you read Gogol it's neither yesterday, today or tomorrow. You ever heard John Coltrane? he asked me. I have *Kind of Blue*, I said (he's on there). Bullshit, he said. You need to listen to *Ascension*. You need to listen to *Meditations*. You need to listen to *Interstellar Space*. You need to wake up to now, my friend. He stubbed out another cigarette. I need to get to sleep, he said. You have no idea the weight of my brain right now. I told Samantha. We have a visitor upstairs (I said).

I got another job (another fucking miserable job forced on me by my goddamn parents). Gardening (they called it). But really it was more about painting creosote on fences, cutting down trees and toppling power lines, talking in circles with insane old people, drinking their fucking tea, lifting slabs, cutting up blocks, delivering coal (eating their fucking tablet). This is the Gulag Archipelago, I told Michael. I don't need another Russian novel.

I split my time between repairing rock gardens, fucking Samantha, sleeping in a great big double bed that used to be my grandfather's (and that I think he died in) and locking myself in the annexe with Michael. Occasionally my father would come up, quiz him on Irish history. Michael was well versed (he had served in South Armagh). But there weren't many hippies in the IRA. It was more like the mods (or the Mafia), you know, clean living under poor circumstances (all of that crap), whereas Michael's whole deal was that you should offend and terrify and appal and undermine (and disgust) at all costs. My dad would bring up Perry Como. What about him, eh? Perry Como doesn't exist, Michael would say. He never has. What the fuck are you talking about? my dad would say. I'll play you a song right now, a good dose (a good dose of Como). Then you'll know he's real. You're a cheeky bastard, my dad would say. And then he would struggle with the stereo, pull out Perry Como's *40 Greatest Hits*, drop the needle on 'It's Impossible', 'For the Good Times', 'When You Were Sweet Sixteen', and secretly, somewhere inside my veins, in the tunnels (long rebel-held) (or so I thought), a little bubble would appear (a little gasp of air) that would fight its way to the surface of my brain

and (for a moment) I was ready to fight for sentiment (to stand by
cliché as profundity), maybe that was as close as I came to any kind
of revelation (I think so now, maybe, a little), and I would go to speak
but then Michael would reach for the tone arm (it only occurs to me
now that he has the name of an archangel) and he would wrench
the needle back like we were in a sitcom or a radio documentary
(the sudden *urrrk!* of the vinyl like the splat of forged ectoplasm, the
disembowelling of some kind of airborne hallucination) and I would
look round and he would be smoking a cigarette (flagrantly) (one arm
behind his head, the other in the air) with his shoes off, his bare feet
mocking my father, every inhalation bringing Perry Como's existence
into more and more doubt.

8. A Beautiful Form of Self-Scarification and Of Course Endlessly
Attractive: *John Bailey recollects Vanity and Glass Sarcophagus in
turmoil and it's true that everyone was in love with Vanity everyone
in Airdrie and everyone in Coatbridge too and after Memorial Device
Glass Sarcophagus were the best live band of the era I saw the shows
and bought the tapes which all go for a fortune now predictably now
that it's all over.*

Of course everyone says it was the tits that first attracted me, that
all I saw was the tits and it was all over after that, but it was
something in the eyes and I don't mean it like some kind of repressed
adolescent romanticising of tragedy and poetry and bullshit or some
attempt to be chivalrous, I'm really not that deep, I loved the tits as
much as the next man but they went together with the eyes, dark
eyes, sparkling eyes, eyes that were alive, not dead eyes looking out,
no, not fake eyes, eyes like a tightrope walker over a deep dark lake,
and those tits, yes, my god, fake tits, and of course all the girls were
mocking her, calling her desperate, a man-pleaser, a phoney, but
really she was the most genuine person I had ever met, at least back
then, and it's what got me into body modification, at least not
personally but as a fan, as something to be appreciated in others,
something to marvel at, because it really wasn't my style, I wasn't
adventurous enough, I'm sorry to say, because to me that's what
those tits said, bring on adventure, a thumb in the eye of fate or God
or whoever dealt the cards in the first place, I wish I could have done
something as daring as growing a new pair of tits when I was
nineteen, like sawing off a leg or getting a tattoo on my neck that
read I-N-D-I-V-I-D-U-A-L so that I could never work in a bank, but
fake tits are the best, a beautiful form of self-scarification and of
course endlessly attractive though when I think of them now, I think

of those dark eyes behind them, I think of the eyes looking up at me, perhaps they're squinting a little, glittering, the dark make-up around the rims, both hands holding these beautiful tits out towards me while I masturbated over them, though really they needed no support, it was all part of the show and she loved to display herself, loved me to come on her tits, some people think it's humiliating, but with her it was like a kind of anointing, there was a spiritual aspect to it and it was beautiful and it was more than tit-worship or eye-worship or greedy sex, although of course it was all of those too, but when I think about it now, the pupils floating on the surface of her eyes like dark lily pads with roots in who knows what beginning of the world and the huge tits in her hands, these creations made to drive me wild, I get a sense of vertigo and I feel myself falling forward and a sense of anxiety comes over me and I lose control of my thoughts, though really it's more like falling backwards, into the past, a past that isn't even there any more, because it was a true romance, I've had plenty of relationships since then, good and bad, with their share of ups and downs, but I can't hand on heart call any of them a romance in the same way, you know that song 'Private Dancer' by Tina Turner, it had just come out at the time and it sort of became our song, I know it's a bunch of crap really but we would listen to it together all the time, we'd play it while we were having sex or sometimes when we were watching one of her videos with the sound turned down, it would be the soundtrack, when you're in a romance that's the kind of cheap music that works for you, that's what the song is about in a way, you know, any old music will do, it's saying that you're no longer thinking with your head, you're caught up, you're swept away, it's the oldest trick in the book and every time I hear it I feel the same way, transported, back to the way we were because there are no photographs of us together, no home movies, no washed-out Polaroids of the two of us at Glasgow Green or on the ferry to Dunoon in December, so the only thing I have to remember her with are VHS copies of her movies, low-budget porn movies, none of which I starred in, obviously, so the only time I see how she was back then, outside of my memories, is with other men, I mean it doesn't necessarily make me jealous, just sad sometimes, when I catch my own reflection in the television, watching her being penetrated by two men on a couch in a council house made up to look like a classy hotel room and for a second it's like she was just a thought bubble inside my head or vice versa but I never saw anyone come over her tits in the movies, you have to hold something back, she always said, you have to keep something special, plus she loved music, she was a big fan of punk and Krautrock and industrial and of course she wanted to get involved, she was an artist, that's how she saw herself, an artist that used sex and her body and gender and stuff like that – though she never talked about it in those kinds of terms, that wasn't her style – and so early on we began doing music together where we would record ourselves having sex, she would get into the zone, there would come a point where she was so turned on, you can hear the moment it clicks on the tape when the voice would come out, this new voice, this automatic kind of voice, not always using words but sometimes, words that you wouldn't expect, words like exhibition and tournament and procession, words that always seemed too long to suit a gasp of passion or an orgasm, words like calculation and expression and verification, sexy words, it seems to me even now and back then, my god, it was all I could do not to blow my load as soon as she began talking these words, these magic words that were like passwords to a whole other kingdom of passion, on her knees in front of me, sometimes with a single thin silver belt tied around her waist and a pair of heels, those eyelashes curling up, nothing else, and next to my penis a microphone so you never knew which one she was going to suck and which one she was going to talk into and we would press up tapes in editions of fifty copies or less and distribute them ourselves, we had a newsletter, nothing earth-shattering but we would write up small descriptions of each release, most of which had a xeroxed picture of Vanity on the front or a blurry scene from one of her movies, deliberately obscured, we were into Throbbing Gristle, Peter Christopherson's use of suspect tapes, Whitehouse, stuff like that, and we'd publish correspondence that we got from people who bought the tapes, reviews, there were a few, and soon other people asked us to start stocking their own releases and we did, if we liked them, or rather I did because music was still a sideline for Vanity, it was still the pornographic work that was her focus, she wanted to be the first intelligent porn star even though I told her there had been porn stars with brains before, but not like me, she would say, and early on we got a letter from Robert Mulligan, the guy that did Sufferage Tapes out of Greengairs, I was the first person in the world, actually, to hear the Steel Teeth cassettes, he had never sent them to anyone, he was just making this racket out there on his own, with no context at all, no idea that anyone was doing anything remotely like it, just completely isolated, but he heard a tape that Vanity and I had made, god knows how, except that we were becoming minor celebrities on the local underground scene, though he never bought it from us and I never asked him how he heard of us in the first place but it was the third tape that we did, *Festival*, a particularly noisy one, that inspired him to write and to send us a cassette and the rest, well, it's history, we started putting out releases by him and he became this legendary figure who worked in a sausage factory in Mount Vernon six days a week and built all of these incredible electronics that he made this

52

ultra-minimal, ultra-lonely music with, so that was one of our early
hook-ups and of course when we met him he couldn't look Vanity in
the eye but she liked him, she said he was handsome, special, which
is hard to believe as even back then he was small and fat and wore
big black woolly jumpers and skintight black jeans and a tight woolly
hat even when the sun was shining but judging by the quality of her
partners in the films, the ones she liked working with, the inner
circle she called them, there was no way of second-guessing who she
would go for and we would go to concerts together, she always
dressed extravagantly, even for the underground, with stiletto heels,
leotards, tiny leather jackets that she wore like batwings, so you can
imagine the kind of stick we got walking along Carlisle Road, heads
would turn, people would shout things from passing cars, it was
amazing and I started upping my own game, I grew my hair like
Dylan '65, dug out my dad's old jackets, some of which were torn and
eaten by moths, and I'd wear skintight jeans and winkle-pickers so
sharp you could have kicked the eye out of a worm and sometimes
she would take her heels off and climb up on stage barefoot and talk
to the band before they even played their first number, no one would
stop her, the bouncers would make way, the band would welcome
her, she would hold her heels in her hand and everyone in the
audience would be looking at her, of course most of the girls hated
her and some of the guys said they did, but all eyes were on her and
she had the stage, if she wanted it, even if in reality it was someone
else's, I had that feeling like I was walking into the future or more
accurately being led into it by its chosen representative, plus she
liked having sex in public places, it never appealed to me before or
since but there was something about being with Vanity that made
me want to be pointlessly daring, we had sex in train carriages, on
buses, once in the back of a taxi, in the park, in the back row of a

concert, at an open window, in the toilet at a party, she had a way before she gave you a blow job where she would very deliberately put on new lipstick and then she would run her tongue around her lips, as if she was moistening them, and it drove me crazy, I can still see it now, it was always an occasion, that was the thing with Vanity, it was never ordinary, it's harder to keep that energy when you are older but I remember it and I still try to practise it, from time to time, and she would look up at me with those eyes, maybe an arm under her breasts, holding them up, and I would think, my god, we're going to die far away from each other and in completely different lives, what a thrill, and that's when she started appearing on record sleeves by local bands, everyone was after her, and for about a year or so it seemed like she was on every second release, all of which had a similar kind of look, you know, band name and song titles written in Tipp-Ex, then a fuzzy picture of her maybe with her legs in the air or kneeling up on a bed with her hands tied in stark black and white, some of them are worth a lot of money now, and her career as a porn star was starting to take off, she fell in with Imaginorg in Glasgow, the company run by Rod Stilvert before he launched Gamma Productions, back when he was based round the back of St Enoch tube station in Glasgow on the second floor of a sleazy walk-up and was still trying to make something artistic rather than the mindless wank fodder that made his name, she made a few films with Randy Jewels and Manda Candy, all of that first generation of Scottish porn stars, I partied with them a few times, it was kind of awkward, actually, there was a boxing match at The Tudor Hotel in Airdrie and Stilvert invited his roster along but the mix was all wrong, you know, all these sexually repressed thugs and slimy businessmen and gangster promoters on one side and on the other side all of us, a bunch of punks, really, and all of these beautiful, fearless women in stockings and suspenders and with their tits hanging out and skirts up to here, it all kicked off when some drunken meathead licked his finger and went to slide it up Manda's asshole as she bent over her handbag, they had no idea how to be around women, simple as that, but rather than cause a scene we all split back to Vanity's house in Gartness but not before Manda got the guy by the neck and smacked him in the head with one of her heels. Vanity lived in a council house in Gartness with an abandoned flat underneath that had been burned out in some kind of domestic dispute, she lived in one room really and it was kind of shabby, for instance she always had an ironing board set up in the corner and that's one of my pet peeves, all of her clothes lay in big piles on the floor, she lived in her bed basically, or on the stool in front of her dresser, she had no phone, that was another thing that impressed me, if she had a booking or you needed to get in touch you could arrange a time where she would wait at the phone box at the bottom of the street or you could write her a letter or of course you could just pop by but popping by wasn't always a good idea, there were a few evenings, evenings where I couldn't resist the urge, evenings where I knew there was something in the air, something that said, don't go, it's not your time, you'll only get your heart broken, but sure enough I would call around anyway and sometimes the light in her bedroom would be on but she just wouldn't answer or other times there would be lights in other rooms, rooms that as far as I knew were empty and never used and once I heard music coming from the back bedroom, a room that she said was just a storage room, yet one night I heard a song coming from it, through a crack in the window, I had climbed the fence after she hadn't answered the door and had been startled by this sound, I call it a song but it wasn't music really though in a way it was still a song, if you know what I mean, it rose and fell like a song, occasionally it would rise a little and then it would die down and at first I thought it was the central heating, then I thought it was a song coming back to me in my own mind and then I had an even worse feeling, that it was the song on the end credits of our romance, a song like something slowly fading, something being very gently deflated, like a dying plastic toy, though maybe that's more with hindsight or cruelty, we played a few live shows together, we discussed having sex on stage but I didn't fancy it, I didn't want everyone to see my penis though it was quite big and I wasn't ashamed of it, also there would have been problems getting away with sex in nightclubs and the next thing we knew we would have been in the papers for all the wrong reasons, which of course Vanity said would have been for all the right reasons but she came to see my side of the story, in the end, but Glass Sarcophagus played that show, the big one, the one with all the Airdrie groups, though I don't remember much of it, there was a fight, inevitably, some kind of incident during the Memorial Device show, something about their visuals causing offence, I knew Vanity had been involved with Lucas from Memorial Device when she was younger but when you saw them together it really made no sense, size-wise, even, it was all wrong, she looked tiny next to him, I remember Nein Nein Nein did one of their refusenik pieces where they refused to change the chord, just this one-chord mantra, it was really good, it was just before they went fully experimental, back when they still had this dirty psychedelic rock thing, I loved it, but people were throwing things and shouting abuse, it was the first time I had been around a lot of the musicians, I was putting faces to a lot of names, people I had corresponded with or whose tapes I had stocked, and it was true that Vanity and I were local celebrities by this point and I still think it was one of our best shows, everyone was expecting us to be very confrontational, we had that reputation, but on the night Vanity did these really soft, heartbroken vocals, at least that's how they seem now, she kept repeating a single phrase, I can't remember exactly what it was and you can't really make it out on the recording but it sounds like Back to nowhere but someone else said it was Parting always and I've even seen it written up as Fucked in no way but that seems too obvious to me, I was playing the guitar with a bow, I had about three strings on it and I was putting it through a Space Echo and then for the second piece, there were two numbers but the second piece was never recorded, the tape ran out or someone forgot to press record, for the second piece I just kept playing these three single notes but in weird rhythms until they started phasing against each other and clanging and clashing, it was really loud and it went on for about twenty minutes before Vanity began singing and again it was just one simple phrase, Do you remember?, that was all, again and again, as it went on it wasn't like she was asking if you remembered a specific thing or a place or a time, it was more like do you remember at all, like it had something to do with space and time and experience and backwards and forwards and our own relationship and I wondered was I living it or remembering it or just wishing it had happened and we both got really drunk afterwards, we were spaced out, we went back to hers where we had really amazing sex but when I came on her tits I noticed that my sperm seemed like it was shot through with silver, like there was a metallic quality to it, oh my god, I said, I'm coming silver, but when she rubbed it between her fingers she panicked, that's not cum, she said, I'm leaking, sure enough, there was a tiny hole under her left breast, a vampire puncture, and it was leaking a sort of gelatinous silver liquid, I looked out the window and it was a full moon, or maybe not quite, something is going on, I said to myself and at first I felt bad, I

57

had been slapping her tits around with my dick and I have quite a big dick, I had really been beating on her, and I half wondered if I had caused the damage myself, don't worry, she said, I'm sure I can get them fixed, but there was something in her voice that told me that this was more of a deluge than a puncture, in the meantime, she said, I can just cover up, do lingerie sex, stuff like that but in my mind I was paranoid, do you remember, I kept thinking to myself, she went to see the surgeon, it was worse than we thought, there were numerous leaks inside the breast and it was causing tissue damage as well as causing the flesh around the side of the breast to lose elasticity and crack apart, she came home from the clinic and we both cried, a rebuild would be a very difficult procedure, they said, we had dinner at our favourite Italian restaurant in town, how about flying to Europe, I said, they have the best clinics don't they, their technology is leagues ahead of our own, but it was an idiot fantasy, we had no money, we thought about a benefit gig, you know, Save Vanity's Breast, but we knew it would bring out all the told-you-sos and the puritans and to tell you the truth, it didn't look too bad and there are a few movies that she made round about the time where you can hardly tell, except for at certain angles where you can make out a thin strip of masking tape just behind the bra strap, honestly though, things had been coming to a head in terms of Vanity's career anyway, she had peaked too young, she said, all the other girls had held back, they hadn't done girl-on-girl right away, they hadn't done anal or double penetration, and so they were able to demand higher fees and gradually move up the pay scale, but Vanity had been doing it all from day one, she wasn't a goddamn businesswoman, she was a passionate artist, and here she was paying for it while all of these cynical bitches, who couldn't even take a cock up their ass without going cross-eyed, were moving up the ranks, truth was she had nowhere left to go, no special trick to turn or ability to unveil, she had given it her all and that was her mistake, at least in the eyes of these maggots.

When I first saw it, I wrote it off, convinced myself it was nothing, that it was something to do with the angle and that I just hadn't caught it properly, he was fucking her under her arm, I told myself, weird, not that sexy but I guess she had to pull something out of the bag. But I couldn't live in denial any longer. I rewound the tape and watched it again. He had clearly inserted his penis into the hole in the side of her breast. I couldn't bear it. I got dressed and walked to her house in the dark. She had dropped the video off without a word at the weekend, told me that she would be interested in what I thought, sealed it inside a jiffy bag, as if the contents might have leaked all over the floor, and when I got to her house the curtains were closed and it seemed like no one was at home so I climbed the fence and stood in the back garden, looking up at the storage room, the same window I thought I had heard the song come from. I could make out nothing but the sound of the wind in the gutters and a straining, constricting noise, coming from somewhere inside my chest, that I eventually realised was the sound of my heart being used as a cock ring.

Vanity went on to star in a bunch more movies, all of which involved tit-fucking, even double tit-fucking, I'm told, but the thought of it makes me want to kill someone, the idea of those tits being torn apart, and the eyes, watching from a distance now, no longer connected to the tits but like ghosts come back to the scene of their own murder, even now it feels personal. Later she became a fairly successful pop star and of course some newspaper brought up the tapes and she laughed them off, in fact it only added to her credibility, then she died in a car crash in the Hollywood Hills on her way back from a video shoot. I read about it in the newspaper. It said that the airbags had failed to inflate. That's the one consolation I take from any of this.

9. He Had Tried to Have His Testicles Removed on the NHS:
*Johnny McLaughlin explains the situation with Remy's father
that it has something to do with ideas of fate predestination and
genital mutilation as the keys to the kingdom or as a secret path to a
holiday on a black beach in your mind somewhere, either way having
something to do with how we all felt back then every one of us in a
way.*

Big Remy's father had walked away from family life when Remy was
in his teens. He was a fairly well-known scientist and philosopher
(though there were just as many people that thought of him as a
crackpot and an occultist). There was a story that he had become
a eunuch in a backstreet operation (though really it was more like
an S&M torture session) where he had hooked up with a group of
subterranean gays that practised cock and ball torture. He had tried
to have his testicles removed on the NHS (the story ran) but when he
was laughed out of his GP's (who suggested psychiatric counselling
instead) he placed a personal ad in a gay magazine offering his
genitals up for use and abuse in return for their skilful removal. Of
course the story only went to prove that Big Remy came from a long
line of homos. But the most interesting aspect of his father's story
(one which I only found out many years later) was the papers he
had written during his short career as an academic (at Coatbridge
College), in particular a semi-autobiographical tract that had been
suppressed by the college entitled 'Fate is Only Once', where he
elucidated his theory of space and time (and their relationship
to thoughts and deeds). The theory ran something like this (and
inevitably I'm paraphrasing and simplifying and maybe even
misunderstanding) but the essence of his argument was that there
was some kind of disjunction between actions and thoughts. It wasn't

that they were parallel occurrences, in his view actions were eternal and forever but thought was something that happened in time and that came to pass only once. He used a really mundane example (which made it all the more convincing).

He talked about a time where he was on holiday with his wife (his ex-wife, obviously). It isn't clear where he was holidaying but we can presume it's somewhere on the coast (not at the seaside, we're not talking Blackpool or Burntisland here), somewhere exotic and eccentric (New Zealand, perhaps, or even Sausalito, the scene of his future castration), but maybe that's just the poet in me. They pull up at a picnic spot (we can imagine that in the distance there are mountains, I see them as being snow-capped, for some reason) and in front of them there's a crystal-clear sea that could even be a lake, a body of water that somehow has the feeling of revelation, of clarity (which may or may not be the same thing), and dark sand, black sand (if you can imagine such a thing). It's lunchtime and they're both hungry from the drive. He rustles something up on the gas stove in the camper van (eggs and salsa is my guess) while she sets up some foldaway chairs and a table on the black-sand beach at the edge of the sparkling waters. At this point he goes into obsessive detail (which is important in terms of his argument). He mentions the transparency of the sea, which he says completely refused to hold their reflections, even though the sun was behind them, and in the distance a group of adventure-sports enthusiasts parachuting out of the sky cast a series of perfect silhouettes across the surface (and at this point he interrupts the text with an odd piece of ornamental syntax, a set of square brackets [[[]]] that also weirdly looks like the view from a prison cell where, of course, it is difficult to cast a shadow, as the sun doesn't have much to go on), and then he describes the preparation of the meal in some detail, he talks of chopping, grating, folding, frying, stirring, melting, he talks about the cutlery, the blunt knife, the silver fork that had already become tarnished and he talks about taking the two plates down to the beach (to this black beach I have in my mind) and of seeing his wife sitting there (disconcerted, as anyone would be, by the lack of her shadow) and of course nowhere does he mention what they actually eat (which seems significant), he talks about the whole process, the preparation, the transfer, the devouring, but not at one point does he mention what it is he has actually prepared. All the while he talks about feeling like he's in a play, following some kind of script that has been written specifically for him (a dream role, in other words), and the whole thing culminates when his wife returns to the camper van and he starts to clear off the plates (plates of who knows what) and he goes to kneel down on the grass (something he would never normally have done, after all he has a nice pair of slacks on and the label says dry-clean only) and just as he does so he notices two small indentations in the grass (just the shape of his kneecaps) and he slots his knees into them, they fit perfectly, so much so that he becomes convinced that he has created the holes himself and that he isn't so much living forward in time as re-living.

He kneels down and settles into the pose (a moment of humility is what he calls it – all the time he maintained his Christian faith, despite the testicles and the philosophy, which either makes it more confusing or elucidates it completely) and as the moment extends, as he lives through it (his wife in the camper van in the distance, the parachutists falling from the sky, the pure clear water, the remains of their lunch on the plates, the precise patterns of rust on the cutlery), it comes to seem as if it was written in eternity, as though

63

his secret self (his guardian angel, he called it) had constructed this total artwork that had lain in wait for him (or more properly that had always existed and that was now somehow revealing itself to thought).

It was right at the moment that he found himself kneeling in the grass and scraping food from the plates (exactly what we'll never know) that he says that he felt like he caught up with himself (briefly, it's true), that he drew neck and neck (let's say). As he saw the red waste liquid streaming down the inside of the white bag (I imagine a tomato salsa in a bin liner as much as a close-up on a tubercular lung) he extrapolated the experience into a Christian outlook. He redefined thought as judgement. You are given this life, he writes, this precise set of occurrences: and you are asked to judge it.

(But think about this.) If everything is already fixed, if we have been here before and set up the whole deal behind our own backs (or if an angel has done it for us in heaven), right down to the patterns on the forks and the shape that our knees make on the (black) sand of a dream holiday that happened long ago and that will live on in eternity, then what thought demands of us is nothing less than that we weigh the will of God itself.

It's a heavy concept (but here's another one). What if the very idea of the will of God exists as some kind of tissue tiger? (What if you trash the great gift?) What if you refuse it altogether? What if this insult, this seeing through of a ruse, this act of rebellion (whatever you want to call it) affords you access to the next level, like a series of interconnecting dungeons whose walls it is possible to think down and for which you are rewarded by a less puzzling interaction (and

then another) until the whole thing comes full circle and finally
you are able to live your life as written (in history and in time over
again), but this time outside of mind, without judgement and beyond
understanding? It may mean nothing (maybe there's no way to be
done with judgement, maybe it's a problem with our brains or maybe
it's just the ravings of a lunatic) but back then, when we were young,
once, forever, it seemed like a genuine possibility.

10. The Golden Light Coming From the Window and Spilling Over the Pavement Like a Perfect Dream: *the saga of Chinese Moon as recalled by David Kilpatrick.*

Hardly anyone ever leaves Airdrie: Airdrie Savings Bank is the only surviving independent savings bank in the UK. That's because it has the least mobile population of any town in Britain. Plus there are six degrees of separation between everyone that lives there and no one is happy until they have established themselves in a complex network of friends, families and distant relations; it's like the Jews, in a way.

Everyone else thinks it's a dump; a horror show; an asylum. That just serves to keep out the curious. Behind closed doors at the back ends of estates, in crumbling mansions in Clarkston and modern flats on the main street, in solitary bedsits and grim flats above chip shops there are hidden some of the most eccentric characters ever to escape from a novel; some of the greatest book collections ever thrown in skips; some of the most overgrown gardens never weeded by a salt-of-the-earth type from the East End; some of the greatest musicians; the most heartbreaking chanters; the heaviest drinkers; the least responsible workers; the slackest teachers; the most committed intellectuals; the oddest astronomers; the most obsessive collectors; the most serious amateurs; and of course the greatest failures. I knew them all in my time. I knew Memorial Device; I went to the shows. I was into all the Airdrie groups. We had a team, we grew up together and we went to all the shows: Findlay, Alan, Duncan and myself.

Findlay and Alan were brothers and they lived with their parents, who were teachers, in Kenilworth Drive, just up from the old Kenilworth Hotel. They were eccentric kids. At the age of fourteen

66

Findlay subscribed to *Newsweek* and Alan was a practising magician who, he claimed, had been initiated into a coven of witches that practised out of Katherine Park at night. Plus they both wore tracksuits with the bottoms pulled right up to their nipples. We were into comics; science fiction; war gaming; role playing; stuff like that. But then we started getting into music. It was Duncan who turned us on. His brother had some albums by The Ramones as well as the most amazing collection of heavy metal albums I have ever seen. Back then he must have had at least thirty LPs. When we would go round to hang out with Duncan, whose parents lived in the flats behind The Kings Cafe on the main street, we would sit in his brother's room, which was completely wallpapered with pages from *Sounds* and *NME* and which had a snooker table in the middle and a permanently unmade bed with socks everywhere and cigarette stubs and which was always dark and creepy and grown up and we would play records and have games of snooker and paint lead figures or plan our next trip into Glasgow, which might as well have been the end of the world.

Duncan's dad was unfortunately an alcoholic. Although he had a good job as the manager of a department store in Shettleston he refused to spend good money on anything except booze so the house was always in a state. There were bare bulbs in every room. I always remember the living room, which had a row of birthday cards on the window ledge from three years previous. His dad would drink at The Tavern, just across from Katherine Park – it's long gone now, don't try to look for it – and he would cycle there and back and once when I was doing my paper round I saw him cycle right into a hedge when he was half-cut. He would come home while we were playing records in the evening and we would hear him coming up the stairs shouting

and cursing and Duncan would act embarrassed and say that his dad
was pretending to be drunk again. He would pretend that he was
just having a laugh and that it was all a big joke on his mother. I felt
sorry for him. Duncan's mother was Jewish and they had a combative
relationship. Duncan bought a PLO T-shirt and when he put it in the
laundry his mum said that she wouldn't wash any of his clothes until
he removed it, which he refused to do, so it was a constant stalemate
and it meant that Duncan always stank as he had to keep taking the
same dirty clothes out of the basket and wearing them all over again,
which were normally skintight Adidas T-shirts and drainpipe denims.

It all changed when we discovered psychedelics. It was this guy called
Scott who was kind of notorious on the scene; a heavy dealer. His
nickname was Sore Arse because he had a series of operations on his
arse for some syndrome or other so that's how everyone referred to
him. He got kind of friendly with us; he was into Tolkien and John
Norman, the Gor books, all that sort of stuff. You couldn't film those
Gor books, he would say, those books would be triple-X in the cinema,
it just isn't possible. Then he would light a joint, with his shades on
and his greasy hair, and we would stare at him like he was an oracle
from the future; an oracle with a penis. Shit, I would think. This guy
is on the edge. I'm holidaying in Erotica this year, he would say, and
he would wink, and we wouldn't even get it. But the point is he began
dangling the idea of tripping in front of us. We came to psychedelics
from the side on, in a way; kind of by accident. We went from
superhero and fantasy stuff to underground comics, you know like
Robert Crumb and *Zap*, stuff that you would hide under your bed in
case your mum saw it. But expanding our minds, hell yeah we were
all for that; we lived in our minds, the more room the better.

On the night of the first trip everyone met up at my mum's house in Caldercruix. I had an empty. We sat in the living room and Duncan put on a Devo record and we each took half a tab to be safe. After a while I saw the curtains wobble a little and there was a drum break on the record that seemed to last forever but that was about the size of it. I heard a rumour that the batch had been cut with strychnine but I tried to keep my thoughts somewhere else even as I had to fight the idea of picking up the phone and asking Sore Arse if everything was okay. Findlay lay on the couch reading that book that Truffaut wrote about Hitchcock; this is back when Findlay was attending the cinema three times a day, crazy about films; a real nutcake. Suddenly I got this huge bulge in my pants; I thought I was going to explode. All I wanted to do was wank off; it was overwhelming. It felt like life was pulsing through me. I could feel the head bulging out, the skin peeling back. I went into the bathroom and dug up my stash of porno mags which I used to hide beneath a loose floorboard under the bath.

Her name was Ginny; I still remember her. She was lying with her legs spread on the bed with one hand holding onto the brass bedhead while wearing stockings and next to her this panty drawer was open and spilling over with lingerie. Oh my god, I said to myself. I looked between her legs and it was like two worlds colliding and it was like lingerie was the highest pinnacle of civilisation; everything we had been fighting for; in Gor and in Middle-earth and in reality. It was a profound moment of worship and afterwards I walked back through to the living room and it was like walking onto the command deck of a spaceship. I told them how great it was, that they should try masturbating on acid, and one by one – all except Findlay – they took their turn in the bathroom so that the magazine was soaked right through and I had to wrap it in a plastic bag and throw it in the bin in the morning. After that it was inevitable that we would form a band.

None of us could play a thing except for Alan who was a piano virtuoso and who had written a book on the history of minimalism when he was fifteen years old and then just stashed it in a cupboard; but we weren't looking for technique and besides he was one of these guys that could play from a score fine but who couldn't improvise to save his life. We were all like that, in a way. So we hit on this idea. Duncan's dad had an endless supply of mannequins that he used in the windows of his store on the Baillieston Road. We decided to make tapes and then organise this show where we would have mannequins dressed up like us, like schoolboys, basically, but looking like rock stars, holding instruments and with wigs on, and we would play tapes of our music behind them like it was a gig. We came up with a name. At first it was Shooting Gallery; then Credible Ring; then Chinese Moon. We called up some bars, got the names of some clubs, but as soon as we explained what we wanted to do they hung up or refused or made some lame excuse. There was only one option. We said to Duncan, ask your dad if we can set up a window display. We'll dress the mannequins and record these tapes and have a musical window in Shettleston. It was like an installation, but a gig too, even though we could go and watch it ourselves. His dad didn't care, he said yes, he was drunk but he was a loving father, as far as I could see, even though Duncan felt embarrassed and obviously at home things were a bit strained.

Everyone got to dress their dummy according to their tastes and personalities. Mine had an eyepatch and a khaki jumper with elbow pads and a pair of beige trousers and brown slip-on shoes and a black guitar – a Les Paul copy, it was all I could afford – and with this long black synthetic hair hanging down. Alan was on drums and he looked like a blue flame; his mannequin had all this make-up on, turquoise eyeliner and blue hair styled in an outrageous art-school quiff like Bryan Ferry on the first Roxy Music album but with a blazer and with grey trousers; it was like someone had set his head on fire or run it against sandpaper and his schoolboy mind had exploded. Findlay just looked like himself and he was the creepiest in a way; a blue tracksuit and a blonde bob and an exaggerated mouth holding a microphone like it was a gun he had just shot himself with. Duncan's mannequin had a black boiler suit with military tags and he was wearing one of those furry Russian hats with a red star and a sickle on the front with this artificial hair hanging down and with painted nails and a bass guitar like a Flying V that he had made out of cardboard and that had a speaker built into the middle of it attached to a rack of Walkmans that would just keep looping the same few tracks so that the music was muted through the window when you walked past and sounded like it was under water; like we were playing drowned in a lit-up aquarium in the middle of the night in Shettleston. The window ran for about a week but then the store owner got a sniff of it and ordered it closed down. Still: what a week. In my memory it seems to stretch all the way across the summer of 1983 and I can still see it now as we approached it in the early hours of the morning; the golden light coming from the window and spilling over the pavement like a perfect dream and then hearing the music as you approached, low, with shouts of people from streets away in the background and the occasional taxi flashing past; and then walking up to it and seeing ourselves, suddenly, or our chosen representatives, more like, in this world and the next, in a way, like it was one step towards immortality or forgetfulness or whatever you want to call it; and the music was good, it was like the sound you hear when you wake up in the night and for a brief moment you are a receiver, like you have forgotten your role as a human being and for one second you catch this strange, high tone, this tone that is communicating on a level that you can only tune into in certain states; and as I looked at the window and heard this long, sustained tone, this slow off-kilter drum beat, I thought to myself, when I die let me wake up here, let me reincarnate into this picture; let me live in this moment forever.

Although we only lasted for a week – and to tell you the truth we had never thought of anything happening beyond that – we generated a lot of interest. People started to get in touch, enquiring inside the store, which is part of the reason it got shut down, I believe: too many crazies got wind of it that had no money to spend on menswear or the summer's latest styles. Luckily Duncan's dad was taking names and forwarding letters – he was very supportive in that way, almost to the point of embarrassment – and so very quickly we became part of this nexus of creative people and weirdos and freaks; which suited us just fine. I got letters from artists obsessed by body parts; a dominatrix; strange reclusive homosexuals; a professor studying robotics at Coatbridge College; people with fantasies about phantom limbs; amputees; lonely CB radio hams . . . but the letter that was the most interesting was from Lucas Black from Memorial Device.

It was weird; it was like he was writing to himself, or to a part of himself, in a way. It was addressed to Mr Downie, who was the owner of the shop; Downie's, it was called. And it was written like he was petitioning part of his brain. I say that now, knowing what I know. At the time, though, it blew me away. It was like a love song.

Dear Mr Downie, it said; I'm quoting from memory here, I wish I still had the letter. Then it had this whole preamble where he laid out his qualifications; as if he had a right to get in touch; as if it was inevitable; like he was touching two wires together, just to get the spark. I remember one sentence in particular; *life has no meaning*, he said, *but it does have resonances, frissons, places, ghosts. Perhaps you would like to see some examples of my work*, he said. *If so, please find the attached* and he had included a photograph of a strange diorama that he had built himself; it looked like a volcano with lava pouring from the top; lava that looked more like feather boas running from the mouth of this papier-mâché mountain and around the four corners there were servitors – that's the word he used – strange mannequins; children with pale wooden faces and silver synthetic hair and sweatshirts with emblems on the front or logos like *I Love New York* or *Coatbridge College Athletics* or, the one I remember best of all, *California Good Guys*; all photographed in this strange half-light that was like a memory.

Of course I agreed to a meeting. By this point I was living in a top-floor flat in a block near Airdrie Academy. I was studying to be an electrician at a college in Coatbridge and I was sharing with some other bozos, just to afford to live away from home, which in reality was five minutes' walk away. Looking back I have no idea why I was in such a rush to leave home. Back then I fled every moment that was laid out in front of me. I could barely wait for the future, which now, to me, is a horrible thought.

I remember Lucas rang the buzzer and normally I had a thing where I would count to thirty before opening the door; that was how long it normally took for someone to walk up three flights of stairs. But this time I just opened it right away and stood at the top of the stairs and watched his approach and I always remember that when I walked out onto the landing I leaned on the banister to get a better look and I put my hand right through a spider's web; right bang through the centre of it. That's significant, I said to myself, I will remember that forever; and I still do, so it must have meant something. I could hear Lucas's footsteps down below. He had a distinctive gait, somewhat lopsided, but soft, like those big boots that Boris Karloff wore in the Frankenstein movie, padding was how I would describe it, deliberate padding, one step at a time, and before I even saw him I could see his silhouette on the wall as he made his way up the stairs and I half expected to see a pair of bolts coming out of his neck or for him to be holding a flaming torch, like he was climbing the staircase of some kind of Gothic castle, which is to say there was something automatic about it, yet deliberate – ominous, in other words – like a suicide scaling a cliff face.

I enjoyed that, he said to me when he reached the top and I wasn't sure what he was referring to but I said, good, anyway, and I held my arm out and I led him inside. He stood stock-still in the hallway and I wasn't sure if he was waiting for me to take his jacket but when I moved towards him he recoiled so we just stood there for a few moments facing each other. I suspect you're wondering why I've come here, he said, after what seemed like an endless silence but which was probably only a few seconds at most. It's about the mannequins, isn't it? I said. Yes, he said, yes, that's it. That would be correct. But what about the mannequins? he asked me. I guess you liked them, I said. I guess you recognised something in them or could relate to them or something like that and wanted to meet up. Yes, he said. I recognised them. But from where? And from when?

It was like having a conversation with the voice inside your head. I went to answer him again; he had me caught in this weird automatic response thing by this point and I started saying something about how maybe it was some kind of presentiment; like some kind of death in life; like you see yourself in the mannequins and it's like mourning your own death; standing over your own corpse; something like that. The point is there's some kind of recognition there. I made it up on the spot, basically; I mean he was demanding answers and suddenly I felt responsible for them. A presentiment, he said to me. Is that something that comes before sentiment? Is that a feeling that you are going to have a feeling? By this point I felt like my brain was being tied in knots. A presentiment is a prelude to a feeling, I told him. What's a nocturne, he asked me? It's a feeling for the night, I told him. That's it, he said, that's where I recognised them from. By this point he was freaking me out. I'm not cut out to be an artist at all, I said to myself.

Let's go through to the kitchen, I suggested. I needed to get out of the hallway; away from all these questions about questions. He walked behind me silently and pulled out a chair and sat on it. He looked at the kitchen table; it was a plain wooden table that we had found in a reclamation yard. That's like my bed, he said. You sleep on a table? I asked him. Of course not, he said. Don't be ridiculous. I made some coffee and we sat in silence some more. How do you know what you look like before you look in a mirror? he asked me. You don't, I said. What you see in the mirror is what you look like. At this point he sighed and held his head in his hands – which were enormous, by the way. I thought to myself, it's fucking Atlas come to smother the world.

When he took his hands away I noticed the big scar around the top of his head. They've had his head off, I remember thinking, what have they put in there? You play music? I asked him. You're in Memorial Device, aren't you? Memorial Device had just started at this point. What is a Memorial Device? he asked me. Are they like markers in the sand? They're a group, you're in them, I saw you play, I told him. Exactly, he said. Exactly. Then he just sat there. Is it like a pocket watch, he said after a while, a pocket watch that you have inherited? Is it like a gravestone? Or is it more like a Dictaphone, where you can record your memories? More like a Dictaphone, I would think, I said, though by this time I was feeling way out of my depth. Do your dolls have names? he asked me. Yes, they have our names, I told him; they're us, in a way. That makes sense, he said, and he nodded slowly to himself. Then he took a notebook out of his pocket. This is how I piece things together, he said, pointing towards the book. I give my dolls names, he said. I name them after parts of my brain. This one here, he said, handing me a picture of a young boy doll dressed in shorts and a T-shirt and with one arm raised, waving; this one I call *The Coast*. This is *The Gully*, he said, passing me a picture of an older male doll with a blank expression and straw-coloured hair photographed sat in a chair in a garden. Then there's *The Pathways*; I don't have a picture of him to hand. He's older still, in poor condition; though he dresses well. Then we have *The Mantle*, *The Lamps*, *The Lakes* and *The Moon*. He handed me a picture of *The Moon*; a small girl, reading from a book, with huge eyes and a sad expression on her face. This is what your brain looks like? I asked him. I think so, he said. I think so.

Would your dolls like to play a concert? he asked me. Where, I said, in your brain? He laughed at that, for the first time. I felt a sense of

76

relief. It'll happen there too, he smiled. But I was thinking more of a show with Memorial Device; maybe opening the show. What is a Memorial Device? I asked him. I think it's like a penknife, he said.

That's how we came to do the shows with Memorial Device. I still get people asking me about them; people who can't remember if they really happened or if they just imagined it. They say to me, do you remember that show where it was just the dolls standing there? I say to them, yeah, that was me; that was my group. They did an article about us in the local newspaper. There was a picture of us outside Alan and Findlay's parents' house with the band playing in the garden and us sat in front of them in the long grass in the summer. Of course they tried to make out that we were creeps or there was something sexually wrong with us. Maybe there was; why deny it? But it was short-lived. None of us really took to the lifestyle; the staying up late, the drinking. I would end up drunk on two cans and start crying. I fell in love with so many girls; it hurt so much. I was just too young and they wanted the older boys, the bad boys or the tough nuts and I would end up making a fool of myself. I couldn't understand why they would want to be with these boys smoking and drinking and treating them poorly. We could be a team, I would say to them; like dark-haired girls with black tights and dramatic black eye make-up; we could be a family. What did I know about family? All we had were the dolls, and they were taking over. Girls tried to get their photographs taken with them but we had a thing where we wanted to limit access, to keep them mysterious, so we would pack them away in boxes and seal them up as soon as each show was over and then go out and mingle with the crowd but of course no one recognised us, no one was interested, even though to us we were the brains behind it, the artists; superheroes in our own eyes. The final straw came for me when that girl Vanity claimed she was dating one of the dummies. And of course it wasn't me. She was dating Alan, she said, but not the real Alan, Alan's double, Alan with the blue flame hair and the schoolboy uniform. She talked Alan into letting her pose with the dummy, or rather her boyfriend did; that idiot. I couldn't believe it. Of course Alan didn't tell me and the first I found out about it was when I saw them pictured together in some dumb fanzine with a caption about true love or something like that. You're pimping us out, I told Alan. You're cheapening the whole deal. I felt strongly about it. That was when the cracks started to show.

Alan had become friendly with this Chinese guy from Petersburn. It was through some astrology course that they were both involved in. There was a Chinese takeaway that the father owned in Clarkston and one night there had been a disturbance – I'm not sure what, the details are still vague – but the upshot is that the Chinese guy's dad had been killed in some kind of incident in the back court. He had been hit with a slab and died on the spot.

Alan called me up. I wasn't there, he said. But I'm implicated. What do you know? I asked him. What did you see? But he just whimpered and hung up the phone. Then Duncan called me. Alan is in deep shit, he said. I know, I said. I just spoke to him. No, not Alan, he said, you don't understand, I mean Alan, Alan's double, the one with the blue hair; our drummer is what I'm talking about. He's out there running wild.

Someone had given the description of a person with blue hair and who was dressed like a schoolboy fleeing the scene. The band needs to split up, Alan said. We need them to go into hiding. We had a meeting at Duncan's parents' house; the four of us sat on the bed with a single bare light bulb illuminating the room and dirty clothes piled everywhere. Duncan's dad came into the bedroom, he wasn't quite drunk yet, just moderately sauced, and he asked us about the killing of the Chinese. I heard he was hit over the head with a paving stone, he said. Who is even strong enough to lift one of those, never mind bringing it down on some poor bugger's skull? We shook our heads and tried to picture the scene and the superhuman effort involved; all except Alan, who just sat there with his head in his hands. Things escalated from there. I demanded to see the dolls, they were kept in boxes in the basement of Findlay and Alan's house, and I insisted that we break them out and examine them. What for? Duncan asked. Are you looking for bloodstains? Maybe, I said. I might be. He looked at me like he was caught in the teeth of something; like a great mouth had opened up behind him and he had felt that first pressure on his flesh; that frisson just before the tooth penetrates the skin; which is the prerogative of young bodies, I realise now; that expectant shudder where doom itself seems like a fair exchange and more worthy of jaw-dropping awe and complete and utter surrender than total weeping despair. I felt like I was pregnant with every idea in the world and that none of them mattered.

We dug up the bodies – almost literally – and examined them for signs of wrongdoing. Aside from some beer stains and some cigarette burns – not to mention the smell of stale make-up, which rots and stinks like high heaven, believe me – there was no sign of anything untoward. If you were involved, I said to Alan, then you need to confess and stop passing it off on these poor victims, people who can't even answer back; though really I meant Findlay and Duncan and myself.

I was with him that night, he said. I was with the Chinese boy. But the killing had nothing to do with me. How could you even think that? How would I ever be capable of throwing that stone? You brought the group into it, I said. The drummer was seen fleeing the scene. Now we're all involved. God knows what I might do next or Duncan or Findlay. Now I can barely sleep for the sake of my shadow.

Then I realised something. Alan's doll was wearing a *California Good Guys* sweatshirt.

Wait a fucking minute, I said. Where the hell did he get that? At first no one reacted. What are you talking about? Findlay said. But then it dawned on them. Oh shit, Duncan said, when did you start dressing like that, Alan? That's not Alan, I said. That's Lucas from Memorial Device and although I didn't say it in my terror I was thinking that's Lucas's brain right there, oh shit, at this point he's *dreaming the entire thing.*

The next thing we knew the police were involved. They interviewed Alan as a witness. The story he gave was that they had been hanging out at the back of the Chinese restaurant; there was a Thursday-night astrology class that they had both attended and with it being so warm, who could forget that summer, they had decided to sit out back in the grass and go over their notes. Some local toughs had turned up; some hoods, basically, and there was some kind of confrontation; it wasn't clear what sparked it off but eventually one of the hoods picked up a rock and threw it and it missed Alan and his friend but smashed the glass on the back door of the restaurant, at which point Mr Chan appeared and began cursing them and threatening them with a mop. Before anyone knew it Chan's brothers had arrived alongside more local toughs – gangsters, who knows – till it was like there were two armies lined up on either side with Alan and his friend caught in the middle.

We were in no-man's land, Alan said. Then what happened? the police asked him. I saw someone pick up a slab, he said. A silhouette, nothing more. And I saw his arms go back and he threw it through the air so that it was spinning like a discus or a piece of shot. And I saw it catch Mr Chan on the side of the head. And I heard a sickening crack. And I saw him fall to the ground. And it looked like his head was caved in. Then what happened? they said. I saw this thing emerge, he said. This guy, this thing; I thought I recognised him. We have a group, we play music, he explained, but it's like an art thing where we have models on stage miming – well, not exactly miming but pretending to be us, in a way.

What has that got to do with anything? they asked him. That's the thing, he said. I thought I saw one of the dolls rising up from out of the ground. Like in a vampire movie, the police asked him, like in a zombie flick? Yes, he said, like in a horror movie, and I saw it glide between the two parties; it seemed to be floating, he said. And it was like it was lit up from below. What did it do? the police asked him. Nothing, he said. That's the whole point. It did nothing. But everyone saw it, he insisted, and when they saw it they fled, screaming. What happened then? they asked him. I watched it for a while, he said, and it kept on moving until it was just a dot on the horizon.

The hoods were never identified; no one would talk. Alan's friend was too traumatised to be a reliable witness. The Chinese gangs claimed they chased the hoods away themselves. But there were reports from bystanders that a schoolkid with a shock of blue hair had floated across the park and down the glen and disappeared like ball lightning over the horizon.

It was Skidz, Alan had told us as we stood around the box. I saw him, it was Skidz. Who is Skidz? I asked him. Skidz is me, he said, and he started crying again. Skidz is me. We looked at the doll in the box, with its legs folded beneath it, its eyes made up like an Egyptian god, its shock of blue hair.

I never found out how Skidz came to be wearing a jumper from one of Lucas's dolls; it was all too surreal and complicated and confused and I couldn't bring myself to ask, that's presuming there was any truth to be found in the first place. But secretly I think we were all impressed. Alan had come alive; he was an artist where the rest of us were just a bunch of lip-syncers. I looked at my own doll and I had no idea what my name was. We cancelled our upcoming shows. There was some talk of us going on tour with Memorial Device but who knows if that would ever have come to anything. Occasionally I would see Lucas in the city centre in Airdrie or one of the other guys in the band but they never acknowledged me or acted as if they knew who I was. We went back to the life sentence, which is Airdrie, for better or for worse. Duncan's dad died of heart failure and Duncan lived there with his mother; we lost touch but I heard he still lives there and that there are still no lampshades to be seen anywhere. Findlay became involved in the Church. Sometimes when I was shopping in town I would see him standing at the checkout area in Safeway collecting for charity. He was the kind to talk animatedly and with genuine interest to dotty old dears for hours; what a waste of an intellect.

But Alan was the one that got away. He left Airdrie for good. Like Skidz he floated away like a ghost or a UFO to who knows where, but every time I make a withdrawal from Airdrie Savings Bank or check a book out of the library or walk up South Bridge Street in the afternoon with its window displays and boarded-up shops, it's like I see myself from the outside for a second and I think my own ghost is out there, somewhere, my own dummy, looking down at me with his one eye and shaking his head.

11. Poor Condition With Promo Stickers: *an informative list of records that Big Patty had and that his ex-girlfriend Maya wanted back after 'the split'.*

Archie Shepp (on Actuel) – You called me in Airdrie while Memorial Device were on tour and asked me if I wanted you to buy this for me.

Louis Moholo – I bought my own copy of this record so you should have two right now.

Great Society – Found it in Edinburgh at Bruce's (by myself, same trip as John Fahey, *Voice of the Turtle*).

Silly Sisters – Found at Virgin in Glasgow.

Big Brother . . ., *Cheap Thrills* – Found at Listen in Glasgow.

Steeleye Span – Only fair that I should have at least one. Your decision.

Julie Tippetts, *Sunset Glow* – We had two copies, remember?

Linda & Sonny Sharrock – *Paradise*

Morton Feldman – dbl LP

Muhal Richard Abrams – Can't remember the label, Nessa? I think I am missing another record from this label. Shelley Hirsch is on it?

At least one International Artists record – i.e. Golden Dawn. This is more of a plead. You know I will never find one of these records again and I would never pay £100 for a record.

Don Cherry, *Mu Parts 1&2* – Found in 23rd Precinct in Glasgow.

June Tabor – Should be two. I found in Belfast, the other here (I think there is a kitty on the front?).

Miles Davis, *On the Corner* – Didn't I find at Bruce's? Could be wrong.

Anthony Braxton – There were a lot I bought at Virgin, seemed like all I was buying for a while.

Jimmy Giuffre – One of the older recordings. Maybe we found on the trip to Wales. Your decision.

Octavia Butler book – Sorry, just thought of this.

Tim Buckley – I specifically remember finding some in London, i.e. *Lorca*, *Happy Sad*. They were in poor condition with promo stickers on front.

12. A Likely Candidate for Sex for Marriage for Kidnap for Another
Kind of Future Altogether: *Valerie Morris takes Remy to see the
gypsies of Calderbank and to get their fortune read when they were
nothing but dumb kids.*

I moved to Airdrie when I was sixteen years old fresh out of school
and with my head full of prophecies some of which were realised
some of which came true in ways that I could never have predicted
and some of which hang over me still not so much like a sword which
any idiot knows is a stand-in for thought, for cogitation, for division
essentially but more like an axe, a blunt axe that threatens to pound
the future into the shape of the past which is inchoate, a blob, a thing
with lots of limbs and tentacles and feet pointing this way and that
where if you're lucky you're able to extricate a single thread, a lone
noodle, a sorry umbilical, a curled pubic hair that might prove that it
was yours in the first place.

We went to see a gypsy I remember that much. This was at the
Calderbank Gala Day. She was set up at the far end of the football
field at the very edge of the village in a field that was only accessible
via a narrow pavement next to a busy road where the cars would blow
dust up into your face and brambles would get stuck to your tights
and where once my grandfather and I had come across enormous
footprints in the earth that were the size of Bigfoot or the Abominable
Snowman.

Because of various superstitions not to say a collective commitment
to the suffering future being the same as the suffering past the
gypsies were not allowed to set up inside the village boundaries but
had instead been relegated to this borderland which was the only

fun in town once a year and where despite the opprobrium of our parents most of the young people ended up by late afternoon where we would make our way past all of the stalls that lined the main street, the Tunnock's tea cakes, the old whisky barrels piled high with tangerines, the stalls with the model airplanes, the badges, the ice cream cones, the smell of chocolate and cheese and hot dogs and the pale blue skies with little puffs of cloud like the vapour trails of daredevils and the smell of gunpowder in the air and gasoline and open fires and in the distance the hazy points of colour that were young men on motorbikes speeding along the summer hills the sun so close that it would curl your hair and turn it fair and there would be young men breathing fire arranged around the perimeter of the football pitch swallowing petrol and letting the flames dance on their tongues and as you passed them they looked you up and down as if you were a likely candidate, for sex, for marriage, for kidnap, for another kind of future altogether.

Me and Remy had been going to the Gala Day for years but it must have been 1979 in fact I'm sure it was because it was the same year that I volunteered to man an exhibition by ASTRA the Association in Scotland To Research into Astronautics that ran in Airdrie Arts Centre and right now I just looked up the date in a book and it all ties in.

For the past year we had speculated about the fortune teller who sat in a red-and-white-striped box that looked like a Punch & Judy show and whose skin I'm not kidding you was green or almost green and who we used to joke was just a torso, a head and shoulders kept alive by wires and chemicals and of course we were in love back then or as much in love as it's possible to be at that age and we would challenge each other you know about the extent of our love. Would you love me if I was just a brain in a jar? Remy would ask me. Of course, I would say. I would kiss the jar goodnight and put a blanket over it and have it on my bedside table and fall asleep next to it. But what if I didn't want to go asleep? he would ask me. What if I wanted to read? I would prop a book up in front of you, I would say, then I would guess how long it took you to read both pages and I would turn it to the next two. But what if you were tired, he would ask me, what if you got the timing wrong? How would I even be able to read in the first place with no eyes in my head? In that case I would read to you, I said, in the hope that you might hear me. They say that hearing is the last to go, he said. But that might be in the presence of ears.

We could see the gypsy looking at us from across the field, The Corpseless Head we called her and we had our dog with us well not our dog exactly but a huge German shepherd called Judy that belonged to someone else in the village but who came to see Remy each day when he was a boy and who would spend the day with him before heading back to his owners for the night and there is a famous picture of us from that day, famous to me anyway, where we are both sitting propped up against the side of a shed with Judy towering over us like a benevolent giant from a children's novel which might as well have been *Anne of Green Gables* now for all that time cares.

I think Remy's father took the picture. He was an oddball alright, quite literally in the end but he didn't care for village gossip or standard ways of thinking and he was brave to me even though he was weedy and scrawny and his face was permanently screwed up like when he looked at you he was staring straight into the sun and of course years later I read the essay that had got him dismissed, the one about fate, and I thought about that photograph and how it captures a moment and how you can return to it with thought all over again so maybe he was talking sense but I don't know, photographs will have you believing anything.

I don't know whose idea it was to have our fortune read. You know how things gradually build up inside your head and things that once seemed frightening become a goad and then a pleasure and then eventually blasé? Back then we were on the tipping point between terror and goad. What a place to be! I wish the adult world was still frightening and unknown. But I can't even remember what she said now which is ridiculous so I've no way of knowing if it came true, which might be for the best, though I think more things came true for Remy than they did for me in the end. I can only remember us making our way towards her crossing this invisible line that separated the gypsies from everyone else and then coming back again. That's as clear as day. What happened in between is just an empty space in my brain. The only other thing I can remember is that we bought one of those spicy kebabs that they would make from a caravan with a full green pepper on the top and the flatbread packed with meatballs and lettuce and sauce and cheese. I had never bitten a whole pepper in my life and I knew if my dad could only see me, if he could've looked down from heaven, he would have shaken his head in protest, which made it taste all the more delicious and painful.

13. Kitty-Catting into the Night Burglarising My Dreams: *Johnny McLaughlin meets Big Patty in Airdrie or is it Belfast.*

There are two types of people in this world (my dad explained to me), persons and non-persons. And Michael is a non-person. And he's fly too. When I first met him I could tell by the way he introduced himself, you know, alright pal, all of this stuff, I knew he was a Bengal Lancer right away.

Upstairs we could hear Michael pacing back and forth, crossing the ceiling and turning back, again and again. He's nervous, my dad said. I don't blame him. It was like living inside a headache. Michael had been a regular visitor (or a regular hideaway) for years now, coming and spending a week or a month here and there, culminating in a three-month stint in the summer of 1983.

Slowly our routines began to mirror each other. The entrance to the secret annexe was in the corner of my bedroom and I was often woken in the night by the sound of Michael crossing the room to use the toilet (or to head out for a late-night walk). He only left the house at night (for fear of being recognised or captured or assassinated, whatever it was) and as soon as I heard him going down the stairs (slowly, playing each step for maximum portent, or so it seemed, like a cat burglar in reverse, kitty-catting into the night, burglarising my dreams of breaking out myself and making off with them, scot-free) I would climb out of my bed and watch as he made his way down the driveway (now furtive), his thin silhouette giving way to the shadow of the gatepost and the fog and then he was gone (like a pot of ink) into the night. I would lie in bed and imagine his route in my mind, walking it myself in exhaustive detail, picturing the moment where he would stop near a gate on the old Colliertree Road (a gate that led onto a path that opened onto a field, a path that is no longer there) and in the distance the lights of the industrial estate, twinkling on the horizon (like a dream within a dream), and often it was like I crossed a threshold, not between sleep and waking, not between death and life (nothing as dramatic as that), but I would emerge (or more properly submerge) into a place where I was the one that was being walked, where Michael's walks became forced nocturnal sojourns against my will, where I gave up my mind, or rather my mind was given, given over to the pursuit of a pitiless phantom that was impossible to make out against the dark of my dreams, but who dragged me round the streets at night and made me stare at closed doors and lit-up third-storey windows and smoke cigarettes and be absent from myself for at least a third of the night (which when you add it up is a potential theft of a third of a third of my life, in other words 0.111111111, where the zero is me and the point is the threshold and the ones are the footsteps in the night and when he came back home he would wake me again as he crept through my room, in effect reversing the third of a third that I had spent dreaming, so that it felt more like 111111111.0, with zero as the cupboard, this secret space, the point as the entrance to my parents' house and the ones as the automatic action of my brain as I dreamed him home, like inverted fish hooks or exclamation marks that refused a point).

I heard about Big Patty before I met him. At the gardening I worked beside a guy called David Nesbitt who would pick me up on the kind of bright, autumn mornings that felt like conduits into the past although back then I was inevitably too tired (or too hung over) or just too tied up in the future to notice the way the past was already impinging on the present. David would drive us to whatever job we had that day, dilapidated stately homes, secret bungalows in the shadow of tall hedges, walk-up apartments in the East End with patches of overgrown grass and wild flowers, Victorian semis with red-chipped driveways and yellowed lawns (dreamy cottages with abandoned bicycles and trees as tall as my expectations of the next year and the year after that). It was David's business and it was going well. I'm taking on someone else, he told me. I've worked with him before. This guy can dig holes like no one else, he said. I once saw him dig a five-foot hole in less than twenty minutes. I looked around and all I could see was the top of his head sticking out with this battered top hat on. He's a real character, he said, a musician. He's a vegetarian plus I think he's a Hindu or a Buddhist or something like that.

Patty actually wore that battered top hat while he was gardening (he looked more like a gravedigger). Plus he wore a jumper with only one arm in the sleeve, so that it looked like his other arm had withered and died. I'm always too hot or too cold, he said, so I thought I would wear half a jumper and that would solve it (why don't you just wear a tank top, I thought to myself, but I said nothing). When we were gardening we would have discussions about music. I've never been to a gig in my life, David told us (we were working in the garden of a semi-detached council house in Grahamshill Avenue that was occupied by a drama teacher called Miss Sweden). Music sounds different when you play it live, David said. Doesn't it? It doesn't sound as professional. Who needs it to sound professional? Patty said. The wilder the better. Who do you like? Patty asked me. I like Dylan, I said. What does she sing? David asked. You've never heard of Bob Dylan? Patty burst, and he dropped his spade in the dirt and sat down on a rock and lit a cigarette. What songs does he sing? David asked.

'Mack the Knife', stuff like that? 'Blowin' in the Wind', Patty said. 'The Times They Are a-Changin''. No, David said, leaning his chin on his spade, sorry. I never heard of them. What about AC/DC? I asked him. You must know AC/DC. Do they sing the one about the train? David said. I fucking give up, Patty said. You are a total space cadet.

Patty had no television in his house and David couldn't get over it. What do you do for entertainment? David asked him. I read, Patty said. I listen to music. I play guitar. I paint. I cook. I play chess. I walk the streets at night. How long would it take you to read an average book? David asked him. How many pages? Patty said. Say, three hundred pages, David said. In that case, one night. No way, David said. That's not possible. Okay, two nights at most, Patty said. Have you ever read a book? Patty asked him. Once, David said. I read the first thirty-three pages then I forgot what I had read and so I had to start all over again. Then the same thing happened and I thought fuck this.

The first time I saw Patty play with Memorial Device I was blown away (I didn't know what to expect). I talked Michael into coming with me. It'll be dark in the club, I told him. Plus there'll be no one there who would ever know who you are. It's a whole other scene. Plus these guys are like John Coltrane on guitar, I said (back then that's what they were saying, that it was like free jazz or improvised music only with guitar, bass and drums). They were playing at a club in Coatbridge. Coatbridge had more live venues than Airdrie, but rather than get a train or a taxi or jump on the bus I suggested we walk there, leaving as soon as it got dark (which honestly was about four o'clock at that time of year) and dropping in at a few choice bars along the way (although I say choice when really I mean terrible,

desperate and kind of depressing). We had a drink in The Barrel
Vaults on the main street and then in The Staging Post (and then in
The Tudor Hotel) and by the time we got to Coatdyke (to The Five
Keys) Michael was acting a little crazy. He ordered two whiskies
and a pint of heavy. One drink at a time, the landlord said. What
the fuck is this, Nazi Germany? Michael said. A few heads turned.
I paid for a whisky and a pint of heavy and I led him to a table near
the door (I was thinking we might need to make a quick escape). The
bar smelled of urine (it was unmistakable) as if after hours they all
got their dicks out and pissed all over the floor and soiled themselves
and passed out and woke up the next morning and went back home
to their hateful wives with no memory (it had that kind of vibe), like
a prison cell or a hospital or a dosshouse (or a care home), a place
where you could just go on the floor and people would mop up after
you, a place to escape every decision you had ever made, except one,
the decision to piss on them all (which is something I understood,
especially in the mornings, when directing my piss, into the toilet or
into the sink, felt like the only thing I had control over, as my heart
raged and my brain beat). This place stinks of piss, I told Michael,
and he looked at me, looked at me like he was seeing right through
me, and he said to me, is that all you have to say? No, I said. I have
plenty more to say. But you're in no state to hear it. He drained his
whisky. Then he sat there like a scrawny stick of dynamite. What
do you think? I said. About what? he said. About it all, I said. All of
what? he said. You need to speak up, pal. I bought him another drink.
At first I thought that the landlord was going to refuse to serve us but
he acted as if he had no memory of what had happened so I ordered
us two whiskies each (I don't know why, maybe I saw the precipice
from a distance and decided to accelerate towards it in the hope that
we could leap the chasm altogether or failing that be wiped out in a

split second on the cliffs) and when I brought them back to the table
Michael grunted and said something about dropping little bombs on
ourselves (torpedoing ourselves, I think he said) and he laughed, this
constricted, hollow laugh, like an overflow on a drain, like he had
spilled himself, accidentally, and I thought of a submarine with a
leak (scraping the bottom of the ocean) spilling air up into the sea.

There was one more bar to go before we hit Coatbridge (a family bar
just next to the fire station). By this point Michael was completely
steaming (he was looking around himself like he was taking his
first steps in fairyland). Oh my god, he said. Did you fucking see
that? There were girls walking past (it was Saturday night, they
were dressed to kill). There was a bouncer at the door. I've got my
eye on you, Michael said, as we walked past him. What did you just
say? he said. Michael had this way of not moving his head when he
was talking that was extremely unnerving and he sort of walked
backwards with his head perfectly balanced (like rewinding a
videotape of a puppet or a wooden doll, like his head was on a string
or on the end of a fishing line and was being reeled back in) until he
was standing right in front of the bouncer (whose bald head reflected
the light from the sign like a birthmark or a tattoo of South America).
You're a chib merchant, Michael said. A squib-packer, a chatterina.
I recognise you, he said. I've never seen you before in my life, the
bouncer said. But if I was you I would take care. Oh, I'll take care
alright, Michael said. I'll take care of business. Not tonight you won't,
the bouncer said. Not with that attitude. With that attitude you're
going straight home. What are you going to do, Michael said, call
me a cab? It's not home time yet, the bouncer said, but when you're
ready I'll drag you up the street by your hair like a gypsy. There was
a moment of silence between them (a split second where their moon

faces were like a pair of empty brackets ( ) in a crime report or a Russian novel). I looked between them like a telescope where you're gazing into time as well as space. If you could stare to the end of the world (I thought to myself) this is all you would end up with.

14. Scatman and Bobbin the Dynamic Duo: *Big Patty's secret sidekick Miriam McLuskie is on the razz with Ross Raymond.*

Is the tape running? Oh my god, this is like making an album. It's never gonna pick your voice up from over there. You'll need to move closer. Okay, whatever.

So I met Patty during his satanic period. He thought he was the devil of Airdrie, the bogeyman in his big cadaver hat like he had just leaped out of a cardboard coffin which in reality was what his house was like or his room was like more accurately. He had this theory about central heating which was like his theory about bugs which was like his theory about urine which was like his theory about sweat; he was always sweating, sweaty hands sweaty palms, so that on those recordings where people praise his slide guitar saying it was like Blind Willie Johnson it's really the sound of the guitar getting away from him like he had lubricated his dick too much and couldn't get a grip on it. Oh my god, he had a room above The Capocci Man on the high street in Airdrie, I'll never forget it, that dump is singed on my brain, a single room that didn't necessarily smell of ice cream more like stale yogurt which was what his bedclothes smelled like. He had all of these glass bottles filled with medicinals he would call them that looked like bottles of milk gone bad but with black herbs rotting in them and olive oil or more realistically urine. He drank his own urine, I'm dead sure of that. If you asked him about it he would just say, give us a kiss. That said it all. I was like that, no thank you. And his windows were always open. He had a single radiator and he claimed that allowing the air to circulate meant it would work more efficiently despite the evidence of everyone sitting on the edge of his bed freezing their balls off. All of his books had

bookmarks in them; sometimes just drink coasters or torn pieces of
cardboard but bookmarks nonetheless always in the exact or really
the estimated middle. It's important to separate the beginning from
the end, Patty would say. Then he would take a drink from one of his
foul concoctions and stare out the open window like he was trying
to hypnotise the horizon or something. How like a book a body is,
he would say. I might be misquoting, essentially, but you get the
drift. Then he would take a volume down from the shelves and turn
it on its side so you could see the bookmark between the pages. It
looks like an ass crack, he would say. I would be like that to him, not
really, an ass has a hole in the middle and he would look at me like
I had just made the worst joke in the world and then he would laugh
and then he would get up and pace around the room. I would be like
that, fuck this, but I stayed with him anyway.

What are we drinking, by the way? An IPA? Fuck is an IPA? Tastes
like melon juice.

I was his secret sidekick, I admit that much, although sometimes
I thought of myself as his sense of permission, like an imp in his
pocket, a wee imp keekin' oot his pocket. It was never anything
sexual. Naw. No way. He was never my type. My taste in men is
quite conventional, depressingly ordinary, murder, actually. I have
no kinks and zero foibles but outside of the bedroom or the restaurant
or the holiday home I'm all ears if you know what I mean. I thought
of myself as a magician, to tell you the truth, someone who had
mastered the most elementary act of magic which did you know is
the practice of invisibility. I could infiltrate any circle, put up with
any behaviour, indulge any eccentricity yet it would never get to me
or affect me on any level. I looked dead ordinary, you wouldn't look

twice at me in the street, but I thought of myself as a punk, as a real punk not as a picture postcard. I was like invisible ink written in the corner of the room so that it would take a candle and some patience to even see me there. I would go on these nights out where people would do pure outrageous things in front of me because I was more like a voice in their head or a pair of eyes in their head more properly, a pair of silent eyes that would watch and wouldn't comment and wouldn't care or judge or report back either way but who at least saw them. Later on I heard that our nickname was Scatman and Bobbin, the dynamic duo. I was pure like that, whatever! That says it all.

You gottae have a can. That's what my faither would say, sitting on the front steps at eleven o'clock in the morning drinking a can of Tennent's, he'd be like that; you gottae have a can. Got any more in the fridge? What is this brand? Never heard of it.

I got to know Lucas, I did. I always felt that we got on dead well. Not that we understood each other. I wouldn't say that. But that's my point. We made no attempt to understand each other if you understand what I mean. In fact we were more like figments of each other's imagination. Right there was this one time where Memorial Device were playing in Kilmarnock, don't ask me why, it was some pure bikers' bar and Richard had phoned them up out of the blue and asked them if they were interested in some live music and oh my god the owner had agreed without even hearing a fucking note of their music and said that it was lucky actually as another group had been booked to play on the same weekend and why not make a night of it. I offered to drive them down, I had an estate car at the time which I got from working a job for a petroleum company entering meaningless data five days a week, meaningless fucking data while

99

listening to music on the headphones, it was a piece of pish. On the day of the show it was pishing down, it was April and it was pishing down, the kind of spring rain that really stings and that makes you feel like you're made of tin. A wee tin solider getting battered aboot in the rain . . . I remember being caught in a pishing storm, not this one but another one when I was much younger travelling back from the huts at Carbeth where we had been fishing for the day and missing the last bus and my mate telling me that it would take two days to walk back but when we eventually flagged a lift in this pishing rain, this rain that pure battered off ma body like a bell, like a rusty bell, and that generated a tone, a low drone (nnnnnnnnnnhhhhhhh like Memorial Device like hhhhhhhnnnnnnnnnn), and that had me thinking oh my god I'm hollow, I'm like a milk bottle or a wine glass, and in the end it only took thirty-five minutes to drive back home and for years afterwards I would be like that, oh my god remember being stranded in Carbeth, several days from civilisation ya muppet? And he'd be like that, remember ringing like a bell in the rain, he would say, remember being empty like a trash can ya plamf?

Do you even know what a plamf is? A plamf is somebody that sniffs dirty knickers.

And as we drove to Kilmarnock in this pishing rain, this pishing rain that was more like a memory than something that had simply been remembered do you get where I'm coming from, it was like the same rain falling again and the car felt like my body and with the rain falling down on it and Memorial Device like my mind, you know that song, *the red light was my baby, the green light was my mind*, although I don't know if it's possible to split your mind up into four, into two possibly but into four seems like a pointless division, what

100

is the point, and as we crossed the moors everyone was dead silent, no one said a fucking thing, no one said zip, do you feel me, and there was no sound except for this rain on the roof that sounded like a hand drum or a heartbeat and I felt pure like a witch with her black cats on the way to a seance.

Oh my god, I'm getting pished already, is this strong? Seven per cent, is that strong? Fuck it. We're in the beer game now.

We arrived in Kilmarnock just as the sun was going down though really it felt more like some cunt had stashed it in a black sock and tossed it into an empty parking lot. Remy was like that, why is it so dark? Lucas was like that, what a question. Why am I rolling my eyes, he said, why is my breath passing through my lungs? Richard was like that, why do I have a huge pain in my ass? I was pure like that to myself, it's like the fucking Three Stooges only the Three Iggys is more like it. Patty said nothing. Dead typical. That was his style. Dead typical. He would separate himself from the rest, aloof, sit silent in the back of the car and never make a move to lift a fuckin' finger or help carry in the amps. If there was food going and most times even that was a rarity he would eat apart from everyone else, either that or he would sneak a sly Pot Noodle when no one was looking. Fuckin' Pot Noodles man, best hangover cure known to man.

I took some flyers, I had printed them up at my own expense. I can't remember what it said now, something about outlaws or feral rock or something like that, I wrote it myself, and I headed into town and handed them out in a few bars including this poncey French-themed bar in Kilmarnock, that was a fucking joke, seriously, in Kilmarnock? They're fucking barbarians in Kilmarnock, give me a fucking break, they're fucking cannibals in Kilmarnock, though they all eat snails mind, that's no problem, they eat fucking slugs too, and they made me pick up all of the flyers I had left on the tables, this woman came out and began yelling at me and halfway through I was like that, I just picked up a wad of them and pure threw a handful of them over my shoulder, fuckin' scattered them everywhere.

You don't crush your can when you finish drinking it? What's that about?

The thing is, right, seriously, and this is between us, right, Lucas had a brother, or so they said. Seriously. Okay listen, seriously, the story I heard was that they were identical twins but of course they were never seen together, you feel me, which led to the theory, the conspiracy theory, that there was really only one Lucas but he pretended or more likely honestly couldn't fuckin' remember that he was sometimes the other brother or even that the other brother sometimes turned up and pretended to be Lucas. Think about it. Fucking think about it. It was feasible because of course Lucas had little to no memory of what had happened at previous gigs or even on previous days outside of what he had written in his notebook so all it would take for either brother was a quick fuckin' glance at the notes and he was immediately up to speed and of course any slip-up or gaps in continuity would immediately be put down to Lucas's illness, the water on his brain, the tragic tributary, that's what he called it once, that's how he described it to me, me and him we were like that back then, it was like it was a delta, that's the way he described it, you get me, and of course I thought of all the blues songs, like 'High Water Everywhere', which was sung by Charley Patton, I don't know if you know that, and of course 'Texas Flood' and 'Flood Water Blues' and 'God Moves On the Water', which was by Blind Willie Johnson, do you know that one, it's a classic and of course 'Goin' Down to the River' by Mississippi Fred McDowell, that's a classic right there if you ask me, and then I thought of Jimmy Reed's 'Little Rain', no rivers without rain, after all, no rivers without rain, no siree, Jimmy wasn't lying man and of course I thought of the damage a little pishing rain can do.

You know what, it isn't melon, it's grapefruit, innit? Grapefruit juice that gets you pished. Bring it on.

Then I thought about how people sang about the Mississippi Delta like it was a snake or more like a basketful of snakes all snaking their way up north through the 1920s and the 1940s, those were its years. Snakes live in decades, someone told me that, do you realise that, the way humans live in years or months or minutes like snakes mark time in terms of decades. They move through time slowly is what that means, like trees though to them it's quickly but it takes a decade for their conception of themselves, do you get me, for their understanding of their existence to come together which is weird but it's no coincidence that drunks take at least ten years to wake up to themselves, ten years of living like a reptile, we've all been there, I'll drink to that, plus Lucas had those wide eyes placed far apart almost as if they were disappearing around the side of his face, you know what I mean, and of course everyone commented on his big feet like flippers and so white, seriously, pure white, which despite what everyone says is nothing like snow but more like yogurt, glutinous. I've got a theory about white. This is my own theory not Patty's. Pure white has a glutinous quality like egg white or like pus squeezed from the eye of a snake. White is a container, is what I'm trying to say, it contains things, bacteria, life, enzymes, it's the opposite of blank, in my opinion, whereas snow is empty like the end of things which is why it's so romantic. Have you ever had a white beer? They call it Weiss beer. But don't get me started on white, I could be here all night. Oh my god now I'm spinning, seriously it's all this remembering.

The thing with the concert in Kilmarnock was that after the support band played, some bunch of mental cases, an old man, an idiot, a middle-aged woman and a creepy-looking guy who together made a noise like a fighter jet tunnelling into a mountainside in the fog at 120 miles an hour which was good while it lasted but was even better when it ended and you had a chance to think about it if you know what I mean, after they had cleared the equipment off the stage and everything was awkward and silent and no one had bothered to put any music on Lucas came up to me, we had barely spoken all evening even though I was unofficially their driver and tour manager and publicist and long-sufferer, let's be honest, and though I couldn't see his big white feet – he was wearing Dr Martens – I could see a large vein in his neck that was as blue as glacier water and that made me think okay maybe snow isn't completely empty, maybe it's just the end before the beginning, do you know what I mean, and before I could even elaborate on that he asked me if I knew how to knit and again before I could be pure like that, what the hell are you talking about are you fucking kidding me you sexist, he was like that, have I ever given you one of my magic squares? I'm like that, no, you have not given me one of your magic squares, though really I was like that, what the hell do knitted magic squares have to do with my own life, and then he took this little knitted square out of his pocket, it was coloured turquoise and brown and baby blue and pale blue and dark brown and had strands coming off it like a fucking Space Invader and he said, here it's a magic square, it will make all your dreams come true. I was like that, oh my god that's mental.

Will we have one more? You gottae have a can. My dad used to play the guitar using a can for a slide. It was mental. Okay, one more for the road, I don't normally drink during the day.

I barely remember the rest of the night to be honest with you. The concert was good, they came up with this song where Lucas enumerated, is that a word, e-num-er-ated all of the subjects of songs, I can't remember exactly how many there were but there were songs about falling in love and songs about being pure enamoured and songs about meeting and songs about falling out of love and songs about being all tore up and then there were songs about despair, complete despair (I may be making that one up myself, I can't remember), songs about God, songs about existential lifestyles, songs about the seasons, about autumn leaves and flowers in the springtime, songs about animals, about wanting to be an animal or acting like one, songs that were more like social commentary, trivial songs, songs about memory, songs about the past and about the future and songs that would bring the two together, songs that were written out of guilt alone, songs that were meant to salvage guilty feelings or salve guilty feelings, one or the other, the PA was cheap, who knows, songs about time, like when will you or what have you or if you or now you or can't you, songs about songs, singing about singing, which isn't singing at all if you ask me, singing about plants growing up or the vagaries of weather, is that a word, vague-ar-ies, and there were more songs, for sure, he listed them all, or it seemed as if he did, and then he had this whole thing where he acted as if he had exhausted songs, he shrugged and he shivered and he cried – it was like rockabilly to me – and then he went into this thing where he started spouting nonsense, like he was having a conversation with himself and talking rubbish, just crazy stuff that made no sense and that's when it struck me. He's singing about nothing. Fuck me. He's writing a song about nothing. It's the only thing that songs haven't been written about. D'you get me? And it was like a love song, it was like he was singing a song to something that was so lacking in love that even the mention of its name would bring it back to life and we would all notice it and fall in love with it like a prom queen or a movie star. Oh god every bit of nonsense was like a poem to nothing from the depths of his heart to the depths of his heart. It's all nonsense, I said to myself, it's all bollocks, then I imagined Lucas lifting me up in his arms, I imagined the pure freezing rivers running through his veins, I thought of his feet, pure writhing like fish out of water.

After the gig we ended up at Patty's flat above The Capocci Man with the windows open to the night sky and I thought of wolves and silence and distant lights and the sound of your heartbeat in the empty cavity of your chest and all that mad stuff and it sounded like the greatest love song that had ever been written but when I turned around to tell Lucas that I could still hear what he had sung and that the open window and the sounds of the street were *playing the same song* he looked at me with a horrified expression, oh my god, like I was some child he had pure given birth to and that he had never known about and that had turned up on his doorstep looking for money and a place to stay, so that I was like that, never mind, I'm talking shit, never mind, and he seemed happy with that and I went next door and lay down on the bed, a bed that was covered with other people's coats, and fell asleep and woke up early the next morning and let myself out and walked around the streets like it was after the end of the world and imagined how I could possibly go on, how the fuck could I possibly go on, which is something I ask myself every day, these days, even while the rest of me pure ignores it and gets on with it anyway. Is that tape still running? Turn it off, I don't want to talk about it any more. Turn it off. One more for the road and then it's

15. The Day of the Frozen Vampires: *the day that Lucas died was The Day of the Silver Sun Ruth Turner says in a letter to the author about the past and the future and about how we invent endings every last damn one of us and how Nothing is Anchored Any Longer.*

We think we're walking into the future. We fool ourselves! But every last damn one of us is walking straight into the past. A shadow passes a low wooden fence. It is wearing a hat and dressed, already, for another time. The pace isn't hurried. It's a pace that says, okay, I give in, I accept it. The movement of this spectre, this would-be ghoul, seems self-chosen, willed from the deepest, most stubborn depths of itself. I heard someone describe it as funereal. Have you ever been to a funeral? The cars are under instructions to remain just under twenty miles per hour. And the mourners too move quite deliberately, instinctually, like a flock of birds flying towards their death in the heart of the sun.

The day of his death, which might as well have been the night of his death, was a day of intense contradictions. It was like a ghost movie, a vampire flick. The sun turned white. The fog rose up, fell back down again, and rose back up. It was like walking through dry ice. I woke up in the morning and I thought, oh shit! All of my pretentiousness, all of my Gothic fantasies, all of my reading is coming true. I cursed every damn book in my library. Then I smoked a cigarette on the window ledge, looking down from three storeys at the street below. The whole damn world is in mourning, I said to myself. This is worse than a Kenneth Grant book. It's more like some pulpy French garbage.

I always had this theory. Men die, women exit stage left. Men's deaths are heavy. Have you ever seen a male corpse? Talk about

108

a full stop! You can't argue with that. The lower jaw becomes distended. The lips widen. The skin hardens. It's like a toad slithering out of the mouth and then taking its place on the top of the skull, an inscrutable toad, a grotesque, undeniable toad, a prehistoric fact. Compare the deaths of women. Women die every day. They lose blood every month. Their blood turns to milk. Their bodies are incubators as much as coffins. Men's deaths look right back at you, dare you to challenge them. And it takes a headcase to do that! But thank god we have many headcases in Scotland, many headcases in Airdrie. Women are indentured to death. Their death is barely a shrug, barely a ripple. I am softer than water, it seems to say, no more forceful than the breeze itself. Women slide into coffins that they never fill, even as the coffins are impossibly narrow, or seem like cots for infants, they dissolve into ashes, are swept up into clouds, are launched in baskets towards the city of the pyramids. They are transfigured by death. Whereas men seem more like monuments, cold stone, prophetic carvings etched in flesh in the aftermath of a landslide. I don't mean to be maudlin. It's just that we have very few facts and most of them seem to be very, very sad.

I heard there was this recording of the dawn chorus that he had made, supposedly on the day of his death, the day of the silver sun, the day of the frozen vampires, whatever you want to call it. The person who told me that is completely unreliable, so I was unconvinced. But then I heard it. It sounded like music for the gallows, *The Morning of the Executioners*, which is what we called it, in the end. I got the tape from Patty.

At the time I was more involved in visual art. I had this house in Gartlea, this house that had been squatted, an old woman had died in it, and I had turned it into a visionary environment that was open 24 hours a day. When I say a visionary environment it wasn't one of these idiot savant-style playgrounds and it certainly wasn't the fucking Watts Towers! In fact, if you didn't know anything about art, like me, woops, you would have thought that it was just an ordinary council house with drab furnishings and the smell of cigarettes and detergent and maybe even urine. I found most of the furniture in skips. I never cleaned the carpets. I blacked out the windows. But the door was always open. I advertised it in the library. *Nothing is Anchored Any Longer*, I called it, and said that it was open for viewings 24/7. I thought of it like a ship going into the night, everyone ageing, imperceptibly, in dark rooms drawn forward on who knows what dreadful tide. I didn't live in the house. You don't sleep in galleries, unless you're some tedious performance artist type. But sometimes I would be present, sitting on the couch smoking a cigarette or opening the door to let people in. I mean, it clearly said above the door, Gartlea Gallery of Geomancy and Geographic Speculation, G.G.G.G.S., which looked communistic, somehow, at least that's what people said, but even then they were frightened to come in, opening the door and peering into the hallway like they had just broken into an Etruscan tomb, and then they would creep from room to room, talking in a whisper, like they were sneaking into someone's actual house, and they would look at things like it was the first time, reading occult patterns into tea-ring stains on the sideboard and describing the position of dish towels in the kitchen as *macabre*. The amazing thing was that it wasn't vandalised. I would leave the door unlocked at all times and okay, sometimes I would come back and find a cigarette burn on a chest of drawers or a crumpled can of beer on a dressing table, but overall it worked pretty well. Once it was obvious that someone had slept in one of the beds.

The covers were all disturbed and the portable television had been placed on top of the cupboard across the way as if they had lain in bed and watched television before falling asleep! That kind of gave me the creeps and thrilled me at the same time, I still think about that person, but overall the installation went comparatively unmolested.

So when Patty approached me, I could see that he was thinking of it more as an artwork than an album per se. He asked me if I would like to present it, this final recording made by Lucas. Now that's an ambiguous term. But I didn't ask him to clarify. I said to myself, okay. Okay, I said, how best to present this? At first I had the idea of playing it in the house, you know, having it on an endless loop in the house as people looked around, but it seemed too pastoral and took away from the atmosphere of uncanny suburban dread in the sea at night that I had fostered by doing not much of anything, really. Then I had the thought of a speaker in a tree, you know, playing night and day, and then I thought, even better, let's have a speaker at the bottom of the swimming pool at Airdrie Baths, you know, have the dawn chorus taking place beneath the waves, like conception itself, in a way, which would make it more like the Song of Songs. I approached the council. They didn't want to know. They were more interested in tortured strips of iron set on low pedestals to signify the miserable industrial heritage of this godforsaken hellhole. Birds rising up like the first morning through the waters was too much like reality for these dull lefties. So we pressed it up on an LP. I had never been involved with anything like that before so it was a difficult process. We found a pressing plant in Glasgow, in some subterranean basement in the Merchant City that smelled delicious, of old newsprint and hot ink, but really they were hopeless. The test pressing crackled and had so much surface noise on it that

it sounded more like a recording of sunspots. We ended up getting
it pressed in Czechoslovakia, in a little town just outside Tábor. We
pressed up 333 copies and Patty came up with the idea for the sleeve.
It was a picture of a page from one of Lucas's notebooks. Of course
the looped letters look like hangman knots and the punctuation
looks like insects, like maggots worming their way out of the text,
but it's all accidental, or incidental, really. In keeping with Lucas's
ordering, there was no significance to the day that we picked. We
simply opened the notebook at random and used the first page we
came across, which was the ides of April, predictably enough. Most
of the text is indecipherable. But you can make out single words
and some distinct phrases. There's a quick zero, like an ellipse or a
bendy halo, above a drawing of what looks like a werewolf or a feral
child. Then there's an e like a foetus, curled in on itself, or a sperm,
perhaps, is that not what the hermeticists say? People say it's Saturn
and a drawing of the stars but I say it's a Q and a couple of full stops.
There are words, clearly, Rose, Earnest, and Artist, Maybe, a little,
December, which is weird, in the middle of spring.

We invent endings, really, which is what it says to me. There is no
resolution, no fixed beginning, no neatly tied-up end. People have
tried to read into it so much, but it was just a moment, passing.
Then of course there's the picture on the back. That was supplied
by someone else. It's a still from a silent film. The figure is walking
away from the camera. The ground is sloping slightly, it's a small
incline. I've heard say that it was taken on the Isle of Man. Someone
identified the vantage point, especially the old tractor that can be
seen on the far right of the shot, a tractor that is known locally as
The Wreck of the Hesperus after the poem where the captain ties his
daughter to the mast in a futile bid to save her life during a ferocious

storm. They say it was filmed in an area known as Smugglers' Cove. I think of Lucas and his bootlegging of memories, his manufacturing of continuity, and then I see him as a pirate, a laughing skull and bones, now, and it makes me want to up anchor once more, to go back to that house that I used to have in Gartlea, that silent gallery, and to cast off for the nearest island, or planet, or lifetime, wherever it is I wash up. But I look at the picture some more and I realise that we are far from land and are missing so much as a dove with a leaf between its beak, so much as an intimation from the future, and so I sit back down at my desk and write this letter and stick it in a bottle and cast it out to sea in the hope that it reaches you. Write back soon. I miss you.

16. Holdin Cells fur Oerweight Ballerinas: *Robert Mulligan aka Steel Teeth talks about Sufferage Tapes and John Bailey and Vanity and living in Greengairs and remembers the warmth of his fellow hobbyists which he remembers fondly.*

Ah started making art when ah was aboot twelve years auld, um able tae say, cause ah huv a big file filled wae alla ma drawins and ma comic strips and ma screenplays, early on ah hud quite a few screenplays, aw unrealised, oviously, aw o which huv a wee date in the corner. Alreadys ah was preparing masel fur discovery, like a body planted in the wids. Aye, ah lived in Greengairs, but lived would make it seem like thir wus actually some kind o life there whereas in reality ma existence wus closer tae a state o suspended animation, a series a frozen gestures caught between the impossibility uv the future and the improbability uv the past.

Durin the day ah worked in a meat-processing plant in Mount Vernon. We made hamburger patties. Ah hud so little money that what ah wud dae is ah wud scrape remnants intae a plastic bag an take them hame an make up ma ane burgers or make a crackin spag bog wae the scraps, which wus made up a horse meat, mostly. It wus like living in the trenches, like lunching at Ypres. Then at night what ah would dae is ah wud draw or write an then eventually ah started makin ma ane music.

Ah used tae buy magazines aboot Citizen's Band Radio and fae there ah startit gettin intae circuit boards an robotics. There wus a group o people who wud meet at Airdrie Arts Centre wance a month, in wan o the rooms in the basement – the rooms wur like holdin cells only wae a widden railing and a wall-length mirror on wan side, holdin cells fur oerweight ballerinas, in ur words – an we wud trade circuit diagrams an programmin languages, maest o which we learnt by going through the bins at the auld Organon factory in Calderbank an rescuing discarded manuals an details o early computer protocols. Ah became obsessed wae the idea o automating, o inventing a form o music that wid play itsel and that wid draw aw its inspiration fae itsel, you know, a form o spontaneous birth that held within itsel the DNA that wid facilitate endless versions an restatements o itsel. Itsel, itsel, itsel, that's aw ah cud think ae.

Early on ah hud this vision or nightmare or mibbe no. Ah read aboot the amniotic night, the strange suspended death in life o the foetus an the terror at the end o night, how when the watrs break and the vigina clamps it feels closer tae death than life an the trauma o the birth canal an the first attempt tae force air into flattened lungs an ah began tae wonder aboot ma ane suspension, how perhaps ah was still unborn, still caught up in the night, an then when ma da died ah wondered if in fact he hadnae finally been born an everyhing that we hud mistaken fur a haemorrhaging in his brain an a failing heart an his bones so weak he was bent double was really just the final moments o expulsion an creation.

Ah realise we've been through this a million times, reading the signs arse-backwards, reversing the logic in the hope that wur just seeing things the wrang way roon, the fervent dream that we ur, but then ah began tae see the dream as a computation, the specifics o the dream as distinct variables what could be slotted intae reality, as intae a circuit board that would then send the whole thing aff on a different trajectory althegether. The point is, if you're gonnae spend yur whole life waiting aroun fur Jesus Christ tae arrive then you'll be waiting furever. But if you decide tae plug Jesus Christ intae the equation, then, well, ye built it yersel.

Ma first build wus a leaping mechanical frog. Then a walking robot that cud bang a drum. Then I went aff on a tangent intae lasers fur a while. By the time ah came back I hud effectively destroyed the wan meaningful relationship in ma life. Not literally but ah might as well huv zapped her wae a dose o electromagnetic radiation.

Ah remember fondly the warmth o ma fellow hobbyists. There wus somethin in their manner that made me want tae live again. Somethin in the comments they wud make, their exclamations, that betrayed a small but particularly focused joy in life, a happy singularity. Wan o them hud invented a magnetic badge wae a flashing LED light on it in the shape o a five-pointed star. That wus nice. They wud pore oer catalogues o electronic parts an wud read specs tae themsel, sometimes aloud, sometimes silently mouthing the details, and I still remember thir wonderful pronunciations, thir knowin nods, thir light-hearted gravitas, which o course is the permanent condition o youth but youth's curse, as well, becuse fae there it's only possible tae topple, tae faw backwards, tae the point where words like oscilloscope and solder and capacitors and boards and modules cease tae huv any meaning or provoke any joy. Obsession is a state o fixation that goes beyond the specifics o relationship tae an analysis o relationship itsel. There's a quote fur ye. Then wur intae symmetry, gravity, attraction and repulsion, proximity, orbits, positive an negative charges. These ur beautiful words too, specially when spoken ur mouthed just beneaf the breaf.

Ah began tae build ma hame-made electronics, boxes that wud generate primitive beats, noise boxes, crude samplers. Ah became obsessed wae contact mics an violin bows. I wud attach microphones tae metal hangers, tae the bars on a gas fire, tae supermarket trolleys that I wud rescue fae the river an drag back hame in the dark, tae auld car exhausts. Ah felt like ah wus bringin hings back tae life, mute hings, metal hings. I wud run ma bow across them and the sound wus like a cracking open o reality, like the voice o the element itsel, in pain or in happiness, who cud possibly tell?

Ah released a few cassettes or rather ah pressed a few up and stored them under ma bed. Nae cunt cared. Ah handed them oot at the meet at Airdrie Arts Centre thinking we hud some fellow travellers there. This is weird, somebdy complained. Ah thought we wur aw weird, ah says tae masel. Ah thought that's whit we hud agreed on. But really electronics wus their only weirdness or rather the single weirdness that took up aw their time. The rest o the time they were just awkward an ordinry which wus sumthin that ah cherished but still it wusnae ma audience.

Ah cannae recall how John and Vanity first got in touch. They might have written tae me. They werny the first people tae hear ma music but they were certainly the first tae express appreciation uv it.

Aboot the same time ah received a cassette fae The Traveller in Black, who wus actually a guy named Peter Solly, who lived in Plains at his maw's hoose, which he hud inherited after his parents hud died and who wus making this extremely minimal electronic music that struck me like a bell, like a bell ringing oot at a funeral that is. Ah found oot he was a CB nut just like me an oor first few interactions were oer the CB radio. His hanle wus Uncle Adolf. Wan day we agreed tae meet at the leisure centre in Airdrie. It was blowin up a storm as ah cut across Rawyards Park, ah remember that much. You hud tae lean furid tae forty-five degrees just tae get anywhere and then the wind wud chinge direction an you wud faw flat on yur face. Still, ahd like tae dae it all oer again, if ah could. Nothin sits better in memory than stormy weather.

When ah got tae the leisure centre ah cud see him stawnin ootside the door in the rain. He hadnae thought tae go inside or rather, it occurred tae me, he wanted tae see ma approach, as ah wus early masel and he hd oviously made a point tae be earlier still.

He hud a heavy mooth and it fell shut wae a clang after every sentence, as if he hud swallowed it, like a fly, never tae be heard again. This is a wance-in-a-lifetime meeting, ah says tae masel. We moved intae the lobby. I suggested a drink fae the vending machine but he looked at me like ah had offended some kind o unspoken agreement so ah quickly drapped the matter. Then we sort o milled aroun fur a bit. At this point ah have tae mention his eyelids, which were heavy and a wee bit bulbous, gieing his hazel eyes the aspect o street lights, as if they were only capable o casting their light doon, o illuminatin his feet, wae his hawns in his pokets, or o staring right intae the heart o the matter. This guy hus scientific eyes, ah thought tae masel. He's wan ae us. Ah wus still wearing ma black woollen cap, which by this point was soaked through, and ah became aware o several streams o watter running doon ma face. I donno whefer he fought he could take advantage o me in ma vulnerable state but at this point he closed in, or appeared tae, that was the kind o sensibility ah hud back then, an he presented me wae an ultimatum,

118

at least that's how it felt tae me, urging me tae stand by ma guns
and tae release his music tae the world. I tried tae explain tae him
that the world, in terms o Sufferage Tapes, hud a population going on
forty people at most, but still he insisted. Yur like a mad dictator in
a science-fiction novel, I wanted tae say tae him, a megalomaniac fae
another planet. But ah nodded and says ah wud dae whit ah could.
Then he took a Mars bar oot o his poket and asked if ah would like
tae half it wae him. Sure, ah says.

On the walk hame the weather hud relented and the sun hud come
oot and ah knelt doon beside the secret burn at the back o the park
and dunked my heed in the watter and held my eyes open, which was
kind ae a personal ritual, but ah couldnae see anyhin but algae an
small specks o matter floating in the pale light, which made me think
ae wet shortbread. Ah read it like the future, a future that looked
increasingly like soggy biscuits in magic ponds ur digestives in tea ur,
god forbid, raw sewage.

A day later ah received a cassette in the post. On the front there wus
a poorly photocopied picture o Benito Mussolini an his wife hangin by
their feet fae a lamppost. The title wus *A Negative Incident Abroad:
Mussolini's Tired Young Halfwit Tongue Lolls.* Beneath it there wus
a pair o brackets with two dots and a comma in between them (. . ,).
As you can imagine I hud nae option but tae put it oot.

It wus the same with aw these guys. You hear the music, you see
the subject matter, you think these guys ur like violent overlords
living in the mooth o hell, staring through the gaps in hell's teeth,
sleeping on mortuary slabs, strange cadavers in unlit basements,
barely functioning savants wae a head ful ae twentieth century, dark

occultists, frog-torturers, spirit-lappers, gunrunners, paramilitaries, supermen, but really they're strugglin just as much as you an me, maybe mare so. Maybe mare so in that they were so feart, this is just ma pet theory, mind, so feart that they hud tae rub their faces in horror every day, they hud tae dunk their heeds in that particular river, like when yur threatened and you seek the challenger oot, you cannae bear the wait, you cannae stan the suspense, you want tae walk intae the heart o the wood and spend the night there, just tae see if alla yur nightmares come true and tae stop the tauntin o yur ane oerworked brain. Then when death itsel rears its ugly heed, or lolls its tongue, you can feel that you've photocopied it tae death, yuv tasted it areadys, in fact yuv bin on the other side ae it, yuv stood on the opposite bank as the ships have pushed aff, this armada o singed skulls and rottin corpses, the unsayable, the unnameable, crossing this reservoir o hate, this lake o terror, this ghastly river that we huv long forded in our mind. You wud think it would take a titan tae conceive ae it, an overlord tae live it, a gigantic courage just tae cast yourself into the watters. But really it doesny. It takes ordinary Joes. After a while ah became used tae the idea that these transgressive types, these avant-gardists, were just as ordinary as embdy else. Look up tae the sky at night, lookit the spray o the Milky Way, and tell me any different. We're aw cosmonauts.

Vanity and John came tae visit. I wus smitten wae Vanity. She liked me and she hud a hing where she wud aways touch me when she spoke, like she wus speaking tae certain parts o ma body, triggering reactions in me, playing me like a set o dice. Darlin, she would call me, an touch my knee, like a butterfly hud landed there, ur a leaf. Ah can still see her tongue, strangulating that wurd, darlin, robbing it o breath. If this is what art brings ye, I says tae masel, then pass me a fuckin easel. John wus the opposite, sardonic, stand-offish, inexpressive. Wan night there wus a car crash. Ah never heard the ful details. They hud landed in a field on the other side ae a hedge in the rain. There wus nae other vehicle involved, as far as ah know. It happened on the road between Rawyards and Greengairs, a terrible back road that wus the preserve o underage boy racers an drunken truck drivers. Vanity turned up at ma door in the rain. She looked like a watercolour. Ah wanted tae reach my hand oot and smear her lipstick or run my fingers through her thick dark hair. She hud an overcoat on wae a belt and heels an dark stockings. A kissogram, ah thought. There's been an accident, she says. We need yur help. Ah took a torch and a backpack wae provisions, it felt like an Everest mission, and we set oot in the dark. Thank you, she says, thank you so much. It felt like an echo, like somethin ah hud heard afore, a voice fae ma childhood. All o the street lights were oot that night, there wus some kinda power cut, and us we made oor way in the rain the beam o ma torch would illuminate stone bungalows an damp caravans. It was like a government experiment, like we were in a model village set up tae mimic an apocalyptic attack. Ah shone the torch in Vanity's face, just fur a second, it was aw ah dared, an she looked like a witch that hud survived a drownin.

When we came across the motor ah thought at first it wus some kinda installation. This is the fascination they exerted on me. It's an art instant, ah says tae masel. It's a wan-aff performance. But then it wus like a sunrise comin up. The light went on inside the motor. John wus in the driver's seat, lookin straight ahead. Is this a set-up? I says tae masel. You have tae understand, it was complete darkness aw aroun us, even Airdrie in the distance wus blacked oot due tae the power cut. And there was John, piloting this motor, which might as

121

well have bin suspended in mid-air, floating through the darkness.
I'm here tae rescue them? I says tae masel.

Whit happened? I asked him. I leapt oer a hedge in the dark, he says.
Why? Because I was goan too fast. That's aw he says, he dinnae say
anyhing else. Ah walked back home and returned wae my maw's
motor and used a rope tae drag them oot. We should probly lie low fur
a bit, John says. Can we go back tae yours? My maw was asleep and
ah hud tae get up fur work the next mornin but ah agreed anyways.
Vanity put her hawn against ma ear, just touched it very softly. She's
tryin tae hypnotise me, ah thought tae masel. Whit the hell. On the
way back John didnae say a hing, though ah noticed he wus still
wearin his sunglasses. How he could see a damn thing ah'll never
know. O course by this time aw sorts o crazy scenarios were runnin
through my heed. Ahm deed, ah thought, ahm crossing the river,
they're ghosts come tae take me hame, it's the Moors murders aw oer
again, they're gonnae kill me and bury me in a field, then ah thought
oh my god, maybe ahm gonnae have sex wi Vanity while John
watches, they're probably kinky like that, and tae tell you the troof
ah got ma hopes up even though ah knew ah would never be able tae
perform, no under the circumstances.

We got hame and ah lit the fire in the living room and asked them if
they wanted a cup o tea or somehing tae eat. Don't you huv anyhing
a wee bit stronger? John asked. My maw hud gin and vodka and
some whisky in the sideboard, mostly there fur guests, and she also
hud a box ae After Eight mints so ah cracked the mints open and
poured all three ae us a glass o gin, even though normally ah didnae
drink at aw. Actually, aw the glasses were durty so we drank them
oot ae eggcups instead. Done any recordin recently? John asked me.

Ah explained that ah hud bin working on a new cassette. Still at it, he says, and he nodded. Vanity climbed up intae his lap and began stroking his chest. I pit my hawn unner ma T-shirt and ma skin wus clammy and ah cud feel ma heart like it belonged tae Edgar Allen Poe and it wus trapped in a box. Whit's the sketch, he says, whit's the big idea behind it? Ah told him the concept wus kind uv like communicatin in the language ae cells, you know, this self-generatin music ah had bin working on. Ah told him ah imagined the communication between the organs, how the heart spoke tae the liver and the kidney spoke tae the testicles and the songs o the organs, these sad songs, in the night o the body, echoing in the veins, vibrating in the blood, at which point Vanity lit oot a high-pitched coo an licked his ear, her tongue wae its perfectly curled tip that made me think o France or Europe, just no o Greengairs. Ah told him how ah had read somewhere aboot atoms, how they repelled each other, how they were on fixed orbits, how when you touch something you're really no touching anyhing, you're suspended above it, hovering in this great force field, this constant attraction an repulsion that wus worse than gravity an how ah hud imagined bridgin that gap wae ma music, that void, where heart could touch hawn could touch eye could touch heed could touch ear, could touch soft ear. The empty music, ah called it.

Ah got up tae go tae the toilet an when ah came back Vanity was on her knees in front o John, in the pale yella music o the candlelight, in the darkness o Greengairs, sucking his cock. John still hud his shades on, so ah couldnae tell if he wus looking at me or no. Ah sat back in ma chair and watched as she coiled her Gallic tongue roon the shaft ae his penis, which was aboot average size, ahm guessing, but really hard. Neither uv em made a sound except fur the friction o her mouth around the heed o his dick. At wan point he held her hair in his hawns, wound it in a tight bunch roon his fist, and ah guess he came cuz his whole body stiffened and then he relaxed though when he got up his penis was still sticking oot ae his zip, still erect, and I couldnae see any cum on it, it wus completely clean, she must have swallaed the lot, I thought tae masel and when he excused himsel Vanity turned roon in her chair and ran her fingers along the outline o her lips, which were noo immaculate and blood-rid, and looked at me with they brown eyes that wur us dark and us glistenin as the past and says, ah love you Robert. I thought aboot the atoms that kept us apart and it was like wan o my ain songs coming back tae me. In the mornin, afore my maw woke up, ah towed them tae a garage tae get their motor repaired. Then ah went back tae processing hamburgers.

17. Chasing a Twenty-Year-Old Girl Halfway Round the World and Setting Up Shop in a War Zone: *Monica Lawson watches Richard the drummer disappear and come back again.*

There was a period near the end where Memorial Device played out as a four-piece with no drums; Remy moved to synth, which of course was his first instrument, and Mary Hanna stepped in on bass. By this point they were kings of the scene and the shows were amazing; the music sounded like it was levitating, spiralling, like it was a vertical construction. People bandied about names; Fripp & Eno, La Monte Young, The Velvet Underground. But it was nothing like any of those. Plus it was birthed from necessity rather than any kind of idea or reference point. Richard had disappeared. Or, to tell the truth, he had run away with a twenty-year-old girl for a job as an aid worker in Palestine. Take it from me, Richard couldn't have told you the first thing about the plight of the Palestinians. He didn't even know they had a plight. But he fell for her nonetheless. Her name was Lubby, which I think was short for Ljubljana or something like that. She was half Arabic and half German. She showed up at a Memorial Device show; a lunchtime show where they played in-store at Our Price records in Coatbridge. She had never heard of the music before. I was at the show; I met her. I saw her buying records, the first Creedence Clearwater LP, *Led Zeppelin II*: entry-level stuff. All the time she was taking sips from this oversized can of cider; which was cute, admittedly, and Richard always had a thing for tiny girls with big cans and that is not a euphemism by the way because she was tiny all over, except for the eyes, which were endless and dark. She had a boy's T-shirt on, a rugby top from some English university, Oxford or Cambridge or something like that, and she wore it with a tiny skirt that fanned out like a Japanese umbrella and suede ankle boots and opaque tights and red woollen ankle socks all scrunched up and falling down. And of course she was sipping from this huge can, which made her eyes seem like dark sunrises, the can like a dolmen or a standing stone, you know, like here comes the summer.

Thing is, Richard wasn't what you would call attractive, per se. I mean I liked him, etc, I spent time with him, you know, I valued him, of course, but it was more out of loyalty to my life and circumstances than any kind of attraction. We were able to be frank with each other, maybe that was it. Early on there had been something between us but it soon cooled off and that somehow allowed us to be closer than otherwise a boy and a girl could ever be, especially at that age, right? Of course I was a little jealous, that was inevitable. Lubby had such young skin, flawless, such keen, clear eyes, lips that looked like they had been drawn in pencil. I saw them talking and I just knew it; I knew they would end up together, though in another way it was the mismatch of the century. Of course she had a big epiphany about the music, how she couldn't believe anyone was making this kind of music, how everything had changed, and it got to the point that she was attending every Memorial Device show, always standing down the front, her delicate lips drinking from a huge can, and Richard would be up on stage, you could see him playing to her; he started dressing differently, he started wearing a cap, for instance, a baseball cap, which Patty hated. What is this, he would say, fucking *National Lampoon*? I had to agree. But of course Richard was going bald, he was losing his hair, and he was overcompensating. The next thing we knew he had grown one of those awful wisps of hair; those little tufty beards that posers grow just beneath their bottom lip. But he was a Leo so it made some kind of sense. Of course his wife never came to

126

any of his concerts. I was his only support from back in the day so effectively he could get away with murder.

I've fallen in love, he told me. We met for a Chinese at the weekend; we used to order from the Lucky Star in Forrest Street in Airdrie and then take it to a park further along the road where no one ever went and where I still return to in my dreams, even though it doesn't exist any more, and in the summer we would lie in the grass and eat our meals with chopsticks out of foil containers and drink cans of beer and debate the future and novels. We set ourselves courses, we had our own club, like, you know, for instance we would listen to all of John Coltrane's albums in order, one a day, until we had gone right through his catalogue, or we would assign ourselves novels, say all Russian novels, Gogol and Turgenev and Dostoevsky and Tolstoy and Bulgakov (*The Master and Margarita* by Mikhail Bulgakov is my favourite book of all time but just so you know you have to read it in the Michael Karpelson translation never the one that Diana Burgin and Katherine O'Connor did where it was like they were making things up for a modern audience really it was sacrilege I couldn't believe it so the message is: avoid) and Chekhov and Pushkin and Lermontov, and then we would discuss them on our Saturday afternoons, which would inevitably turn to evenings and late nights and sleeping in the park. His wife was a real bitch, she didn't care, though she was good-looking, I'll give her that, which was odd, you know, as in what on earth were they doing with each other, and this particular Saturday we had been reading Chekhov, inevitably, and that's when he told me that he wanted to stop reading, that he had no further need of reading, in fact. I've stepped into a novel, he said. I might as well be Rimbaud going off to Palestine. Are you really going to go? I asked him. I want to be adventurous, he said. I want to live. Books aren't living, he said. Music isn't living. Staying alive isn't living. Chasing a twenty-year-old-girl halfway round the world and setting up shop in a war zone: that might be living. It was hard to argue with him, even though I knew full well that books were alive and music was alive. I saw her pussy, he said. That disarmed me, I admit. It wasn't the sort of thing we usually talked about. Damn it, he said. I saw her pussy. She took her panties down and she let me see it, he said. She didn't want me to touch it, but she wanted me to see it. I want to show it to you, was what she said. And the thing about it was, it was completely bald. It wasn't shaven, there was no stubble, no nicks or spots; it was just this bald fact. You know how they say that everyone has a fingerprint that is uniquely theirs? This was like someone with no fingerprint, someone without a curl or a wrinkle or a flaw, and I thought to myself, what the hell, I'll follow her to the end of the world and that way no one will ever find us.

When the rest of the group heard about it, well, at first there was a big hoo-ha but when Remy suggested getting Mary Hanna in they started coming round to the idea. Patty said, yes, let's continue, but with no drums, that way when they ask us what happened to our drummer we'll just say he ran away to Palestine, he left his wife for a twenty-year-old and now he's somewhere on the West Bank, precise location unknown, and he's a better drummer for it. It beats dying or going off the ball or being told to pack it in by your wife. He remains a member, Patty said. In fact he's more important than ever.

It was the moment of his elevation, in the eyes of the band, in the eyes of his friends, in the eyes of the gossips and the bitches and the hangers-on, in the eyes of the commentators and the journalists and the hagiographers to come, though not in the eyes of his family, and I admit that even I was unsure. Throwing it all in with a twenty-year-old was bound to end in tears, I thought. But who knows what the point of tears is?

In the end it was me who drove them to the airport. Richard's family would have nothing to do with it. His estranged wife had been on the phone to his father and convinced him that he had lost his mind, that it was some kind of crisis, as if any attempt at escape was equated with biology at its most pathetic.

It was an early-morning flight. Lubby had arranged everything. They were to stay with a friend who lived in a suite in a hotel on the shore at Tel Aviv and from there they would make contact with a humanitarian organisation and relocate to a distribution hub on the Gaza Strip; though when I looked at them both in the rear-view mirror they looked more like Jackie O and JFK on their way to Dallas. She was wearing these big dark glasses and a floppy hat so you couldn't really see her face, which was a blessing, in a way, because it was true that she had the kind of dark eyes that would bring out the high diver in everyone and who knows I might have ended up in Israel myself.

Still, the atmosphere was awkward. They didn't say much. It was like a first date, in many respects, and there didn't seem to be much of a rapport between them. As we drove along the M8 the roads were completely empty except for some slow-moving trucks and the occasional taxi. There was the sound of birdsong, of the sun coming up. Occasionally I would catch a light in a window, the hopeful glow of a new day in a block of flats or in the high glass of an office in an industrial estate, and I thought to myself that life was beginning all over again, that every day was a clean slate. Everything is forgiven, I said to myself, though under my breath. I didn't want them to think that I was judging them. When we pulled up at the airport Lubby made a big deal about thanking me and telling me how wonderful I was, to the point where it seemed phoney and unreal but that might just be me, typical me. With Richard, we just shook hands; it seemed more appropriate than a hug or a kiss, you know, like shaking hands with someone that was just about to go over the top. As I watched them walk off, Lubby was walking a few steps ahead of Richard and somehow that bothered me. It made me think of my own bickering parents and the space between them and I felt sad. On the way back home I had the urge to waste my day, to write the whole thing off. At this point I had a job as a cleaner in the eye infirmary in Sauchiehall Street in Glasgow, working nights cleaning the building from top to bottom, part of a staff of three, and I thought to myself, bugger this. Will I really remember, at the end of my life, another dismal day wiping door frames and hoovering up syringes, will I ever recall getting my pay docked and getting served with a written warning? Well, here I am telling you about it, so I guess I did, but whatever. I thought of that character in the Russian novel, the one that Richard and I had read and had talked about in the park, the one that had inspired us to sleep out at night, in the wild, that had made us want to throw ourselves over precipices and flit across rooftops while everyone else was asleep, and it was as if he had finally stepped out of a novel, and I saw my own chance, in a way, though it was chump change, really, small beans, more like clambering out of a paragraph, what was the name of it now, it was the one where someone is writing a diary, a diary that when he comes to read it the next day is filled with all of these miraculous events, all of these forgotten deeds, some criminal, some wonderful, all of which are beyond recollection, even the writing of them, and he comes to the conclusion that he is no more writing his own life than writing his own diary, which results in a great sense of freedom.

It was through writing that we kept in touch, letters with postmarks from all around the Middle East, names like Nuseirat and Ashdod and Hebron and Yatta and Halhul, postcards with clenched fists on the front or children dancing in the street or silhouettes of Bedouin encampments at sunset near the Dead Sea, and I began to feel as if they were writing themselves, like somehow Richard had been swallowed by history, by geography, drowned in distance, and each missive was like a gravestone, each letter like a carving in marble, beloved son, dearly departed, sweet, sweet friend. He wrote about the street food, the view from the window of their room, of his first impressions of Jerusalem, of the sight of the men leaving the mosque after prayer, flooding through the tiny ancient streets (which made me think of fish or sperm), the pressure and volume of which left him pinned against the wall, of meeting a Scottish Rabbi at the Wailing Wall, which seemed improbable, but there you go, that's the stuff that happens, of the metal detectors and commuter tunnels and checkpoints and of the children subsisting on nothing but dirt and the Israeli raids and the kidnaps and the held-without-trials. I tried to lighten the tone. How's her pussy? I asked him. Sprouted any hairs yet? But he never took the bait. We're doing a lot of good out here, he said. We're changing things for the better. I had my doubts, I'll admit it. One thing that I did notice was that over time his handwriting improved. It became much neater. At first when he would send me a postcard it was barely legible, like a single flowing line, as if his hand couldn't keep up with the speed of his thoughts and had just become fed up and stopped trying. It looked more like a cardiograph than handwriting. And when it changed, when suddenly I could read each word without guessing or squinting or moving it back and forth in front of my eyes, I thought to myself, something in his heart has changed.

Meanwhile Memorial Device had been offered a record deal. It was one of these indie labels that were surreptitiously funded by a major and they were looking for a few trophy signings to maintain credibility. At least that's how it seemed to me, cynical me. They paid for them to go down to London and Patty asked me to go with them, he wanted me to be the band archivist, he said, to document the trip. Plus he had fallen out with their unofficial manager, Miriam McLuskie, on account of her being a mental case. I handed in my notice at my job. I wrote to Richard. I'm going to London with the group, I told him. They're being courted by a record label. He wrote me from a cafe in Jerusalem. He had started smoking and had shaved his head. I've lost a lot of weight, he said. You would barely recognise me. Right now the world of record contracts is another planet to me.

We took the sleeper to London, Patty, Remy, Lucas and myself. The record label had booked us first-class tickets so we had access to the bar and we sat up drinking all night. It had been snowing heavily and the weather had affected the power lines, which meant that throughout the night the electricity would go on and off, leaving us drinking in darkness with the whole world outside the windows illuminated in white, like we were speeding across the surface of a wedding cake. There wasn't much conversation; mostly we just drank and looked out the window. In the morning we were half drunk and hung over but we got in so early that nowhere was open so we walked to a park at Soho Square and brushed the snow off the benches and

132

tried to sleep. Afterwards we visited St Patrick's Church and then we had breakfast at a place just off Charlotte Street, where the record company was.

The label boss had his feet up on the desk when we walked in and he immediately offered us some beers. He was trying to be cool. Lucas was on good form and he asked him some spectacular questions, like if we were to exhibit an uncommon degree of zeal during the recording of our first album – that's exactly the words he used, *exhibit an uncommon degree of zeal*, I'll never forget it – could we then take what was left over from the budget and use it to fund a performance in Timbuktu? My mum always said she would send me to Timbuktu if I was bad, he said. I think I've been bad enough by this point. The label boss, I think his name was Sidney something or other, seemed a little uncomfortable. Then Lucas asked him about Roger Daltrey. This was a recurring obsession with Lucas. Everyone else hated The Who. I mean, who could blame them? Has there ever been a more depressing vaudeville take on rock n roll to this day? But Lucas loved them, especially Daltrey, and he had heard that Daltrey had never written an original song in his damn life, yet there they were sharing the stage at Woodstock with Jefferson Airplane and The Grateful Dead. It wasn't even true, Daltrey had written plenty of songs, but there was no point telling Lucas that. Do you know if Roger Daltrey is looking for material? he asked Sidney. I don't know Roger personally, Sidney said, but I know his publishers, I could certainly put you in touch. Done, Lucas said, and he leaped from his chair and offered him his hand, this huge hand that looked like a flatfish from the bottom of the ocean. Sidney took his hand and shook it gingerly. I got a shot of that. I was crouched by the side of the desk the whole time. I was small enough for no one to take any notice of and I think

133

they all forgot I was there, which made for some great shots, believe me. They were all in black and white; I had the feeling that I didn't want to make it obvious that it was a particular time – to me it might as well have been a blues band or Southern boppers or a punk group or anything. Plus because I was crouched on the ground all of my shots were taken from below so everything in the pictures seems to loom and to suggest and to be full of meaning, I think.

I was amazed that they didn't ask more questions, actually. To be honest they seemed a little overwhelmed by the occasion. I thought they would have been demanding this and securing that and laying down the law, but no, if Lucas hadn't been there I doubt they would have asked a single question. Later on, Sidney took us all out for some drinks at this club in Soho where we knocked on a door at the bottom of a flight of stairs and where a hatch was drawn back and a pair of eyeballs appeared. It was quite boring, actually. He introduced us to his assistant, I can't remember his name now, a name like Simon or Richard Sparks, a name like a daytime radio presenter, and he was just so tiresomely upbeat that it was tedious. At one point he sort of cornered Remy and put a hand above his shoulder, leaning on the wall, so that he had him hemmed in. I couldn't catch most of the conversation but I heard them debating the merits of fake blood versus real blood, that old chestnut. Then a few girls appeared; Sidney's sister and her friend Jemima and some hangers-on. Jemima was striking, with long black hair and dark eyes and a freckly complexion and with tight leather trousers and a sculpted, body-fitting top that was turquoise and black and that pushed up her breasts. She made for Lucas immediately and Sidney suggested we all go back to his flat, which was in a block that overlooked the Thames on the south side.

134

His flat was a state. There were still the remains of the morning's breakfast on the table. In the distance we could see speedboats and barges and small steamers making their way up and down the river in the dark. He put on The Velvet Underground, *Loaded* not *White Light/White Heat*, a safe bet, basically, and then he passed around some joints. No one offered me one; by this point they had forgotten I was even there, insignificant me. I saw Jemima unbutton Lucas's shirt and slide her hand inside as everyone sat around talking and it looked like there were scars on his chest, or burns perhaps, and that she was massaging them. Lucas kept writing things in his notebook, but surreptitiously, he had a way of doing it that no one else would notice. I looked out at the river and I could see St Paul's and the Post Office Tower in the distance and in the sky planes were circling, their flashing lights, and the boats moving both ways at the same time. I had this feeling, it's hard to describe, but something in me was disappointed, in a way it seemed like the same old nonsense, the same old temptations, the same old rotten garbage. I had thought more of the group, and myself. Then I had a guilty feeling, like I was on the run from pleasure, so I lightened up. I stood up and asked for a joint. Lucas looked at me like I had just materialised out of thin air and passed me a stub from the ashtray and I lit it up then lay back on some cushions next to the window and began taking pictures out the window at random and of my hands and of the light fittings above my head that were meant to look like old-fashioned candelabra but were all bent like spider's legs. All the while Patty had been sitting silently on the couch with his shades on and his battered top hat but then he came over to the window and asked me to stop taking pictures. I'm not taking pictures of you, I said, I'm taking pictures for myself. Still, he said, it's making me uncomfortable. I should never have asked you to come. I was quite stoned by this point and I think I read it wrong, thinking that he was concerned for me and my values and of disappointing me somehow, and so I said to him, no need to apologise, my dear, we're all human, but he just looked at me blankly and asked me for the camera, which I gave him, I don't know why, sunglasses after dark have a power is all I can say.

Then things started getting crazy. Jemima had her top off at the breakfast bar. A friend turned up in a taxi with a block of opium. Sidney put on this music, this awful disco music, and Jemima began dancing with Sidney's sister until the two of them were topless and rubbing their breasts against each other. Then he produced a microphone and an amplifier out of nowhere and the two girls took it in turns gasping into the microphone and singing things like I'm going to take you higher and higher while the other one crouched down on the floor and rose back up again. By this point it was a fully fledged party with strangers coming and going and people shaking the band's hands and patting them on the back. This is messed up, I said to myself. I found myself a quiet room in the dark and fell asleep.

In the morning there were bodies everywhere. At first I couldn't get the door of the bedroom open for a girl who was slumped against it on the floor. It looked like someone had ejaculated in her hair. Remy and Simon Sparkles or whatever his name was were sitting together at the breakfast table and they looked up and sniggered conspiratorially when I walked in. Look what the wind blew in, Remy said. The only thing that's blowing anything is you and your new boyfriend, I said, and I stuck my fingers in my mouth and pulled my best frog face. They went back to talking rubbish or whatever it was they were doing, nudging each other and making a big deal about grabbing each other by the shoulders and mock wrestling and all the sorts

136

of things that repressed drunks get into. I took a seat at the other side of the table and peeled a tangerine. The remains of the previous day's breakfast had been used as an ashtray, with a bit of fried egg and some rashers of bacon covered in a mound of ash and butts. Tell you what, Sparkles said. I'll pay you fifty pence if you eat that. No problem, Remy said, put your money on the table. Sparkles put fifty pence down, two twenty pence pieces and a five and two twos and a one, a real insult, and Remy went at it without a second thought, gagging occasionally, trying to wash it down with water, eating the fag ends and all. It was disgusting and pathetic and really quite sad. This is the big time, I said to myself as Remy let out a huge belch that stank of stale cigarettes.

I spent the rest of the day by myself. I visited the Jewish Museum in Camden and thought of Richard and what he would make of it all. I smoked a joint in the grounds of the Imperial War Museum then I walked along the South Bank of the river. I'm the princess and the pea, I said to myself, as I sat on a bench next to London Bridge. Here I am, living the life, hanging out with one of my favourite groups, in the inner circle, and yet it all seems so vacuous and pointless and demeaning. Is everyone the same? I asked myself. Is everyone full of it?

No one was talking when we met up for the night train home. The bar was out of the question. We all had separate cabins and we went to bed without a word. When we arrived in Glasgow the next morning I was dressed and ready to go and I jumped off the train and took a taxi back home without even saying goodbye.

I wrote to Richard. What you're doing is a good thing, I said to him. You were right to get out. I put on one of their cassettes, *Give Us*

Sorrow/Give Us Rope, and I lay down on my bed. It sounded so good.

Things started to get back to normal. I guessed I had been dropped as their archivist but I didn't want to look for another job, I wanted to take time out to discover my own values and to reorientate myself, you see. My mum and dad, I miss them so much just saying this, but they were so cool and supportive even though they had their own troubles and when I told my dad I had lost my dream job, that the group had gotten rid of me, which wasn't strictly true, he just hugged me and said, good riddance to bad rubbish, and made me a cup of tea and some toasted scones.

I started taking long walks; I'm a walker, I always have been, it's how I cogitate, actually, like the movement of my legs, the happy scanning of my eyes somehow moves the thoughts along and provokes conclusions. I walked to the Botanic Gardens in the West End of Glasgow. It was a beautiful spring day and the daffodils looked ready to explode and the snowdrops were so sad and white and forlorn and hopeful at the same time that it made me think of roses. There was a group of paraplegics picnicking with their carers on the grass. One of the boys, who looked to be in his mid-thirties, was giggling over a sandwich. I want to laugh at sandwiches, I said to myself, I want to cry over leaves and eulogise starlight and write poems about car parks and about ice cream being cold and coffee being hot. Not exactly a career, I know; but maybe I could invent it.

I received a letter from Richard. He had been involved in a skirmish during a demonstration outside an access point where an old man had collapsed and died after being held by Israelis. They dragged

me away, he said. Then they beat the crap out of me. There was a
bloody bandage in the envelope and a picture of him being carried
away by four guards, his arms and legs extended like a starfish. I'm
earning my stripes, he said. What about Lubby? I asked him. I didn't
hear back from him for a few weeks. In the meantime I slept with
the bandage under my pillow. I don't know why; maybe I thought it
would make my dreams braver.

Lubby's fine, he said, when he wrote back. Busy. She's working as an
assistant to a human rights lawyer. We're both very busy. I volunteer
part-time at a radio station, Radio Free Hebron, it's a pirate station.
I spend most of my time befriending firemen and security guards in
order to get access to rooftops where we can set up transmitters. Of
course we have to keep moving and if we get caught, what then?

Lubby was on television, he told me. Very briefly. The lawyer who she
works with is representing the family of a man who died in detention.
She was on the news, standing next to him as he read a statement
from the family. She looked great, he said, she was holding a sheath
of folders under her arm and she was wearing sunglasses. She looked
formidable, he said, but soft too, like the front would melt behind
closed doors. Things are changing, he said, you'll see. I got a job
selling perfume and I sprained my ankle, I told him, that's all I had
to report.

Memorial Device played a show in Bellshill. I went to see them but I
kept out of sight and just mooched around until they came on. They
were supporting some dreadful old folkie who had enjoyed a critical
rethink because he had combined Eastern tunings and raga guitar
with Western folk songs before anyone else. This was the debut of the

new line-up with Mary Hanna on bass and Remy playing keyboards. The drum stool is still free, I wrote to Richard. But they have a new member and it's a girl. I had never heard of Mary but someone told me she had built a stone circle or something like that outside Greengairs and that she was an artist, in secret.

They sounded so good. It reminded me of standing on a hill, in the dark, with a big industrial plant in the distance and just feeling this roar, this massive unearthly vibration, like the silence had been taken over by something that was even deeper than silence itself, something that silence implied, in a way, like silence was a sound and here was its underpinning, this terrific gridlocked noise that sounded like a complete standstill even as it never stopped moving. They're going nowhere, I said to myself, and I felt relieved.

Ever since you left, I wrote to Richard, they've lost direction. The music just sits there and vibrates. It's amazing. It's like the soundtrack to my life.

Richard wrote back. I smashed a window, he said. I lay down in the street. I rode on top of a lift to the twenty-first floor. I resisted arrest. Lubby and I got photographed for a newspaper. I headed a campaign. I drove a truck. I stood up for what was right.

He wrote to me with a new address in Tel Aviv. Keep it vague, he said. I think my mail is being tampered with. It wasn't hard to be innocuous; that was the story of my life back then. I told him about taking walks, about my dad's health, which had deteriorated, about my sister's gymnastic displays, my brother's financial success. I feel like an ugly troll under a bridge, I said.

140

In July my dad died. I don't want to talk about it too much except to say that everything seemed pointless until one night I came to him in a dream and he was wearing the same sky-blue shirt as in the picture we used for the Order of Service which was taken on holiday in Salou in Spain, his dark skin, his smell, and I reached out and touched him, as in a dream, and I kissed him on the forehead and I asked him if I could always come to him, if we could still share affection in dreams and if he was still alive there and he said yes and he smiled and he held me, caught in that state of double-mindedness that we take for dreams, and I asked him how it was possible and he replied with a word beginning with the letter P that instantly slipped my mind but that at the time I took to mean being omnipresent, like he had given himself to life so completely that he now resided in every part of it, but it was more than his self speaking, it was like his revealed self, and at the same time there was a new sense of calm, or an old sense of calm, more accurately, like he had given up the ghost of being anything but himself. He said it's because I am prevalent or pervading or permeating, something like that, and it was a great source of comfort and strength to me. I wrote to Richard. I have opted for a career in magic, I told him. I have discovered my true calling.

The letters stopped for a bit and when they started back up the tone had changed. They were more like anonymous postcards, bog-standard stuff. Occasionally there would be a postmark from Lebanon or Jordan or Egypt. I saw the pyramids, he said. It's hot here. How's Lubby? I asked him. I was getting a bad feeling, I admit it, but he never replied. It turned out that he had been sleeping rough, mostly living on the roof of a two-storey building in downtown Jerusalem while taking itinerant work wherever it was available. It all came to a head when his mother had a stroke and the family asked me to get in touch with him and ask him to come back home. I can't come back home, he said. I'm destitute. That was the word he used, destitute, and of course I began to suspect all kinds of things. I've done some things I'm not proud of, he said, things I'd sooner forget. Then he quoted the opening of *Notes from Underground* by Dostoevsky, one of the books that we had studied together. I am a sick man, he wrote. I am a spiteful man. I am an unpleasant man. I think my liver is diseased. Adios for now, he said, and with that he disappeared from my life.

By this point I had formulated my idea of walking cures and I published a few booklets and articles on the subject in the New Age press. I had this thing where you would identify points, much like in acupuncture, but instead of linking the organs you're joining the dots between parts of your life in the past and in the present, realigning things, basically, but the key thing is you have to add somewhere new, you have to extend your walk into the future, symbolically, by wilfully getting lost, by being attracted by signs, by ambiances, by the voice of silence itself, it's a two-sided thing in that you rewrite your past while embracing the future, and like all of the most efficacious magic, it's related to the physical processes of the body itself, to physiology, so it's not just idle thoughts in thrall to themselves. But the point is you create your own alignments. The idea of there being fixed ley lines in the earth that have this undeniable power no matter what is ridiculous to me, it's like saying there's one fingerprint that we all share or that our veins all have the same shape as the London tube map. The point is to fix personal correspondences in space and then grow from there, which leads to the kind of magical thinking that proves that you were living in heaven all along, but that's far away, at first the basic point is that you walk the distance between feelings and memories so that you establish circuits that come alive, as if you are generating language from your movements, like writing a love letter to the specifics of your own life with great gratitude – that's important, that's key, in a way – but it's more like hieroglyphics, really, hieroglyphics that are designed to be read from a great height, from beyond the earth, from beyond our lifetime, really, and so it becomes a page in this book, this book that we get to write, which really is an endless book, or an endless series of books, every one of us, if we're awake, and sometimes when it snows, when it snows all evening and in the night when you walk out and there are no footprints but your own and in the orange glow of the street lights you look back at yourself and see your movements and look forward and see nothing but fresh snow and for a moment you feel like an artist or a writer and there's this canvas in front of you, this blank page, and your movements become light and deliberate, which is grace, really, which means being graceful, and that's why calligraphy matters, to a walker most of all, and why I dream of the snow, the soft white snow falling on my father's grave, and I want to tread on it gently, purposively, and then light out for wherever the spirit takes me and never look back except to orient myself towards the future, which I think is some kind of cure, I think.

I did a series of talks. I had a night at the Theosophy Society, a weekend at a festival organised by a company that made soap, a workshop in the basement of a herbalist in the West End. I did a series of walks. I walked a heart shape around the Isle of Man, where I got some vacation work in a cafe on the seafront. I had visited there as a child and I lost myself on the island for a whole summer. On my return I grew particularly fond of the old Monkland Canal, which I would follow from Coatbridge all the way to Calderbank, where my grandparents had lived and where my father had grown up, and on to Gartness and Plains and Caldercruix, where once I was caught in marshy ground behind Easter Moffat Golf Club and reduced to tears about how lost I was, and like anyone, from time to time, I wished that I could go back home, that somewhere there was a jumble sale to attend or dinner to be late for but then I would pull myself together and curse sentiment for what it was or at least I would try to.

I had few friends at this point. When Richard disappeared from my life it had been like watching a body disappear beneath the water from a tiny raft on an endless sea, a sea without waves, or currents, or birds in the sky, a sea without evenings, even, without night, which is an unbearable thought, really, but which somehow sustained me, don't ask me how.

Then Richard wrote. It was almost a year to the day since my dad had died. Something has happened, he told me. I've been arrested, he said. I've been charged with GBH. Lubby's husband, the lawyer, helped me out. It means they're sending me back to Glasgow to serve my sentence. You can call me on this number at a certain time, he said. If you still want to, that is.

I called him the next day. My dad died, I told him, but I walked my way through it. Your dad was an honourable man, he said. He sounded like a lawyer. Listen, I said to him, where are they sending you? Barlinnie, he said. Lubby's husband pulled some strings. The prison system here is deplorable, they're having me deported. Legally I shouldn't even be here. I didn't know Lubby got married, I said. Yes, he said. She did. What happened? I asked him. I was attacked on Christmas Day, he said. I was asleep in an alleyway and they tried to rob me. On Christmas Day, can you believe that? I woke up and I went at them and they both ended up in hospital. I got seventeen stitches in my head. They got off scot-free. It's a travesty, he said.

I couldn't think what to say. I stood there in silence and I could hear his breathing, as if he had just run up a flight of stairs, but that seemed unlikely. Where am I calling you? I asked him. A detention centre, he said – well, not really, more of a halfway house. I have my own cell, he said, as if that was something. Have you told the band what happened? I asked him. That world doesn't exist to me any more, he said. Then why call me? I asked him. I don't know, he said. I don't know. Then I heard someone say something in the background and he told me he had to go. I'll write when I touch down, he said. Tell no one. Come and see me.

Barely a month later, I set out to walk to Barlinnie. No one walks to jail; they drive there, take a bus, get picked up by a friend. But no one walks there. The streets to the west of the jail are laid out like the sun, a semicircle bisected by the horizon or maybe it's a wheel, slowly turning, a Ferris wheel. Whether it's deliberate or not, I don't know. But on the east side of the Cumbernauld Road, next to the prison, it's a different story; the streets are more like a spider's web on caffeine. There is a hairdresser's, a library, a Jehovah's Witnesses' Kingdom Hall, everything that you might need on your release, and in the air there's the smell of foul bread and beer, the presiding demons of the east.

When I walked in, Richard looked like a ghost, sat behind a small wooden desk in a windowless room, a piece of my past that had finally caught up with me. At first neither of us said anything. We sat there, almost unable to look at each other. It isn't how we thought it would end up, is it, he said, finally breaking the silence. Maybe not, I said, though when I thought back to the drive to the airport it felt more like delivering him and Lubby to the future than seeing them off. Deliverance, he said, is that what you're thinking? I was taken aback. I don't know what you mean, I said. Then he shrugged and asked if he could borrow five pounds. I got a job in the kitchens, he said, which means more food for me, but I could do with something to get me started. I felt a sudden pain in my head, like he was shining a torch into my brain. Listen, I said to him. I don't think I can do this. You mean the whole visiting thing, he said. Yes, I said, it's too much. This place is too much. Tell me about it, he said. Do you want me to let anyone else know that you're home? I asked him. You think I've come home? he said.

I gave him some books to read. Use these for sustenance, I told him, and then I blew him a kiss across the table in an attempt to turn around the atmosphere. You don't have to come here any more, he said. We can still write to each other. Okay, I said, it's a deal. Let's pick up from where we left off.

In his first letter he talked about the Beasts, that's what he called them, the paedophiles and the sexual offenders. You wouldn't recognise one of them in the street, he said. There's no particular look or style or approach. They all know each other and talk away with each other instantly. Sometimes you'll find yourself talking to a guy, a real nice guy, you'll think, and then you'll walk up the stairs with him and he'll turn off to the right and you'll realise he was actually a Beast. Plus they get much more privileges than us, we need to earn television time and things like that, whereas they get it when they want it.

Early on he told me that he now had his own private cell. My cellmate decided to leave, he said, that's all. I thought to myself, I don't know this person at all.

Music is always more than life, he wrote. His thoughts had been turned around. It's life's duty to live up to music, he wrote. When is life the equal of music, except in memory, except in dreams?

I could relate to that.

Music is another world to me, he said. No need to remember the music but think of me, he said, in your dreams, tonight. Goodnight, he said, as I scanned his letter while smoking a cigarette out of the window and listening to music and wondering what the hell it had to do with memory or prophecy or the past or the future. I imagined him looking out through the bars of his now-empty cell, at this upturned wheel made up of streets and houses and people's comings and goings, this endlessly repeating past, and I thought of the music of Memorial Device without him, this music that never changed, it seemed, but that still relied on time and I thought of performance art and nonsense like that and I thought he's wrong, you know, it's life that we need to live up to, it's art's duty to rise to the occasion.

I came across some photographs of my father as a young man; it must have been sometime in the fifties. He was sitting on a low wall and behind him there was a rose garden. Something told me he had planted it himself, something in the way he was sitting, straight-

147

backed, with one leg crossed casually over the other, a cigarette in his hand, not looking at the camera or at anything around him, really, but staring slightly to the right, not focused on anything, at least anything that could be seen.

I told Richard about it. You might as well be mourning one of the clouds in the sky, he said. I started to think that he was some kind of Zen master sent to taunt me but that didn't stop me resenting him. I met some Rosicrucians in jail, he said. Some Masons too. I covered the metal frame of the bunk above me with mottos and drawings and phrases. Whoever goes in there next is in for a treat. Then he told me he had decided to read the complete works of Shakespeare while he was in confinement. No better time for it, he said. He gave me a running commentary as he went along. He hated *The Tempest*, couldn't stomach it. He had always liked *A Midsummer Night's Dream*. *Hamlet* was good. He would trade sonnets with the prison guards; who knew they were such a well-educated bunch?

He heard a rumour about his assailants, how one of them had lost an ear in a fight. I might turn up with an ear in my pocket one day, he said, that's all I'm saying. He fell for the moon in a big way; I know that for a fact. I keep moving towards the light, he said, no matter what. Then one night he wrote me this amazing letter, which I lost, unfortunately, but where he talked about how he had watched the moon rise over the houses in the distance, in the corner of the window, through the bars, rising over the semicircular estate and casting it in a strange silver glow that made it seem like it was on fire, like ice on fire, he said, something like that, and that he stood by the side of his bed and put his head back and outstretched his arms and that he felt like a crystal being cleansed.

148

He got out in October and had nowhere to live. His parents still didn't know whether he was alive or dead, never mind back in the country and fresh out of jail. His wife – well, god knows what she was doing with her life. I had no contact with the music scene by this point, so I had no one to tell, although I did see Remy in a chemist in Sauchiehall Street one afternoon but I resisted approaching him. Of course I thought things would all go back to normal once Richard was released, that we would resume our afternoon hang-outs, that once more I would have my study partner back, my walking companion, my sweet friend. That's typical of me. I'm always wishing things back, despite all of my talk. But it wasn't to be. Richard put his name down on a waiting list for a council flat but in the meantime he lived in a hostel near Glasgow Green where he had to wrap all of his possessions up in his jacket at night and use it as a pillow in order to prevent them from being stolen. We met up for a few afternoons in the East End, we took a few walks along the Clyde, but he wasn't the same person any more. Not that he seemed unhappy; it was more like he had become porous, like there was no longer any barrier between himself and the outside world. He would constantly mishear things so that conversations would be either extremely frustrating or extremely magical, depending on the mood you were in. He would come out with words, single words, like he had just plucked them out of the air or from your thoughts or the world's thoughts, more likely. Stranded, he would say. Did you just say you feel like you're stranded? Or, one afternoon, an avowal, he said, an avowal? At first I thought he was talking about a woman but then he just took a long drink from a carton of milk, that was another new development, and said, no, I just thought you were about to assert something. Plus he had all these plukes on his face which frankly made him look disgusting.

How can I put it? It was like standing at the very edge of a precipice, at the top of a waterfall, and hearing all of these sounds echoing below and picking out a word from this distant roaring that might have been language, like language itself was vertigo-inducing, and sometimes when he would pluck these words out of the air I would feel a tremendous sense of anxiety, like the floor had just been pulled from beneath me and I was running like a cartoon character in mid-air and I would feel the way I did when I visited him in prison that first time, that I had to get away, that I could never come back, that there was a final step that I was unwilling to take, a final leap that was just too terrifying to contemplate. Still, I did what I could to help. I filled in some forms for him, loaned him a fiver here and there, tried to maintain our friendship. My dad was my example. But sometimes the story is not about you. One day I disappeared from his life like a cloud, like a cloud that nobody would mourn, just as he had predicted. It wasn't the end of either of us but sometimes I think back to that waterfall, that torrent of language, and I have an image of us together, lying next to each other in the grass, quizzing each other over books, in the open air, and I wonder if the rot didn't set in right there, if we didn't catch something from those books that made it impossible for us to be happy. Of course I kept his letters and I cherish his memory. But listen to his music again? You have got to be joking.

18. This Is Where I'm Gonna Sit It Out and Then Impregnate the Future: *Airdrie and Bobby Foster remember Teddy Ohm.*

There was this guy called Teddy Ohm. He called everyone groover, you know, like, alright groover? But he was hip. He had been in some group in the sixties, I dunno, some local beat group that had dropped acid and blown their minds and that were famous for staging an anti-Vietnam gig in Airdrie Town Hall. I mean, we weren't even in Vietnam. Plus he had published this really early fanzine where he would write about The 13th Floor Elevators and The Chocolate Watchband and where he would talk about rockabilly and the blues and shit like that. He said that Eddie Cochran was a psychedelic avatar, whatever the fuck he meant by that.

He was everybody's connection. Pills, blow, you name it. He looked like Edgar Winter crossed with Frank Zappa crossed with Cher in the 1970s, effeminate but tough and kind of scarier for it. Yeah. What I'm trying to say is he was striking. He would walk down the road wearing a full-length leather jacket, sometimes white, sometimes black, with this long grey hair flowing down, and besides the drugs he made his money supplying props to movies, mostly historical shit: he had a crazy collection of swords and maces and daggers and chainmail and all that kind of shit. He was a hard man alright. They say he was on first-name terms with Mel Gibson. What the fuck would I know? I heard he wore floor-length leather jackets because he was always packing a shotgun in the inside pocket. But the other thing is that he was a record dealer. He had golden fingers. He could uncover all of the rare shit. His speciality was weirdo private-press shit, bombs like the Fraction LP, Circuit Rider, D. R. Hooker, garage stuff like The Bachs and Index and rural shit like Relatively Clean

Rivers and Hickory Wind, you name it. At some point I picked up all of these from him, insane shit, and most of it in at least Ex+ condition.

You would go round his house. He lived in a house he had designed and built himself outside Caldercruix in a field, smack bang in the middle of this featureless field with nothing but a motorcycle track leading up to the front door, it was weird, and with a view out to the reservoir where he would fish for his dinner. That's another thing: he had a deep freeze in his garage that was packed to the gills with fish. Anyway, yeah, you would go out there and his house was totally like an early 1970s crash pad, you know, with like a lower-level living room down a couple of steps that had shag rugs everywhere and wicker chairs suspended from the ceiling and brick bookcases with books about the zodiac and pharmaceutical catalogues and the occult, shit like that, and of course beat literature and science fiction and even more weird shit like books on biker cults, what the fuck. So you would ask him for a particular record, say you were after like a mono copy of the first Red Krayola album. Okay. So he would sit you down, all the while in complete silence, like a heavy fucking deal was going down, like a ritual was taking place, this fucking occult ritual, and he would make a big deal of getting out this vaporiser, he was the first person I ever knew that had one, you know what I'm talking about, like made of glass and you plug it in, and he would load it up with this grass, this grass that was time-killing, that's the only way I know how to describe how strong it was, that it would actually kill time dead – no question – and then he would pass it to you and take out the record you had requested and he would sniff it: he would sniff it and he would grade it visually and by its smell. Ah, he would say, taking a big dirty sniff, that's a fine pressing, groover. It was unbelievable. Ever since then I got into sniffing records. It's like fine wines, in a way.

So somehow I got into his confidence, don't ask me how, maybe it's because I was naive and clueless but enthusiastic and also I had a little bit of money because I had left school at sixteen and got a hotshot job in financial services, which I basically used to fund my hobby and my weekends, so that I was regularly buying shit from him.

Okay so one day we were sitting around sniffing vinyl, I think we were spot-checking like a copy of John Fahey's *Days Have Gone By*, which is actually my favourite record of all time, cards on the table, when he asked me what I was going to do about the end of the world. What do you mean? I asked him. What you gonna do when it all comes down, groover? he said. I've never thought about it, I said. I guess I'll run towards the blast and hope I get blown to pieces or dissolved, whatever it is this shit does to you. I intend to sit it out, he said. Then afterwards I'm gonna impregnate me some women. Then he sold me the record and shooed me out of the house because he said he had a party later and that I should leave before I got myself incriminated. That was the exact word he used.

Okay so he keeps banging on about this end-of-the-world business every time I see him and eventually I ask him how he intends to survive. This bungalow will be blown sky-high, I say to him, and there will be no skanks left to impregnate. That's where you're wrong, groover, he said. Then he asked me if I fancied a drive. I sat on the back of his motorcycle and at first I put my arms around his waist but then I realised I had made a major faux pas and that it was kind of gay, so instead I put my arms behind me and held onto the metal bar at the back. The drive was exhilarating. We weren't wearing helmets and the wind was messing up his hair and it was blowing back in my face and whipping me and wrapping itself around me like fucking Medusa or something. We drove for a few minutes before he pulled up next to another featureless field somewhere outside of Slamannan. We jumped the fence and I followed him across the damp grass where we came across what looked like a simple manhole cover sunk into the ground. Check this out, groover, he said, and he opened the cover with a dagger with specific nicks cut into the blade and we climbed down a metal ladder into a deep dark space. He flicked a switch and the lights came on. It was an abandoned nuclear bunker that he had bought from the government for £15,000. Wow. Okay. The place had its own filtered air system to deal with radiation and poison gas attacks and it was reinforced with a steel Faraday cage and with twenty feet of concrete. All around us there were piles of decommissioned electronics, crazy shit, Second World War communicators, shortwave radios, oscillators, you name it. The room was half the size of a football pitch plus he was growing marijuana down there. It's undetectable, he said. It's the dream set-up. Plus he had doublers of every LP in his own collection, all Mint or Ex+, in alphabetical order on a shelf that spanned the length of one wall. This is where I'm going to sit it out, he said, and then impregnate the future.

Don't ask me to take you there. I mean it. I couldn't find it again. Besides he's probably sitting in there as we speak, in the pitch black, sharpening a fucking Viking axe. Okay so one day I show up at his house, I'm looking to buy a copy of the Savage Resurrection LP. Teddy turned me onto Blue Cheer and told me about their producer,

Abe 'Voco' Kesh, who was involved with this whole subterranean biker scene based around guys like Allen 'Gut' Turk, who Jack Kerouac wrote about, and of course I became obsessed and began collecting everything I could that had anything to do with him, thinking to myself, in a way, that Teddy was like the Lanarkshire equivalent and that I was buying into some kind of fucked-up psychedelic biker lineage.

Okay so Kesh had produced this album by The Savage Resurrection that was reputed to be like two guitarists soloing non-stop for about forty-five minutes and of course I had to have it. Teddy had two copies, inevitably, one in the bomb shelter and both Near Mint. I turned up for the spot-check and the sniffing session and the whole ritual and there was this young guy sitting kind of awkwardly on a hammock by the window and looking kind of sheepish, with like big spots on his face and a runny nose. Who's this doughnut? I thought to myself. Then I was like, wow, wait a fucking second here, is this his bitch or something? Okay. I have no idea what kind of taste these gays have. But then I remembered him telling me how he was going to impregnate himself some women after the apocalypse happened but of course, who knows, maybe that was just so they could give birth to more boys that he could imprison in his shelter. I hope to god he never reads this, by the way, otherwise I'm a fucking dead man. Okay so the guy with the acne turns out to be Big Patty, or Patrick Pierce as I knew him. He must have been about fifteen years old at the time. What are you buying, I asked him? The Velvet Underground, he said, *Live 1969*. Amateur, I thought to myself.

Teddy took out the vaporiser, loaded it with the grass. As he passed it around he took both the Velvet Underground LPs out of their sleeve – it was a double album – and held them under his nose. Then he put the first LP on the turntable and cued 'What Goes On'. Okay now there's a keyboard solo at one point and that was when I lost it. It was like someone had pulled the carpet from underneath my feet and I was freefalling into Teddy's underground lair. I saw Patty on the hammock, rocking back and forth and grimacing and with a little bit of drool running from his mouth. There was a poster on the wall, it had a skull on it, some horror poster, and the skull began to melt and run down the wall. Jesus fucking Christ, I said to myself. I need to move. Okay so I can't remember what happened next but somehow on the way to the toilet I walked into a cupboard instead, a cupboard with all of these empty cardboard boxes used for packing records. And I climbed into a box and just curled up and lay there. The only thing I can remember is the face of Jesus bleeding through the ceiling in silver and dripping onto me and stinging my flesh with every drop. Wow. It really fucking stung but it felt good. I must have been in there about an hour or so, just curled up in this box with this face with an agonised expression melting at me but when I started to come down I pulled myself together and walked back to the lounge where no one even said anything about where I had been or how long I had been away. Okay but the thing that had changed and that freaked me out was that Teddy and Patty had swapped positions. Teddy was now sitting on the hammock and Patty was sat on the chair and all the while this Doug Yule organ solo on 'What Goes On' was still going. It was impossible. Right? These people are trying to fuck with me, I said to myself, there's more than meets the eye here or something like that. Anyway, I bought the Savage Resurrection record and split and left them to their gay-boy scene, maybe, but don't print that.

I can't even remember how me and Patty hooked up. Naw. I think I might have met him again at a record fair where he was with this beautiful little blonde that I had seen at gigs and who was one of the hottest things on the scene, I couldn't believe it, but later on I slept with her and it was a big disappointment, she didn't even take her tampon out before we got into bed, but it was enough to pique my interest, you know, what the fuck was this guy Patty's story? Okay so we start hanging out, we were kids, into the usual shit, comics, porno, music, drugs, booze. Booze was a big problem. We couldn't get enough of it. We had this one connection, this guy called Assif, who was the son of the guy who owned an off-licence in Clarkston. We were underage but when his dad wasn't around he would slip us the merchandise and we would slip him the readies next time we saw him and then go drink in the park or at whoever had an empty. At the time Patty was living in this big sprawling haunted bungalow in Forrest Street that was hidden from the road by twenty-foot trees and that was perpetually gloomy and dark and where in the back garden there was the remains of a mine and an old chimney and these great dilapidated greenhouses which is where we would often drink in the hot summers and it was where he kept his stash, his porn stash, he was so paranoid about getting caught he would bury the mags in the soil or secrete them in the grow bags for the tomatoes, which was crazy as they were often soaked beyond use or at best soiled and covered in dirt but try telling him that, that was just his style. Still, to this day I like me a soiled porn mag. He would buy them from a vendor who had a stall outside Queen Street station in Glasgow. No one bought porn in Airdrie, okay, it would be like pissing on your own doorstep, plus this guy knew the drill and so made it less embarrassing, immediately folding the magazine in two, wrapping it in brown paper and sliding it beneath your arm. Patty marvelled at his technique. What a pro, he would say. Okay so there's a day when your cock is hard for things like that and there's a day when your cock isn't, what can I say.

The other thing we used to do was we got into petty thievery, just stealing shit for the hell of it, that kinda style, breaking into back gardens in the neighbourhood and once even creepy-crawling a house up on Grahamshill Avenue and stealing some books and burying them in the ground, pointless shit. Then there was the night of our big escapade, our teenage retribution. Okay. We had a falling out with Assif. I can't sell you any more, he said, my dad found out, he's going to kill me. We're going to kill you, Patty told him, don't worry about your dad. We are a much bigger problem. The whole thing blew up, the way things do when you're a teenager, and soon we had a vendetta out for Assif and a score to settle, even though we were obviously the ones in the wrong. Alright so one night we go to this gig in Airdrie, some depressing washed-up punk show but with live-action painting by this naked guy and his wife who were eventually dragged out by the promoter which was good stuff actually. Afterwards we're half-cut and looking for a fix. Fuck it. I come up with the idea of burgling Assif's shop. Yeah. I know.

We arrive about 2 a.m. The place is all shut up. Okay so I give Patty a lift and he manages to get onto the roof. I climb up after him. There was a single skylight right above the cash desk. The shop was completely dark. Patty puts his foot through the glass and the whole window just falls in, wow, alright, smashing all over the desk. Holy shit, I'm thinking, we're done for now. But we climb down through the window regardless. There were no alarms or CCTV or shit like that back then; everything was more honest. We were too scared to switch a light on and bring attention to ourselves so we walked around with our lighters held up in the air before us. We got some booze, some good booze, a bottle of single malt that was as expensive as fuck and we sat down on the floor in front of the fridges and started passing it back and forth. I filled my pockets with cigarettes and batteries, I don't know why, pure greed, and then we sat there, smoking and drinking and reading porno mags. There was a microwave oven in there so we started heating up snacks – ravioli, shit like that; fucking instant hamburgers, remember those? They always came out like damp. Yeah.

Patty told me about his dad, which I never knew about, how he had drowned at sea after falling off the deck of the ship he had worked on, somewhere on the approach to Jeddah, or so they said; he was a chef on an ocean liner and during a storm he had been swept right off the deck, that's how they reported it, though no one knew for sure. There were rumours, he said, that it might have been a suicide. Even then Patty was a big reader, into poetry and shit like that and he said he thought of his dad like Hart Crane, just getting up and climbing the railings and taking this calm step off into the waters of oblivion, deliberately, matter-of-factly. Where's the poems? I asked him. Yet to come, he said. I want to be like my dad, he said. Like Hart Crane. Okay by this point he was steaming drunk. I want to disappear, he said. Then he started crying and his nose was running and it was disgusting, big yellow snots all over his face. Wipe your nose, I said to him. Unpuff your eyes and pull yourself together. We're living the high life, I said to him, the low life, you're a criminal poet right now, come on. I was humouring him for sure but I needed to get that snot out of my sight. The drinking continued, the tears subsided, the food went cold. I drank until I puked then I passed out.

I was woken in the morning by Assif's father shaking me awake. You bloody arseholes, he kept saying, you bloody arseholes, in this mad accent and pacing up and down. Okay it was funny, actually, in a surreal way. Of course he called the police. At first we couldn't wake Patty and we thought he might be dead or in a coma but eventually he came round and when he realised what had happened he started crying again. I'm not saying this to make him look bad but he did, he was a real softie. Anyway, Assif's dad decided not to press charges, luckily enough, but Patty's mother was furious. My parents couldn't care less. They were both serious alcoholics and pretty much hands-off aside from the occasional pathetic beating but it was decided that we weren't allowed to see each other, that I was a bad influence. Fuck it, I thought, and I remembered his snotty nose and his cry-baby bullshit and I was glad to be out of it. Then my parents died, one after the other, just like that, and it was as if they had taken that same step out into the air and into the water. Into this great big ocean that we all sink to the bottom of as easily as going on holiday or taking a day off. Their deaths were very light, is what I mean. It was like they floated away or drowned on thin air. Does that make them poets? Afterwards I travelled for a while, just around the UK, I wanted to see what this place was like where I lived, and I inherited a fair amount of money as well as the family home, which I immediately sold and never went back to; handed over the fittings, the furniture, the photographs, the lot. Occasionally I would call up Teddy and ask him what the fuck was kicking, you know, what was hot, and one day he tells me Memorial Device are kicking, groover, Memorial Device are hot, and I'm like, who are Memorial Device, and he says, remember Patty, your partner in crime? I couldn't believe it. I felt it should have been me somehow. I was into this shit when he was still squeezing plukes in front of the mirror. What the fuck was that about? Okay so I bought the record, I always listened to Teddy's recommendations, but I didn't hear anything new in it. I saw them play live a few times but I stayed at the back and didn't introduce myself. I was a bad influence, remember?

19. A Minor Cog a Small Life a Little Bird: *an anonymous mother writes about bringing up Lucas Black and love at first sight (the kind that only happens in the past) and the etiquette of the tête-à-tête and dreams of being swept away like in a science-fiction novel or a fantasy while always coming back to the snow the unimaginable snow again and again.*

I don't want you to print my new name. Things have changed and I live a different life now. Not that it matters but anyway, I don't want you to print it, if that's alright with you. I'm a minor cog, a small life, a little bird. Even if I did give you my name it would mean nothing, less than nothing, even, it would just be another name without a face, another Carol or Philippa or Elizabeth. What would that tell you? But still, I prefer to withhold it. As I'm writing this I'm looking out the window, on the third floor, at Paris in the snow. Can you imagine that? Of course you can. I mean, Paris in the snow: it leaves little to the imagination. Imagine if I had said Budapest in the spring, or even better, Arran in the autumn, or let's push the boat out, Nigeria in the winter, which will figure later in my story, so start imagining it now, if you can, and let's see where we end up.

At first there's not much to tell, at least not much that would interest an outsider. I grew up happy. I did well at school. I couldn't get a job. I moved around a lot. I took menial jobs, minimum wage. Then one day a man came into the shop – I was working at a shoe shop, an average shoe shop on Dumbarton Road in Glasgow. He guessed my shoe size; I was a size 3. I'm the one that's supposed to have the expertise, I told him. It's not expertise, he said, it's intuition. Do you like music? he asked me. I had always dreamed of liking music, of being carried away, which is what music can do to you or so they say.

162

Am I going to be swept away like in a novel or in an old-fashioned film? I wondered. My tastes were old-fashioned, even then. I read books, I liked crossword puzzles, in a way I was a spinster before my time. And here was my suitor, ready to rescue me from a future that I might have found in a word search or a board game. I was naive, too. I kept up the discussion of shoe sizes long past the point where it should have turned into the first awkward manoeuvrings of a romance. You like music, he said to me, this stranger who was dressed so well, but you don't like to dance. I took this as a personal affront, although deep down I knew it was true. I can dance as well as any of them, I said, and I intend to prove it. I was surprised at myself. This was an outburst, there was no other word for it, something that I had never experienced except when I was alone, walking in the park near the university, where I would often accost myself with sudden outbursts that would alarm me and point to some kind of inherited madness, perhaps.

The scene of our challenge was set. We agreed to meet at the Barrowland Ballroom, at five past eight, on the following Friday. In the meantime I attempted to brush up on my moves. I remember I attended the Mitchell Library and enquired as to whether they might have a volume that would alert me to the latest footwork, the correct amount of give and take appropriate to a man and a woman engaged in a tête-à-tête, which I believed to mean a secret assignation with a particular choreography but of which I was immediately disabused by a brusque young man at the enquiry desk who informed me that a tête-à-tête had nothing to do with dancing, though he was forced to concede that it did imply some kind of discretion. In my lunch break I studied diagrams, attempted to decode movements that were indicated by curved arrows and solid footprints. I combed through the back stock of the shop until I settled on some elegant kitten heels that allowed for maximum mobility while providing an appropriate pedestal for my legs, which were lovely and comely and much commented on in my youth.

On the evening it was love at first sight. He swept me from my taxi cab and my feet barely touched the floor all evening. So much for my dancing lessons! It was a time of great romance, the kind that only happens in the past. He was knightly, courteous; for instance one night he missed the bus back to Glasgow from Calderbank, where he had paid a visit on me in an attempt to win the favour of my parents, and instead of accepting their heartfelt offer to stay the night he had insisted on walking back to Glasgow himself, a journey through the nocturnal city that took him all of five hours but that impressed my parents no end. Here was a real gentleman with an athletic sense of values, my mother exclaimed. I sat in front of the fire and rubbed my hands together and thought abracadabra, here comes the future in top and tails.

I left my job at the shoe shop for a course at Glasgow University. I was the first member of my family ever to take advantage of higher education. I would meet my suitor on the campus and leave him to play pool with the boys in the Union while I attended lectures. Some nights I would study so late that I would hear my father rising in the morning and leaving for work before I had even finished taking notes.

My suitor, it turned out, didn't have much money. That was the first disappointment. He was living in a bedsit in Kirklee Circus near the Botanic Gardens in Glasgow that consisted of a simple mattress on the floor, a cupboard where he hung his beautiful suits and a few

164

candles scattered here and there for when he ran out of money for the electricity meter. He had recently arrived from Northern Ireland, he informed me, but he wasn't giving much away. What are your intentions? I asked him. I intend to unwrap you like a present, he said, and threw me roughly onto the bed and proceeded to devour me. I was quite the tasty little thing back then.

We made the decision to start a family and were married in fifty-nine. Some of his family from Belfast attended the wedding, three brothers and two sisters, but I was unable to strike up a rapport. We held the reception at The Tudor Hotel in Airdrie and for our honeymoon we drove to Italy and back in an old Morris Minor, which I would not recommend, as driving in Europe is extremely perilous and our trip was fraught with incidents. We tried repeatedly for a child but without success and so made the decision to adopt. Family was very important to my husband, it was his raison d'être, if I understand the phrase correctly. We jumped through the usual hoops, ticked the usual boxes. Our little angel was delivered to us, our little package from the stork, by a group of pasty-faced nuns who ran a refuge for unmarried mothers in the West End. There he was, staring up at us with those big blue eyes, eyes too big for his head, his dad said, and I held out my finger, it was all his tiny hand could take, and he wrapped his hand around it and held on for dear life. I thought of the part in the Bible where Jesus talks about making his disciples fishers of men. He's the one for us, I told my husband. I'm his dad, he said, and we held each other, the three of us, and had a little cry.

An angel touched him on the head when he was born, that's what his dad used to say, and of course it was true in more ways than any of us ever knew.

We moved into a ground-floor flat just off Woodlands Road in Glasgow. On the corner there was a large second-hand bookshop, which suited me fine as I was a big science-fiction fan and you could trade in books you had read so we were never short of entertainment. My husband wasn't much of a reader, he had barely been to school, his dad had insisted that he go out and get a job to help support the family, so at night I would read to him and our little baby, who we named Lucas after an old uncle who had been lost to the mists of time and who we thought we might resurrect. Sometimes I wonder if those strange worlds and alien planets set it all off. We'll never know. My husband was a very literal man, a straightforward type, and he would ask questions like, in what year is this set or what language do the aliens speak or how long did it take them to reach Mars, practical stuff like that. Whereas for me and for little baby Lucas, we were caught up in the fantasy.

He wasn't particularly musical as a child. I think his music teacher at school might have put him off. She was rather severe and chastised him for singing out of tune in the school play, which made him feel self-conscious. He had a group at school with some chums, 7-Up I think they were called, but they never got past the planning stage.

He was fine all the way through primary school. The summer before he graduated to secondary school his dad took him shopping and bought him books on mathematics and the constellations and Egyptology and later that night he came downstairs in his pyjamas and said he couldn't sleep because he kept thinking about death, about his dad dying and me curled up like an old leaf in a coffin. That won't happen for a long time, his dad told him, which was the wrong thing to say because that just set him off and he began crying and saying, so you admit it, it is going to happen. Looking back we should have kept up the facade. What child needs to be told about death? You might as well tell them Santa Claus doesn't exist.

It seemed there was a morbid streak in him, one that he couldn't have inherited from me because I was as dizzy as a chorus girl. He went through a religious phase, which we both encouraged. We thought it might give him some kind of solace. You had to watch what you said with Lucas, you had to be careful, he was the most endearing combination of earnestness and naivety, which meant he was ripe for brainwashing.

When he was seventeen he left home. We didn't want him to go, couldn't understand why he would want to leave, but all of his school friends were getting flats in town in preparation for university and by this time his dad was high up in the shoe trade and we had bought a pleasant semi-detached house in Airdrie. He seemed to settle in well, at first. He began to phone home less and less. Then there was the suicide attempt. It was all over some darling girl with circus tattoos on her arms and long red hair and who wore leather boots and could speak three languages and play the cello. When he was recovering in hospital she came to visit but he refused to see her so I took her for a sandwich in the canteen. You can't blame yourself, I told her. You can't fall in love with every needy puppy. My boy's special, I told her, he's the kind to scream and cry a lot. That seemed to make her feel better.

He came home to recuperate but he was quiet and withdrawn plus he had started smoking and at night he would sit in his bedroom with his favourite music playing and stare out at the street lights in the distance while smoking one cigarette after the other, these awful strong cigarettes that he would roll himself. Sometimes I would send his father up to check on him and later when I went to investigate his dad would be laid out asleep on his bed while Lucas still sat there, staring out into space, looking out towards Glasgow and smoking cigarettes from the side of his mouth, which is how he drank Coke or beer too, always out of the side of his mouth. It was one of his foibles.

Lucas always had big feet, big feet and big hands. His nickname was The Man from Atlantis or sometimes Luciano. Plus he had a large, regal forehead, you could almost imagine a coat of arms on it or a jewelled turban. It made him look very exotic. I would say to him, these people don't have half your intelligence. You're a highly educated person. You're a special boy. You shouldn't let them get to you. Sometimes I would picture him getting up from his chair and floating through the window, swimming up through the night sky like we were stranded on the bottom of the ocean and breaking through the bright clouds and waving his hands in the air, his big massive hands, like a distress signal or a beacon, and bringing back a group of angels with masks on and breathing apparatus that would take us to heaven or happiness or whatever it was that eluded us.

Things got worse from there, unfortunately. While Dad and I continued our great romance, Lucas went downhill. He became involved in a cult that owned some property in the Borders. I never fully understood what they were all about. But there was a leader, someone with a name like Sri Abergavenny, I think that's correct, a religious name, and they practised total renunciation, brain death, they called it. They whittled away at compassion, empathy, love, concern, common decency . . . They saw them as things that got in the way, like bugs on the windscreen that mean you have to slow down and can't go forward. Lucas shaved his head, which was a tragedy as he had locks to die for when he was young. They believed in sheltering their followers from the world so no one was allowed to leave the compound. Lucas wanted to leave, I know that. Later he talked about beatings, sexual impropriety. But he was stuck there. I think they did things like meditate, garden, eat lentils, walk around naked, stuff like that. They had a thing where they repeated clichés or commonplace sayings, the sort of thing that his dad and I might have said to him, until they became nonsense. They called it whirlpooling. That was hurtful. Occasionally we would receive a letter from him, though it was always typed and never signed so who knows who was really writing, and it would say things like, I am speaking to you from a dream or I am sat on a lonely balcony facing the sea, which was nonsense, as they were landlocked, but obviously it had something to do with the teachings, like they had risen above the sea, something like that, which made me think of Lucas smoking at his lonely window. And then suddenly he was back home. He had been gone for about eight months. The story goes that he was at a lecture, there were these mass lectures every day, The Precepts, they were known as, and there would be hundreds of people in this great hall come to see Sri Abergavenny sat on a cushion, and at one point this fellow, this complete stranger, just collapses in front of him, complaining about a terrible pain in his chest. Lucas picks him up and carries him to the stage. This man is dying, he says. I need to take him to the hospital. The whole room goes silent. Isn't this exactly what they were programming themselves not to react to? But the permission is given and Lucas walks out of the room, carrying this stranger in his arms, and delivers him to hospital. He never goes back.

But then his behaviour alters. He wasn't depressed, he hadn't lost his enthusiasm. Rather, it was misdirected. He started talking to himself, running commentaries, describing everything he was doing, you know, like, I peeled an apple and now I am eating it. I am making a tea for my father. For my breakfast I am sucking the juice out of an orange. His name, his address, his date of birth. It was like someone who was slipping in and out of a coma and who was holding on to facts for dear life.

Round about this time his dad had been offered a partnership in a lucrative business venture, though we later found out to our cost and, it must be admitted, to our profit, that it was actually a criminal network masquerading as a charity. We upped and moved to Nigeria. A salt sea cure is the term, I believe, a holiday in the sun. We moved to Jos, north-east of Abuja. It was like a speedway and a shanty town and a slum and a casino in the desert. We lived in a small adobe building with a rooftop terrace. At first Lucas seemed to take to it. He made friends and played dice on the street in the baking sun and worked for a while as a driver, moving farming equipment and sheets of wood, and sometimes whole families sat on the back of his truck to here and there and back again. By this point Dad was up and running with his charity work, which I'm ashamed to say involved photocopying banners and fabricating licences so that back home we could collect funds from hapless passers-by on Sauchiehall Street that were supposed to go towards a phantom genocidal conflict in Africa. Not that there wasn't trouble. His dad got burns on his thighs and on both of his feet after an altercation at a village meeting somewhere on the plains, but we were there as figureheads or links in the chain, this terrible economic chain that fed on suffering, I'm afraid, rather than missionaries. Then the winter came down and finished his dad off. Can you imagine that?

As I sit here in Paris, on the third floor, in the bleak midwinter, it's hard to picture. I see my husband, Lucas's dad, asleep beside me. I see the Sunday papers, English editions, weeks old, hand-delivered by a mulatto boy named Kenji, spread across the bed. The only sound is of the fan, spinning, and of the hissing of the earth outside in the distance. From next door, through the wall-length wardrobe at the foot of the bed, I can hear voices, a running commentary. I am, I was, I always will be, he would say, though not in so many words. I was brought up in a quiet household, with a sense of calm. I had no experience of this. I had never heard my father raise his voice. My mother had died at a young age from a problem with her kidneys. My baby sister passed away at three years old. I had looked forward to the same, a quiet life, then death, but with culture. Now here I was in a monastery for the insane, in the winter, in a country where snow was a memory or a dream.

20. I Thought They Had Cut the Top of His Head Off and Were
Spooning Out His Brains: *The Clarkston Parks had a time of it in
Airdrie.*

We had a group called The Clarkston Parks, me, Alan, Dougie and
Goosey. Good, innit? Mod, innit? My old man was a lorry driver;
my mam worked at a baked potato place in Airdrie. I was a mod.
I became a mod. Me and my pals were the mod squad. We lived in
one of them shoeboxes in Mull, in Petersburn, which of course now
seems really romantic, innit, now that I don't live there any more
and my mam and my old man are gone. I remember lying awake in
my bunk bed, I remember it to this day, the wee one asleep beneath
me, listening to cassettes all night long and staring at the street
light outside, sometimes hearing footsteps in the lane or drunken
conversations or even one night live sex, which was a thrill, believe
me. And dreaming of smoking cigarettes and drinking and imagining
my future wife being out there somewhere and what she was doing
and all that kinda stuff. Oh baby, I'm dreamin' of Monday, oh baby,
when I see you again. That was me: portrait of a young mod. I
would listen to things like The Pistols, The Stranglers, The Jam. I
remember walking all the way to Coatbridge one summer afternoon,
cutting across these empty parks, looking sharp as hell, that was
me, right then, what a moment, you only live once, there wasn't a
soul around and all the time the sun was beating down and it was
like a mission or an initiation, just to buy a cassette of The Damned's
Machine Gun Etiquette. From there I got into sixties stuff, like
mod and psychedelia and freakbeat. There was this club night in
Glasgow, Joy of a Toy, it was called, where they played classic sixties
soul and garage and British psych. We were all over it like a rash. I
started sending away for fanzines that had things like pictures of Mr

172

Spock or Twiggy or Brian Jones on the front or you know like Roger McGuinn looking cool with a bowl cut. I got into the whole thing of clean living under poor circumstances.

My old man would drive us into Glasgow in the evening and pick us up afterwards, no matter what the time. He was great like that, my old man. I would borrow his suits, he was a sharp dresser in the sixties, and I would say I bought them myself or even better that I had my own tailor, innit? I had this girlfriend at the time, Mary Bell, not the child-killer but of course everyone said that so they started calling her Mad Mary Bell. Mad Mary Bell the modette. She was pretty crazy, actually. Once she picked up some pills that were just lying in the street covered in dirt and ate them. We were walking down the street and before I could stop her she had snatched them up and swallowed them. Happy days! They could have been anything but in the end nothing happened. Once she drank a bottle of plant food just for the hell of it. I was impressed. She was mental. She didn't like to have sex, that was one thing, well, not penetrative sex, she just liked you to rub your leg or your penis over the front of her panties, that was all, and she would moan and lick her lips like crazy. It was a real turn-on but obviously frustrating at the same time. She had a great look, though, long white coats, tiny handbags, blonde hair curled around her face like Mary Quant. We looked the part, me and Mad Mary Bell, absolute beginners, classic.

The Clarkston Parks became kind of big on the scene. We had a residency at a place in Calderbank, a working men's club that burned down long ago. We built up quite a scene out there, in this weird depressed mining village that was actually a hotbed for mods back in the day. Who knew? And they would run buses from Coatbridge and Airdrie and Shotts and Greengairs and sometimes even Glasgow and they'd all be singing on the way there and being Calderbank you would get a mix of people turning up alongside the hard-core followers, a right bunch of loons. Sometimes you'd get rockers and metallers looking for a fight; sometimes locals looking for a fight; sometimes even locals that weren't looking for a fight. We had this whole thing where we were working-class hardmen with style, innit, so we could handle ourselves, even if it meant getting our shoes scuffed or spoiling the cut of our suits.

One evening a local biker gang turned up, looking for trouble. They called themselves The Fenric Wolves or The Wolves Of Fenric, something like that. They were all ugly, a real rogues' gallery, with beards and long hair and sweat stains on their stupid T-shirts and with their sneakers on. I can't stand leisurewear to this day, it really distresses me. They made a big deal about pulling up on their bikes and skidding around the car park with their lights on before we played. Of course there were a lot of mopeds parked outside and later we heard that one guy, this notorious biker called Teddy Ohm, had picked up a bunch of scooters – and these were classic scooters, authentic 1960s Vespas – and taken them and thrown them over the bridge into the River Calder. Years later, when I was walking the length of the Monkland Canal from Coatbridge for a cancer charity, I passed beneath the bridge and you could still see a rusty moped sticking up from out of the water.

Our bass player, Goosey, had greasy curly hair. It's an affliction, innit? The rest of us had classic bowl cuts, sharp as you like, whereas he looked like a darts player or something. He was a cool guy and a great musician and he died from some kind of lung problem when he was only thirty-two years old, long after we had lost touch, although I would still see his brother from time to time, who was a nutcase. On the night the bikers all filed in and stood at the front of the stage. It was like Altamont or something. They were breathing really hard, I remember that, there were a lot of flared nostrils. They were like bulls getting ready to attack. I went up to the microphone. We did that song by Tinkerbells Fairydust, classic British psych, innit, 'In My Magic Garden', and so I just said, this is a song by Tinkerbells Fairydust, and it was like a rag to a bull. I saw one guy bite through one of the cans of beer he was drinking in a rage. This massive fight broke out. I kicked a guy right in the face – the stage was perfectly at eye level. People were throwing tables around like in a Western brawl. The bikers had chains and hammers and Stanley knives and chibs. Goosey leaped off the stage. He took about three guys down with him. I took off my guitar and fucked somebody right around the head with it. There were bottles flying everywhere. I saw them going at Goosey and then this crazy thing happened. I will never forget it. They scalped him. One of them knelt on his chest while another held his head back and a third guy took a blade to his scalp. It all seemed to happen in slow motion. There was blood everywhere and for a second I thought they had cut the top of his head off and were spooning out his brains. But then one of them held up this mop of grey curly hair attached to a thin layer of flesh and it was like they had beheaded a Gorgon in a snooker club. It was grotesque and I just completely lost the plot and went haywire. There was a screwdriver lying on top of my amp and I grabbed it and launched myself at his assailants. I stabbed one of them in the back of the neck and he began jerking around like a puppet or a broken-down robot, like when they stick one of them electrodes in your brain and you start acting crazy. His friends backed off, though one of them still had Goosey's scalp in his hand like some kind of Greek myth. I waved the screwdriver around, like I was going to do anything, and they made for the door, but not before one of them grabbed hold of Mary and dragged her kicking and screaming out into the night. It was a total nightmare. No one called the police, I couldn't believe it, not even the owner, who was more worried about vengeance and getting closed down than he was about justice, lucky for all of us, in a way. We had someone drive the guy that I stabbed to an industrial estate outside Holytown where we dumped his body on the pavement. I had no idea whether he was alive or dead. We had to take Goosey to hospital but we said he had fallen down a brae next to the River Calder and somehow scalped himself on the cliffs, which they believed, amazingly. Where's his hair? they asked us. We lost it, we said, it must have fallen into the river.

Then we had to track down Mary; Mad Mary Bell. The next day went past and no one heard a peep. Luckily enough her parents lived in St Albans and couldn't give a toss whether she lived or died so there was no pressure on that front. Alan's address was on the back of all of our records. He lived with his mum, who got 24-hour care on the social because she was basically doolally, so he could do what he pleased. Two days later he called me. They had posted a ransom note. It looked like it had been cut out of the *Daily Record*, a classic newsprint threat. If yOU want THE GiRL too lIVE, it said, tHen MeEt us hEre on SaTuRDay aT 12pM. Then there were the coordinates from an Ordnance Survey map, if you can believe that. None of us had any idea how to work it out but we had a teacher at school who was interested in orienteering and the classics and all that sort of thing that we still kept in touch with. He was kind of a local legend; Mr Scotia. We called him up and he invited us over

to his house for lunch. He lived in a modern flat just on the corner
of Forrest Street and after soup and bread made by his wife and
some coffee and a brief history of the parks of Clarkston – he was
a local-history buff as well – his wife cleared away the dishes and
he spread out a map on the table. There's your location right there,
he said. It was beneath a disused railway bridge in the glen behind
Katherine Park. Ah, Katherine Park, he said, and he mock swooned
and the monocle popped out of his eye and fell into the pocket of his
oversized dogtooth suit. Katherine Park, he said, the paramour of
my youth, my mistress, my pride! What are you boys up to? he asked
us. Some kind of derring-do? I was eager not to break the spell, I was
always impressionable that way, so I told him I had been challenged
to a duel for the hand of a young woman. I'll be your second, he
announced. You're seventy-four years old, his wife interrupted, you're
seconding no one. Do not be disabused, he whispered, as soon as she
left the room. I'm handy. Don't let the cut of my jowls fool you.

I thought about it for a minute. Alan looked at me like I was crazy
and mimed slitting his own throat. But then I thought screw it, the
whole thing is getting crazier by the second, let's up the ante. Okay,
I said, you're my second, at which point Scotia's eyes lit up, eyes with
cataracts like strawberries, almost brimming over.

The next day we visited Goosey in the hospital. It'll be wigs from
here on out, lads, he told us, that's what they're saying, and secretly
I thought at last we can have some coherence in this band but then
I felt bad, his head was mangled, he looked like a skinned beetroot.
We've located Mad Mary, I told him, we're meeting them down the
glen for vengeance and for a handover. Don't do it, he said, don't
get involved. Let's just call the police, we did nothing wrong. You're

forgetting something, I said. I may have killed someone. None of us have any idea if the guy I stabbed is dead or alive.

I was scared; there was no denying it. I sat up at night on my bed and looked out the window and held my breath at the sound of every siren in the distance, coming to get me, innit, coming to take me away. What was I thinking, I asked myself. Why did I get involved in any of it? Isn't sitting here at home, safe, at night, with all my cassettes, with the music playing low, in the first flush of youth, looking good, being one of the faces of Airdrie, isn't that enough? Of course not, I knew that, and even then I felt an invisible hand which I knew was really my own, or God's own, or Paul Weller's own, whatever you want to call it, pushing me past the tipping point, urging me on.

I called Mr Scotia. It's more complicated, I told him. Death has reared its ugly head. He told me a story about being in the army, about soldiers tossing coins to decide who gets to disembark and who gets to stay on the island. This was Crete, near the end of the war. It all comes down to the toss of a coin, he said, in the end. These people are serious, I told him. I wanted him to understand. These people are dangerous. Young man, I am retired, he said, but not from life. Then there was this long silence on the line. The entire phone call was an education.

On the day there was the four of us, Dougie, Alan, Mr Scotia and myself. Scotia had armed himself with an old Irish walking stick with pointy nodules up and down it and an iron tip that would send off sparks every time he declaimed and struck it against the ground. It was like some ancient god of thunder had our back. A god that walked at a pace of about two miles an hour; a god who insisted on stopping to smell the flowers or gesticulate wildly in the air or point out some haunted place of childhood memorial or pseudo-historical significance every few steps, innit. In the end we were twenty minutes late but they were all still there, waiting for us, all spread out underneath this bridge like it was a photo shoot and not a potential murder scene. It was a warm summer, memorably warm, and of course Scotia was decked out in a full suit and with a bunnet and a tie and I remember his face was streaming with sweat by the time we arrived and he kept mopping his face with a hanky. He was wearing a shirt and tank top and a jacket and god knows probably a vest too. An old mod at the helm, I says to myself.

As soon as he caught sight of the bikers he broke ahead of us, leading us into the melee. I could see that everyone was taken aback. What the hell was this? That's when I saw Mary; Mad Mary Bell. She didn't look dishevelled at all. She didn't look kidnapped. In fact when I saw her she was stood there smiling, talking to this pluky-looking young guy with long hair swept back and a pair of Ray-Bans on and with her finger in her hair like she hadn't a care in the world.

This ends amicably or not at all, Scotia burst, and he cracked his walking stick against the ground just like that so that it echoed all the way across the bridge and back again. I thought to myself this is more like a seance than a duel. Teddy Ohm stepped forward. At first he seemed reasonable. He started out with a long preamble about honour and territory and the code of the warrior and guff like that but Scotia interrupted him with another crack of his cane. Cease and desist, Scotia said. I know you. You're Edward Thom, I remember you. I taught you at primary school. Look at you, he said, passing the stick around the outline of his body like he was casting a spell.

What did I tell you about tattoos and earrings and long hair? Didn't I say you would get into trouble? There were a few titters coming from the crowd. Listen, old man, Teddy said, but Scotia cut him dead. Old man? he said. Old man? Let me educate you, sunshine, in the true code of the warrior. First off, he said, the girl comes with me, and he pointed his stick at Mary who by now was paying rapt attention and who walked over to him like she had been magnetised. A warrior goes into battle foreseeing probable loss, Scotia said, and he mopped his brow again. That always stuck in my mind. Mars is a dead planet, he said. But there is that which remains. We long to taste of each other's flesh, he said, and he nodded at Teddy and looked straight at him. I saw a few bikers recoil but he had Teddy's attention for sure. Now Teddy seemed kind of nervous. What about the Mars behind the Mars? Scotia asked him. What about the star behind the stars? Teddy looked dumbfounded. Then Scotia cracked his stick one more time and sparks flew out in four directions at once. The pluky-looking kid with long hair let out a gasp and at a signal from Scotia we turned our backs and I took Mad Mary by the hand and we walked off, slowly, with Scotia at our head and all of these bikers struck dumb, standing around us like statues, afraid to make a move in case he just zapped them on the spot. It was amazing. Later on I found out that the pluky kid was Patty Pierce. This was years before he became a big deal on the music scene. Back then we taught him a lesson, though, that's for sure.

21. Every Disappointment Was Like Something Awarded You in Heaven: *Street Hassle in a rare face-to-face interview with Ross Raymond.*

RR: Do you have a history of drug use?

SH: A history would imply something that could be pieced together and that could be made sense of. In that case I have no history of drug use to speak of.

RR: What were your early influences?

SH: Rising late. Lighter fluid. That book, what do you call it, fuck knows. That film too. Questions, generally.

RR: What questions?

SH: This and that.

RR: Why?

SH: Do you mean for what?

RR: What age were you when you first masturbated?

SH: Thirteen, fourteen, something like that. I was a late starter and have been playing catch-up ever since. The first time I ever came it was so shocking that I thought I had broken my dick. Though for a while I was mixed up between urine and sperm. But that's another question entirely.

RR: If you could sum up the Airdrie music scene in one word, what would it be?

SH: Pointless.

RR: Was punk important?

SH: No. Well, yes, in a way, because a lot of people that might have been doing something else with their lives suddenly realised they could get away with being themselves and still survive or even thrive, but also die, which was coming anyway, which was inevitable, but punk was a way of aggrandising weird character traits and specific tics and making levels of ability interesting because it got rid of any notion of a norm so everything became fascinating and every failure became a breakthrough and every disappointment was like something awarded you, in heaven, which suddenly was these back-room gigs and wash-out art-centre shows and rehearsal-room jams, which were like new routes to immortality, man, like for a moment everyone was beatified or forgiven but of course then everyone began trying to play like everyone else and grace was suspended and there was a whole new standard that got in the way of everything. Punk was supposed to deliver us from rock n roll but in the end it took rock n roll to deliver us from punk. Less specific orthodoxies are more interesting in lieu of the destruction of orthodoxies altogether.

RR: But what about all that blue-denim, we-mean-it-man rock n roll bullshit?

SH: God saves.

RR: Are you religious?

SH: Oh yeah, sure, very much so. I'm like one of those hermits in the desert hanging upside down from a cliff with one toe. Only normally it's the cenotaph in Coatdyke and I have fallen on my head.

RR: Name three groups we should know about.

SH: The Pin Group. Steel Teeth. Chinese Moon.

RR: What was your first group?

SH: Rat Tattoo.

RR: What was the story?

SH: We formed at school, this would be 1978. We dubbed cassettes from one player to another, released about five cassette albums. Our whole thing was, you know how there was like a gay channel on CB Radio? What if there had been a metal channel where everyone met up to play metal at each other? What would it sound like if you put a cassette recorder right up to your CB receiver and recorded it straight to tape? That's what Rat Tattoo sounded like.

RR: Primitive?

SH: I would argue that it was pretty sophisticated.

RR: What do you think about Memorial Device?

SH: I think a bunch of things. I think that guy Remy is a clown and if I was him I would slip out of town fast and never come back. You can fucking print that. I remember him back in the day, it was at this party, and he was sitting around in these tight silver leggings and with all of this eyeshadow on and he was playing his crappy songs on an acoustic guitar, lying on the floor, slumped up against a wall and everyone was ignoring him or pretending that he wasn't there. He was trying to reinvent himself but everyone knew about his synth-pop bullshit. I couldn't believe it when he turned up in Memorial Device and everyone was saying they were hip. My balls are hip, I would say, but they ain't making albums, although they have appeared in public on several occasions, all of which were outside my own control, I admit.

RR: Your balls appeared in public?

SH: You know how it is, you have a rip in your trousers, they fall through, what you gonna do?

RR: Don't you wear any underwear?

SH: That's the thing. I have a big sister, quite a good bit older than me and more experienced in the ways of the world, etc. She was always bringing boyfriends home, mods, rockers, punks, goths, trendies, you name it. One time she brought this guy home, a guy who was a DJ at this night in Glasgow that was a big deal at the time, Joy of a Toy it was called, it had been going since 1977 or something like that, they played punk and psych but also, like, classic rock and soul and alternative, it was schizophrenic, and it was New Year when she brought him home and they had split a taxi from town and my mum and dad were drunk themselves so they didn't care, neighbours were falling all over the floor, it was that kind of night, so he got to stay the night and I remember hearing them having sex really loud next door, heaving and panting and begging and all that shit. The next day he was sitting at the breakfast table pleased as punch. He was wearing a pair of jeans and a black V-neck T-shirt and one of those checked seventies lumberjack jackets and a pair of baseball boots, I think, and I sat down next to him and asked him about music. He went on about Wire, *Pink Flag*, which was fine with me, but then he had this thing about Neil Young, he kept going on about Neil Young, about how his *Harvest* album was like the true country, none of this Acuff and Rose bullshit, he kept saying, which meant nothing to me at the time, and he had this weird thing that he would do with his eyebrow where he would just raise his right eyebrow for a millisecond and it was like a bird shrugging, a bird flying away and shrugging and saying, you know, what do you expect, it's what I do, something like that, and I was impressed, this guy is living it, I thought to my teenage self, living what, I don't know, but then the thing that compounded it was when my sister told me that when he took his jeans off the night before he had no scants on, no underwear whatsoever, just his naked balls underneath the denim. It blew my mind, just naked balls, I thought, what an idea. I had been brought up on things like combs and toothpaste and socks and vests and underwear. It was crazy to me. I asked her, doesn't it stink, I said, doesn't it leave a stain? He said he washed his jeans when they got dirty, she said. Besides, she said, he doesn't care about stinks or stuff like that. Then she smirked and said that she thought it was sexy, this penis so near the surface, just ready to strike, not caged up or anything. I admit I was a convert. From that day on I threw all of my scants in the bin and just walked about with my bollocks hanging carefree. After that it was every man for himself.

RR: What was your first exposure to the music scene in Airdrie?

SH: My mum had some records by Sinew Singer. She claimed she had dated him briefly in like 1960 but that he couldn't betroth himself to any one woman because he was married to rock n roll, so he had all these partners and it didn't work out, it couldn't, my mum was the monogamous sort and besides there were all these women claiming that Sinew was the father of their sons, god knows how much of Airdrie he populated but he was my father for sure, spiritually. I used to do these dance routines to his records, you know like 'Who's Responsible?' and 'Tracing Paper Moon', shit like that. Mrs Grey would come over who lived a few streets away with her husband Alec and I would put on a dance display in the front room and they would look at me with their jaws on the floor, not knowing what to think.

185

I'd be flipping out all over the place. I guess that's where I started associating art with madness or high energy or something.

RR: What was your first instrument?

SH: Bass. It was all I could manage, one note after the next. Plus it left space to, like, fall on the floor or jump off stage, stuff like that.

RR: Did you ever see Memorial Device play with Mary Hanna on bass?

SH: Let me tell you about Mary Hanna. I knew her at school. She would wear these tights. Fuck me, it was incredible, I can feel my bare dick in my jeans right now. Like pale blue nylons or once even red nylons. People used to yell at her stuff like *Bedknobs and Broomsticks* because it was rumoured that she had been caught masturbating with a bed end or the pole of a brush, something like that. But she didn't care, she was above it all, at least that's how it seemed. I always remember one time in chemistry where she was sitting on the floor next to a radiator, I don't know what was going on, but she was sitting there and she had her legs pulled up against her chest and her arms wrapped around her legs with these heels on and just for a second I caught a glimpse of her stocking tops and it was unforgettable, it was seared on my mind forever, the tiny centimetre gap between the blue of her nylons and the black of her skirt. Oh my god, I thought to myself, that is a gift right there. Sometimes you would see older boys waiting for her after school but there were rumours that she was a lesbian, I guess because she was unobtainable. Then there was this time that I got into a fight. I wasn't a tough guy, it wasn't my style, but I was walking home one day across the fields and this guy, this older guy, sort of pushed into me and knocked me aside and I just lashed out instinctively and banged him one. He grabbed me by the throat and said, you're in fucking big trouble, just like that, and he arranged for a fight the next night, up on the spare ground at Craigneuk. I didn't want to do it, I wasn't that tough, but it was on my way home and there was no way out of it. On the night I cut across the grass with some friends that I had talked into backing me up but they were no help whatsoever and this guy came out of nowhere and just cuffed me one and I fell back on the grass and saw the clouds coming up and birds zooming across my eyeballs. I managed to pull myself up on my elbows in time to see my assailant walking away with a leer on his face, they called him Spike, what a joke, and with him was Mary Hanna. At one point she turned around and looked at me and shouted, fuck off, you loser. I'll never forget that.

RR: Have you ever had a normal job?

SH: I worked in a shoe shop in Coatbridge for one day and got fired. I couldn't be arsed going into the stock room and finding different sizes so I would just automatically tell people that everything was out of stock. You genuinely can't be arsed, the manager said to me, can you? He seemed kind of impressed, in a way. That's well observed, I said, and after that it was all over. Of course I had a paper round, my dad was always putting my name down for paper rounds. Everyone in Airdrie had a paper round at some point. That's a real job right there, he would say, and of course I would just go dump all of the papers behind a fucking hedge at Easter Moffat Golf Club and be done with it.

My best job was as a postman in Holehills in Airdrie. That was a fucking eye-opener. There would be human excrement on the stairs inside the flats and you would hear all these crazy fights going on behind closed doors. Plus you would be delivering court orders and shit like that and often you would knock on the door and there would be this slamming noise round the back and you would see the guy who lived there fleeing across the back garden, leaping the fence and just disappearing into the distance. You were constantly being harangued, though, people would come up to you and say, you got my giro there, mate? I have to post it through the letterbox, I would tell them, it's the law. I can't just hand out fucking cheques in the middle of the street, what do you think this is, the ice cream van? But then they would start getting antsy, giving me shit like, I won't be in all fucking day, I need my giro man, I'm fucking skint, I need to visit my maw in hospital, my dad's a fucking diabetic, shite like that, so that I would just give in and give it to them on the spot, who knows if it was even genuine, but I was a soft touch and they knew it. Anyone with messy hair is a fucking liberal and will eventually give in to pressure, that was the philosophy of Holehills. Plus shitting on your own doorstep keeps the other dogs at bay. That was another one. It was like a fucking social experiment. What was that documentary where they all went to prison? It was exactly like that.

I actually got bit by a dog there. I used to have this old mod parka that I would wear and this fucking dog just leaped at me in this guy's driveway and attached itself to my arm. I lifted the fucking thing up and it was still hanging on by its jaws, just clamped around my arm. Luckily the parka was thick enough that it couldn't sink its teeth in but when I got back to the post office they were all really cool and the head man sent this letter out, it was brilliant, he had it delivered to every house on the street, saying that until this guy got his dog under control no one would be receiving any mail. You could never get away with that now. But back then the post office had your back, it felt good, even though the head guy was the dad of my first girlfriend and had banned her from seeing me because I was a Protestant and she was a Catholic, which is fucking nonsense. I wasn't even an atheist. I wanted

nothing to do with the whole fucking deal. Maybe you know her, Maya
McCormack, she played in that all-girl group Dark Bathroom?

RR: Whatever happened to them?

SH: It's a long story. They started out as a kind of jangly sixties girl-
group thing, you know, like The Shangri-Las meets the Buzzcocks,
that kind of thing, it was happening all over in the early eighties.
Actually, I think they were called something else back then,
something like The Ladybugs, something cute like that. I was getting
the train into Glasgow once and I met these girls that I knew, this
kind of notorious pair, and Maya was with them. I don't know if she
had ever been into Glasgow before, or if she had it was only her second
or third time, but there was an air of expectation as we pulled out of
the station, the four of us. I looked at her legs, I can still remember
them, she had a short black-and-white go-go dress on with dark
woolly tights and ankle boots and she had her dark hair all pulled up
in a wild beehive with loose curly strands all hanging down in crazy
corkscrews. She seemed nervous and delicate but also poetic and a
little unhinged. In other words she was ticking all the right boxes.

They were going to some club in town, maybe it was Joy of a Toy, I
can't remember, but I decided to tag along, even though Maya told
me she was meeting her boyfriend there. What a joke, I said, this girl
is mine. Her boyfriend was the typical sensitive intellectual feminist
type that is completely unattractive to women. I sat with the three of
them at the table and made deliberately vague comments designed
to undermine him. It worked and soon the tension was palpable. At
one point Maya and her boyfriend went outside to talk and I'm not
really clear what happened but it seemed he was getting more and
more wound up and that he went to hit her, though probably not

really, maybe he just lunged at her or something out of frustration, who could blame him, but the next thing I knew the bouncers were restraining him and she came rushing back in with one of the other girls from her group, Megan, I think, and all the while I could see him shouting and banging on the glass outside. I felt evil, like I had just trapped an insect in a jar or something. There was a big fuss, the bouncers said they could smuggle Maya out of the back door to keep her out of harm's way. What a joke, they were leading her right into harm's way, really, ha ha ha ha ha, but soon the three of us, me and Maya and Megan, were making a dash for the train back home. When we got to Airdrie we jumped in a taxi but then Megan lost the head when Maya insisted on going home with me. If I had known that's what it was all about I would never have helped you in the first place, she screamed, and then she beat her fists on the door and leaped out of the taxi and ran off crazy in a huff. That was the end of The Ladybugs right there, ha ha ha ha ha ha. We went back to mine. I had this flat just above Benny's, this chip shop in Clarkston where everyone would hang around outside and get up to no good. The previous tenant had died in his bed and the body had lain there for weeks undetected, it was a big deal at the time, so it meant I got it cheap. No one else would live there. But it was an artist garret for me, although I did nothing but stare out the window at the park and drink beer sitting on the edge of my mattress and have sex with confused girls, like on this particular night, and if you're reading this, Mr McCormack, we even used a condom, so fuck you.

Three things I remember about Maya. Number one, she had the firmest buttocks I have ever held in my hands. They were a marvel to behold, her tiny skirt literally stuck out behind her at forty-five degrees and I remember her lying on top of me with her skirt pulled up above her waist and me with a hand on each cheek like the first man on the moon. Number two was her eyes. She had green eyes, like a cat in the corner of a dark room. Number three was her skin. Kissing her neck was like running your tongue along a cold marble pillar.

It didn't last long, her father was having none of it and one day I got a note through my door, hand-delivered, saying that she couldn't see me any more. She had walked all the way from Plains one summer afternoon, which isn't that far, but somehow the thought of this journey and her sad determination really got to me. When that sort of thing happens to you when you're young it feels like it was written in a book before you were even born and that the next chapter will be even more beautiful and tragic than the last.

In the short time that we had together I tried to educate her about music. I played her tapes of Pere Ubu, Peel Sessions, shit like The Only Ones and Suicide, and I turned her onto free jazz, Albert Ayler, Ornette Coleman, Frank Wright, stuff like that. I gave her an education that summer, that's for sure. That was my own part in the story, as far as I'm concerned. From then on it was awkward.

RR: What do you mean?

SH: She got an older boyfriend and she would avoid me. I would bump into her in Glasgow, say walking down Queen Street, and her new boyfriend would walk on and not even stop so she would be left to say hurried hellos and then tear off after him and I would see the two of them shaking their heads as they crossed into George Square like I was just so much rubbish to be shot of.

RR: You were going to tell us what happened to Dark Bathroom. I had that demo tape they made, *June 1941*, and it was amazing, songs like 'Easter Island' and 'Harm That Foot Down', stuff like that.

SH: Yeah, okay. You know, I always wondered about that title. That was another summer, I suppose. When I get my shit together I'm going to get another band going as well. Plus I want to write a novel, a ghost story, probably. One morning I woke up really early and couldn't get back to sleep and it was one of those weird really foggy autumn mornings and I opened the curtains and looked out the window and across the road in Katherine Park I could make out all these figures dotted about across the park, stock-still, motionless, just standing there, not looking at me but like looking away into the distance or just staring down at the ground, not even looking at each other. I'll never forget it. There's a story there somewhere, don't you think?

RR: You were telling us about Dark Bathroom . . .

SH: That's another ghost story. The whole place is full of ghosts.

RR: What place?

SH: Katherine Park. Airdrie. You name it.

RR: What happened next?

SH: Then I cut myself. This was right after the split with Maya. I took a knife and cut right into my arm. No reason. Except I felt like I was coming to a place where I was dying, the old me was dying, and all I could see ahead was everything that everyone else in my life had experienced, you know, peace and quiet, this kind of like-it-or-not sense of fulfilment, preparations for the grave, that kind of shit. It outraged me. It wasn't a suicide attempt, far from it. It was an attempt on life. There's an ancient myth where the arm is severed or the hand is sacrificed, something like that, you must have heard of it, where you give your hand, like in marriage, but to a new life instead. At this point it felt like there was a magnet stuck under me, that my body was metal, and that it was impossible to move forwards or backwards. So I stuck a knife in my fucking arm to see if it would bend or if it was still possible to give myself away to something new.

RR: Did it bend?

SH: Did it fuck. So Maya got with Patty for a while. At the time I thought he was kind of a ponce.

RR: How come?

SH: He was the sort of guy who would always have a novel conspicuously sticking out his pocket. In fact one time I saw him walking along the road and reading at the same time.

RR: What book was it?

SH: *Under the Volcano*. He was holding it up right in front of him so everybody could see it, as if anybody could fucking care less what you were reading in Airdrie. It just made you look like a three-speed.

RR: What's a three-speed?

SH: A three-speed gear, a queer. As soon as Maya got with him everything changed. He always wore these boots, I don't know if you saw them, these quasi-military leather boots that almost went up to his knees and the next thing you know Maya is kicking around in thigh-high leather boots and smoking cigarettes and acting moody as fuck. They would walk down the main street in Airdrie and everyone would be turning their heads, Patty with his glasses on, these little irritating Lennon specs, the kind you would never tire of smashing, and with a fucking top hat and this floor-length trench coat on and Maya next to him, only she's wearing a white fur coat and fucking white leather trousers and boots and a pair of shades, looking round with this total disdain for the world but still trying to impress it, if you know what I mean. I saw her in the chemist's one day, buying white mascara or some fucking thing, and she was wearing these ultra-tight leather trousers and you could see the thin V of the black thong she was wearing coming out the top of the trousers and I thought to myself, when the fuck did she start wearing lingerie? She made me feel like a rapist when I bought her lingerie. Of course I was annoyed at myself. How come I couldn't turn her?

RR: But weren't you in Occult Theocracy with Patty for a bit?

SH: That group was completely bogus. If I hadn't been such a fucking otherworldly channel it would just have been pub rock.

RR: What about Dark Bathroom?

SH: I mean, Dark Bathroom, come on. Who the fuck came up with that? The next thing you knew she had this band, this all-girl bathroom band, I can't remember the names of the other two but Maya was on guitar and vocals and Mary Hanna played bass with them for a bit. Mary was in all the good groups, the bitch. They had this thing where they all dressed really severe like dominatrixes with skintight PVC dresses and long hair with blunt fringes and white skin and red lipstick and they would have like a chair sitting centre-stage and they would play this music, it was all improvised, in other words they made it up on the spot, using metal slides on electric guitars, just this screaming electric noise, and they would build to these insane crescendos where it sounded like a magnetic storm and then their sacrifice would appear, usually some young damaged boy, some clueless follower, and they would strap him to the chair and then torture him. It got them banned from venues. Sometimes they would tie him up and break eggs over him and then Maya would push him

194

backwards, the chair was suspended by ropes, and she would put the heel of her boot in his mouth and he would suck it and they would play this music where it was like the mother goddess tribe were back to take over the world and then they would cover him with feathers or jam or melt candle wax on him and sometimes Maya or one of the other girls – I never saw Mary do it – would wear a strap-on plastic dildo and they would ejaculate over him, god knows what was in there, I heard it was yogurt but who knows. I saw them play and my jaw was on the floor. I felt like I had been dating a five-foot-high black hole.

RR: Wasn't there a thing with a cheesegrater?

SH: Yeah, I saw that, it was mental. They took a cheesegrater to this guy's dick. All that was left was like this wilty blue vein, ha ha ha ha ha. I spoke to Maya a few times, after shows, I was still friendly with Patty, but she was always stood there looking at me like I wasn't even worth torturing. Who knows, maybe I wasn't, or maybe I was just doing too good a job myself. I got another group together but it was a heavy scene, we were into shit like Wire, Gang of Four, Eyeless in Gaza, This Heat, scratchy shit basically. Keith Levene's guitar playing on *Metal Box* was massive. The lead singer – I was playing bass – was into new wave French movies and art and shit but he was a user, they all were. We got a few gigs, we played at this pub in Finsbury Park in London, this big show where there were journalists from *NME* and *Sounds* turning up but we were so incoherent and fucked up that they scrapped the idea of even reviewing us. I thought it was a plus, that we had pulled off some kind of ultimate coup, but that shows just how completely fucked-up I was. I started using myself, a bit. Of course we had no money to get back home and the singer, I won't mention his name, he's dead now, you know who he is, he fucking pawned our guitars to pay for a prostitute in this fucking bum-dungeon in King's Cross, which is where we were staying. We were there for two nights and had left our guitars in a back room at the venue but when we went to pick them up the bar staff told us the singer had been there already and taken off with the lot of them. We confronted him and he was totally matter-of-fact about it. I needed my hole, he said. What a line, I'll never forget that, and then he just shrugged, like it was fair enough and we could all understand it and sympathise with it. This guy was like five foot one and with greasy hair sticking to his face and a biker jacket that was about three times too small for him. I don't know how he did it. The lead guitarist and the drummer, whose name was James Begley, maybe you know him, they just split immediately, walked out and left me holding the cat, as it were. We had no way of getting home so the two of us had to hitch a lift. We stood up near the exit to the North Circular Road, right next to that sign for Hatfield and The North, but the first night we only got so far as St Albans, where we slept in the park next to the cathedral. The next night we thumbed our way to Carlisle, where the singer talked this truck driver into dropping us off at the services outside Hamilton for the price of a blow job. I couldn't believe it. He came back totally calm and collected, like he had just negotiated the greatest deal of all time, like he had taken this guy for a mug. I just have to suck his cock, he shrugged, while he's driving the truck, that's all. That was a bridge too far. It has to be while he's driving? I asked him. It's the only way he'll get off, he said. C'mon, he said, like I was a total prude, live and let live. I couldn't believe what I was fucking hearing. And where am I going to be while you're slurping this guy's dick beneath the steering wheel? I asked him. You'll be right there, he said, watching me. That's part of the deal.

Sure enough, we drove from Carlisle to Hamilton with the singer on his knees choking on this truck driver's rancid cock while the trucker, who seemed to be on amphetamines or something, did like a hundred miles an hour up the motorway, occasionally looking round at me and nodding, you know, like this is how it's done, son, now we're living. Fucking hell, I thought to myself, I'm in a rock n roll band at last.

Then he died, maybe you heard about it? He found this credit card, he didn't steal it, he found this jacket in West End Park, just across from the hospital, and there was a wallet inside it and there was a credit card in there and I think he took it as a sign, like a blessing from God, and like a good soldier he spread it out amongst his friends. There was this famous day, this last day, where he took a group of his friends on a trip to Edinburgh, all expenses paid on this found credit card. I wasn't there myself but I heard they were all drinking on the train in the morning and buying records and had a slap-up meal in a restaurant and then a tab at a bar in the Pubic Triangle, where everyone was dancing with strippers and getting it on. He must have known that it was a final blow-out, that he had effectively dug his own grave. Before he could even be arrested he hung himself from a tree on the Carlisle Road. There was a piece about it in the newspaper and of course I thought about that song, the one about strange fruit hanging from the branches.

RR: What are you working on currently?

SH: I'm writing lyrics, writing songs. I've had a few bands since then but nothing has gelled, nothing has really felt right. I've become very interested in Aleister Crowley and the occult and as soon as I clean up my act I intend to start practising the rituals and get serious about my life and my magickal practice. And of course there's that ghost story I want to write. It's in there somewhere, I'm sure of that.

22. Ships Rising Up and Passing Through the Water Full of Sunlight and Memory the Tricks That It Plays: *Bruce Cook on Autonomic Dreaming with Lucas and Vanity and all the baggage that comes back to haunt you like ghostly ships at the bottom of the ocean in a graveyard beneath the sea breaking free and rising to the surface.*

If I remember it right Patty's mum and dad were Italian – or half Italian – or something like that. I could be wrong. They owned a little shop on the main street in Airdrie that sold Italian chocolates and cigarettes and ice cream. Stuff like that. You would see his mum every night when she closed up, walking along the road with these boxes of cigarettes under her arms. She never left them there at night. It was too much of a temptation for burglars. They'll kill you for a fag in Airdrie.

The first time I ever tried a Turkish Delight, it was in there. I bought it with my pocket money and I almost spewed my ring, man, seriously. But I kept going back for more, maybe it was seeing the advert or something but I got it into my head that it was romantic and sophisticated – you know, like garlic or pasta. Sometimes I would see Patty – he was just a boy then – sitting at one of the tables in the back, eating a sherbet dip or a tube of Smarties and I would think man that boy lives in heaven so he does.

We ended up becoming friends, I was coming in that often, and we would hang out at his house, which was this amazing gloomy mansion – you shoulda seen it, it was freaky – with toilets that had sloping floors and a basement playroom that was just like an open wooden frame that led off into the darkness and that was really creepy and that was good for watching horror movies or science-fiction films late at night on his black-and-white portable. His mother would bring us down sandwiches, though really they were just single slices of bread with cured meats on them and olives and hummus, and it added to the feel of being somewhere else completely.

Our friendship didn't last long – it was one of those things, man, no big deal either way – and then my parents moved to Shettleston and that was that. I grew up and went to college – total waste of time, why bother – then got a job at a cooperative grocer's in the East End. I was produce manager and I enjoyed the work. I rented a small house with a garden where I grew my own food – or tried to, man. We were a total bunch of hippies back then, we were into solar panels, grains, Buddhism, incense, yoga, cushions, ha ha . . . know what I mean? But we were socially plugged in too – it was important for us to be in the East End and change what we could there. What is it Gary Snyder says about seeing where you are and what can be done? That was a big thing with us. I started teaching a martial arts programme in a back room at Shettleston Library in Wellshot Road on Saturday mornings. It was a funny bunch, man – old retirees looking to stretch their muscles, a couple of serious headcases, some pregnant women, the kind of strange hermits that lose themselves in the East End of Glasgow, a few of my hippy friends – then one day this guy shows up, this huge guy with a scar on his head – that wasn't uncommon in the East End – but with these huge hands and feet. I remember when he first came in – he was dressed in a white T-shirt and a pair of long white shorts – and I caught sight of his hands and they were like shovels. If I get hit by one of those, I thought to myself, I'm a dead man.

It turns out he couldn't fight to save his life, which was lucky for me. I asked him why he had decided to start training and he gave me this whole story, man, this whole thing about how he had dreamed a dream where he had been given some Sanskrit name that meant The Defender, The Protector – something like that, seriously – and that now he had to live up to the title. I asked him if he had any experience of fighting and he talked about manning the front line in his brain – straight up, this is how he talked, man – about how he was well up on strategy and theory, he started talking about historical models, man, these gambits, what did he call them – things like The Oslofjord Gambit and The Lundtoftbjerg Compromise – and I realised he was talking about the Second World War. Wesertag, he said, pointing to the scar on his forehead. Weserzeit. He kept referring to a small notebook that he kept in his top pocket. He said his organs were in bad shape and asked me if I could do anything for them. I told him that martial arts would definitely streamline his body and bring his organs into a more harmonious relationship – that was what it was all about, you know what I mean, at least the way I taught it. He seemed relieved. My organs have been giving me nightmares, he said. Then he told me that dreams were the language of the organs. Wow, I said, that's pretty heavy, man, tell me more. Then he said that dreams were actually your own internal organs talking to you. Like, for instance, certain organs speak in certain ways. The kidneys, he said – and I remember this in particular, it was way-out stuff – the kidneys don't talk the way you think they would. They don't talk about water or deserts or whatever. No, he said, the kidneys were more like panthers, man, like jackals and lynxes prowling in the light of the moon. Heavy, right? Or like sex with very feline women, he said. That's your kidneys talking. I was blown away, man. I had never thought of it like that and I recalled the old maxim, you know, as above so below. I pictured the bloodstream as a network of voices, man, information-rich, tides of this and that, it just came to me right there and then – tell me more, man, I said, tell me more. Then he told me that the heart was the ocean beneath the ocean – you believe that – that the genitals were represented by elephants. Speak for yourself, man, I joked, but he was deadly serious. No, he said, not just elephants – check this out – but circus animals and beasts of burden with heavy eyes. What do you have to learn from me, man? I said to him. You're the man. Movement, he said. Balance. Coordination. We need to get this guy teaching, I thought to myself, we need to get a class going.

So we began training together and the two of us put together this class – we called it Autonomic Dreaming.

The heart is tried every night, Lucas said, that's how he would introduce each workshop – it was mind-blowing, it was insane – he would read all this stuff from his notebook. It is taken from the body and it is weighed, he would say, it is stalked like a lion, it is examined for vulnerabilities, we track it, we put it through its paces. The heart is also a hotel, he would say. More particularly, it is luggage, baggage. Recurrent dreams of hotels, more especially of left luggage, of checking out and of leaving all of your effects behind, that is the heart speaking. I was like that, shit, if you say so, okay.

We came up with breathing exercises – visualisations. We travelled along the secret byways – that's what he called them, the white and red veins running up the spine, he said – and we spun off into realms of fantastic creatures – great buildings, wildlife, feral activity – all this shit. I realised that the organs were literally dreaming the world. Seriously, I came to this conclusion. At the same time, Lucas's martial arts skills blossomed. He would flip partners into the air with his big hands like tennis rackets, send them cartwheeling across the room. I felt like I had a future champion on my hands.

Inevitably, we began to socialise. I drove out to Airdrie to see him and visited him at his mother's house, where he lived in a caravan in the driveway. He was always a record collector and always had music on the go – weird music, way-out music – and I remember one night when I was sitting in the caravan and he was playing a record – this is before Memorial Device, I don't know if he was making any music himself at this point – but he went out to the kitchen to get us some drinks and I overheard a conversation between him and his mother. It broke my heart. Seriously it fucked me up, man. It looks like you have a friend there, Lucas, I heard her say. Then there was silence for a while and I heard him ask her – have I ever had a friend before? A male friend, she said, I don't believe you have, no, unless you count school friends, but really, they're so unfussy they're barely friends at all. Seriously, I felt so much responsibility at that point I almost upped and fled.

I only found out about the whole memory thing gradually. Of course I suspected something was up but I guess I just thought he was some kind of savant – is that bad, man? What I mean is I didn't question it, man, I just accepted it, you know what I mean, this otherworldly aspect, this flimsy quality, if you like – which I don't mean negatively – just that he didn't seem as bolstered by personality as most people. He was the most endearing combination of, like, startling intellect married to this weird childlike quality – his great hands and his massive feet married to this very peaceful, angelic demeanour. I heard it got worse, man – that he became more isolated, more dislocated – but back then he just seemed touched, as the Irish would say.

Everywhere there were synchronicities – that's another thing about being with Lucas, he just sort of set them off, like his very presence would trip all of the world's presets. As soon as you mentioned someone's name they would appear. Like for instance, man, I was telling Lucas about an old girlfriend of mine, Vanity – she became famous later in her life and died in a car crash in San Francisco or something like that – but the thing is, man, I hadn't seen her for years and I told Lucas this story about our first date, how I had been at a concert in Glasgow and was cutting through the kitchens in the back – I was looking for a fire exit where I could smoke a sly joint – and there she was doing the dishes and she saw me and presumed I was in one of the bands that were playing. Were you just on stage, man? she asked me. Yeah, man, I said. Which group were you in, man, she said, the one with the hats? Yeah, man, I said, the one with the hats. I felt immediately emboldened. We should go out sometime, I said. Yeah, man, she said and she wrote down her phone number on a piece of paper before I was chased out the kitchen by her boss. It was that easy. But of course from then on I was caught up in a web of lies and the relationship went nowhere, man, especially when it became apparent that I was a member of no band and had no talent whatsoever as well as no friends and no prospects, ha ha, if you know what I'm saying. Which wasn't so bad really, man, as she was the worst kisser of all time, seriously – she was all teeth – there was no soft to her whatsoever. And her taste in music was awful. Shocking, man. She came back to my pad and wasn't even able to choose an LP to play – she said she had never heard of any of them, if you can believe that. That was pathetic, man. Seriously. We had

sex a few times – oh it was awkward, really bad – her mouth shut
tight, breathing heavy through her nose the whole time – seriously –
which was off-putting. You're having sex, I thought, not giving birth.
I can't really remember how it came up – maybe there was some
overenthusiastic chick hyperventilating in one of the classes and I said
to Lucas that it reminded me of sex with Vanity – but sure enough,
less than a week later, Vanity shows up for one of the classes. I hear
her outside talking to Lucas and I recognise her voice immediately,
I hear that phrase, man, *that is a total deal-breaker*, she says. Who
else talks like that in Glasgow, know what I'm saying? She walks in
and it's like she's a ghost, a sexy ghost taunting me. She's looking
great, man, I'll give her that, she has grown into her body, she was
like a stick insect when I dated her, seriously, all angles and degrees
but here she is now, in tight jogging pants and a leotard, looking like
Olivia Newton-John sent down from heaven. I went in brazen, man.
Wow, I said. Heaven must be missing an angel. Hell is certainly
asking questions, she said, looking me up and down. She had a mouth
on her too by the way.

We took the class. By this point we had a method of teaching that
combined guided meditations, bodywork and a short knowledge
lecture. The classes would focus on certain organs as the locus of
certain images or words or states of mind. On this particular night it
was the pancreas – which of course is associated with the goat as well
as amusement parks, destruction of household goods, hallucination,
nothingness and certain vegetables, as well as total bodily paralysis.

Under my tutelage Lucas had come up with this motion – that's what
he called it, it wasn't quite a dance – this motion that he thought
mimicked the movement of speech associated with the pancreas,

a turning round and a lifting of one foot after the other, a sliding forwards – it's a helter-skelter, he said, that's how we work on the pancreas. We had a full class that night – older women, a few recovering drug addicts and alcoholics, a guy called Akbar that I would occasionally play chess with in a flat on Alexandra Parade – and to be honest, man, I was secretly pleased to see that despite Vanity's blossoming she was as graceless as ever. She flopped around like a baby elephant though maybe that's just my genitals talking, know what I'm saying.

I could see that Lucas was watching her closely. He would move around the room, correcting people's routines. I had taught him well. But when he came to Vanity he took both her hands in his and he kissed one of them. Man, it was remarkable. This is like Shakespeare, I said to myself. Phew. Everyone else was caught up in their own motions but I saw it clearly, man, saw the look on Vanity's face, how taken aback she was, how bowled over, and then Lucas reached down and lifting one foot after the other he put her bare feet on top of his and held her around the waist. Seriously. Her feet looked tiny on top of these huge plates of meat – I remember her chipped nail varnish and her bunions – and then he began to lift his feet, slowly, one after the other, guiding her around the room, as if she was a puppet in his command, honestly, man, and I saw her lean back, I saw her body respond – seriously, who knows what was going on inside – and he led her in this slow looping movement – it's like DNA, I said to myself – her head lying back over her shoulders, her hair hanging down – and she closed her eyes, man, he had her completely in his power – *completely in his power* – and I watched as he licked his finger and ran it down the length of her exposed neck. Seriously. He might as well have slit her throat.

205

Then McManus joined the group – Adam McManus. I should have seen it coming, man, in retrospect. He had all the hallmarks of the kung fu guru – know what I mean – shaved head, toned body, teetotaller, vegan, so completely balanced, man, and nice to everyone, that you just knew there was a seething well of resentment and hatred and madness that was ready to spill over at any moment. He got big into Lucas's thing about the organs, man. He would come to the martial arts classes and he had this whole thing where he claimed he was ex-SAS or Special Services or something like that. I've heard it all before, man, every bouncer in Glasgow, every security guard claims Special Ops duty. But then he said he had been active in Northern Ireland as an agent provocateur. He let it slip to Lucas, man, who wrote it down and told me. There was no point in telling Lucas anything that you wanted to keep secret – you had to presume that he would immediately go and tell someone else. He had nothing to keep secrets in.

He told Lucas about an IRA bank heist that had gone wrong. They had set up it up in painstaking detail. They had mapped the bank – the positions of the cashiers, the exits, the alarm system – the whole deal, man. McManus had been chosen to lead it. When you go in – he was told – you turn to the left, where the main security guard is seated. He holds all of the master keys and can let you into the vault. Everything was set. McManus kicked the door in and swung to the left, screaming, Don't fucking move! There was nothing there but a blank wall. Seriously, man, that's what he said. Someone came up behind him and hit him over the head. When he woke he was tied to a table in the outbuildings of a farm in South Armagh. It gets heavier, man. There were three guys with balaclavas dressed completely in black standing round him. He recognised their voices, he said. He was pretty sure they were the same three guys he had gone into the bank with. You fuckers, he said – at least that's what he claimed he said, who knows, man. You stitched me up, he said. And he began calling them snitches and grass bags and scabs, apparently, or so he says. Then one of the men took out a hacksaw and ran it, really gently, between his legs. Seriously, man. Who's talking now? the guy said to him.

Then the leader – the taller of the three – stepped forward. We're not here to represent sides, he said. We have evolved beyond this petty partisan mindset but we are here to settle disputes, something along those lines. Then he brought something up, man – something that he could have never possibly known about McManus's past – something that had never been resolved. You've sinned, he said, matter-of-factly, just like that. Then he took a raw vegetable from his pocket and started munching on it, seriously, that's what he says. McManus started crying, man, he lost it, basically. Then the main guy takes his balaclava off. He looks like an older McManus. I came back for you, he says.

He wakes up again, man. This time he's driving a car on the way to the ferry in Belfast – seriously – who knows how he got there. He reaches into his pocket and there's a one-way ticket to Troon. Never thought I would be glad to see that, he says. He drives from Troon to Glasgow. He arrives late at night. He's driving without purpose, man, who knows where he might end up. He pulls up at the gates to Kelvingrove Park at the top of Kelvingrove Street. There's no one else around. He gets out of the car and starts running into the dark, just running, man. He gets to the fountain – which back then was going 24 hours a day, it has been fucked for years – and without a thought he launches himself into the water.

At first he survives by stealing vegetables from outside fruit and veg shops and sleeping at the top of the park. Then he starts hearing this voice, this voice from beyond. It's his future self, he claims. Seriously. That's what he says. It's an attempt to turn his life around. He cleans up his act, changes his name. He was a vagabond, he said, but there was something in the blood that was speaking to him. You believe that?

In Lucas he found the perfect combination of living guru and willing student. I'm telling you, man. Vanity became involved – it became this threesome – this secret kung fu cell. They were into body workings – extreme diets, fasting. I would take them through the moves at my martial arts class and it was like they were humouring me – like they were already beyond it or were on some fast track to complete body gnosis. But when Lucas and I hung out together it was like nothing had changed – we were still best buddies, man. We would go to concerts – we even took a weekend to Leeds together to attend a martial arts conference where Lucas and I demonstrated our organ-linked combat stances, and while some people labelled us as fantasists there was a strong reception for what we were doing. We stayed in an old hotel that was like a stately home with its own grounds in the university area. At night we sat on the balcony and drank beer and Lucas read me some poems he had written, which were more like ultra-condensed diary entries, like 'Waking/light from the window/a confluence of birds/with/names' and 'Your name/is/Lucas/you/fool' or 'Planets above the/horizon/each one of which/stars too/the same'. Are you sleeping with Vanity, man? I asked him. He read me another poem which basically said, 'Yes/who/yes'. This is bullshit, man, I thought to myself, I'm being taken over by a cult and my best friend is sleeping with my ex-girlfriend and talking like a Chinese hermit.

One day Lucas plays me this tape – I want you to listen to this, he says – I'm keen to get your opinion on it. We're at the studio – working late – fitting a new central heating system. Lucas puts the cassette in the player and takes out his notebook. Okay, he says. He presses play and this sound comes out – this low-level drone but with a pulse somewhere in the depths, know what I mean, this distant orchestral sound that had been smudged somehow, sunk, perhaps, know what I'm saying, like a shipwreck rocking back and forth on the bottom of the ocean. We kept working away – neither of us said a word. Then Lucas obviously forgot what he was playing, man, and eventually he turned and said to me, do you hear that? What is that sound? I decided to wind him up. It's the sound of a graveyard at the bottom of the sea, I told him. I've been there, Lucas said in a panic, and his eyes looked like they would pop out of his head. Seriously. He was taking a total frenzy. I recognise it, he said. I've been there. What's it like, man? I ask him. Oh, he says, and he shakes his head. Oh. He's like that, it's like being stranded, he said. Marooned, he said. It could be an island, he said, it could be a sunken ship. Or wait, yes, it's a graveyard, yes, he said, I can see it now, all these ships swaying in the tide, tiny fish swimming through them, angel fish, he said, silver streaks of light. When did you hear it before? I asked him. When I was sleeping, he said. Or when I was silent – at night, alone – or when I had an operation, maybe, I think so, I remember floating down through the waves as I went under and finding the ships, these great ships, like ghosts, all scuppered but lit up, illuminated in the dark.

I couldn't keep it going, man. Lucas was becoming agitated. I confessed to him. That's your recording, man, I said. You put it on. Look in your notebook, I said, find out what it's about. Yes, he said. I remember. The ships, he said. The sunken ships. I put a contact mic on my forehead, he explained to me. Seriously. Right on the ajna chakra, he said. And I recorded it while I slept. I wanted to play it for you. The nightly descent, he said. It's right there. I was like that, man oh man.

We continued working while the tape ran in the background. Everything sinks, I remember thinking to myself, fuck me, everything sinks.

McManus, Vanity and Lucas began teaching a class together on Saturday afternoons – I let them do it against my better judgement but it proved a success – and soon they moved it to three times a week. It was more like interpretive dance, know what I mean, modern dance like Merce Cunningham or something like that but with kung fu moves in there and with it keyed to the music of the organs, you know, which by this time they were all recording with contact mics and choreographing movements to it and all that. They had great results, man – old spinsters dancing for the first time, newly flexible rheumatics, even drug addicts and alcoholics kicking it in favour of this new way of relating to their own bodies. I never attended a class myself. I was too proud, in a way, but sometimes I would walk past and stick my head around the door and it was like they were floating in there, man, seriously, it was like an aquarium in there and they were all these weightless blooms of colour floating this way and that.

Then one day I got a call from Vanity. Someone was looking for McManus – someone from his past life. They're after him, she told me. If anyone turns up looking for him tell them he has left and you have no idea where he is. I was furious, man. Just totally fucked off. What are you doing covering for McManus, man? I asked her.

We're trying to do our best here in the East End and you're telling me that thugs are going to come in and turn over the whole place looking for this prick? Listen, she said. It's not McManus's fault. He was kidnapped and he still gets flashbacks and nightmares all the time because of it. That's what she said, man. He was doing his duty, that's what she said. I lost the head at that. Just fucking lost it. His duty, man? His fucking duty, man? Explain to me in what way a human being's duty involves spying for the state, man. You know what I mean? She said she didn't want to hear it and she hung up the phone. I called Lucas. He told me the same thing – in so many words – but it was as if he was reading it from a piece of paper with no real idea of its import or even its meaning. Okay, I said to myself, I'm caught up in a web of madness here, man – I need to protect myself.

Sure enough, not even a week later, two guys show up at the library on a Saturday afternoon. I'm coming out of a beginner's yoga class and there are these two guys – maybe in their forties or early fifties, both with grey suits and silver hair, lots of gold rings, smelling of Old Spice. Excuse me, son, one of them said. Can I ask you a question? I said, go ahead, man. You see that sun out there in the sky? he asked me. Would that be the same sun that we see over in County Armagh? You're fucking with me, man, I said to him. I have no time for this. I'm setting you up, he said. That's a very different thing. What you're supposed to say, when I ask you about the sun, is that you wouldn't know, that you're a stranger here yourself. At this point they both patted each other on the shoulder and made a big scene about slapping their legs and falling about in laughter. What can I do for you? I asked them. There is nothing you could possibly do for me that I couldn't do myself, the other says. Then he hands me a photograph, a Polaroid of McManus. You wouldn't happen to know this gentleman, would you? he asks me. In the photograph he looks different – he's out of shape, he has long greasy hair plus he's wearing glasses. Never seen him in my life before, man, I said. I heard he was teaching class here, the second silver-hair says. I heard he was a vegetarian or something like that. You heard wrong, man, I said. Now kindly leave the building. They both looked at me for a second and then one of them took out his wallet. All we need is an address, he said. And you'll never be bothered again. I don't know what you're talking about, man, I said. I need to take a shower. Excuse me, gentlemen. Then I walked away.

There was a communal shower room in the back of the library and as I entered I could barely see anything for all of the steam – the odd foot, some dark curly hair, a belly sticking out from the mist like a Chinese peak. Then it was like everyone disappeared and I was on my own in the clouds. Someone came up behind me with a garrotte and wrapped it round my neck. Seriously. I felt it cut into my throat. I tried to fight him off but he was too strong and I was so slippery from the soap and the steam that I couldn't do anything. I fell onto the floor and my assailant knelt on my back with both legs and pulled hard at my throat. They're going to fucking decapitate me, man, I thought to myself. Then I came to a point where it felt like I was at sea – where everything slowed to the pace of the ocean – and I began to lose consciousness but so slowly that I felt myself sink under. But here's the thing, man. Beneath me I could make out shapes – black shapes, that I took to be rigging, torn through, high masts with fish running up and down – and they were illuminated, man, phosphorescent, lit from below. I thought to myself, is there something that I've forgotten, man? Is that what this place is? Know what I mean? Did I set it up myself and then forget about it or abandon it? My thoughts were infinitely clear at this point, man – seriously. I felt my body go, felt the tension in my limbs give out and I slumped, head first into the depths. I fancied I could hear voices and that I could make out what they said. But it all came out as numbers which I began to hallucinate as the coordinates I was free-falling through. It made so much sense at the time, man. Then I saw the ships – I actually glimpsed them – and although they were wrecks they weren't free-floating, rather they were anchored in place, all of them, which exaggerated the pull of the tide on them – rocking their black shapes back and forth in this deep green water that still seemed suffused with the sun. Every so often – way off in the distance – a pillar of bubbles would rise in the water as one of the anchors released and a boat took off. A ghost galleon, man, a skeleton crew, I said to myself as I flew over the tops of the sails and listened to the endless numbers in my ears. I'm in a children's book, I marvelled, seriously, in a true adventure.

When I came to I was in bed at home, sitting upright with a cup of tea, still warm, on my dresser. I picked up the phone. McManus, I said. You're an asshole, man, but all the same I think I may have given away your whereabouts to a pair of Irish hitmen. I was strangled and kidnapped and then dumped in my own fucking bed. Did they make you a cup of tea? he asked me. That isn't funny, man, I said. But yeah, yeah, they did actually, man. Did you drink any of it? he asked me. No? Good, good. Why what's in it, man? I asked him. You never know, he said, but anyway I need to flee for my life, I think. Cancel my classes, make my excuses, he said. I'm out of here. Are you taking Vanity with you, man? I asked him. No, I don't think so, he said. She has nothing to do with it. Somehow I felt relieved, man, seriously.

I called Lucas. I got kidnapped man, I told him, and it's your friend McManus's fault. I could've been killed, man, I told him – I don't even know how I got away. They must have access to my flat, I babbled. Who knows what they did to me in the meantime, I fretted. This might not be the end of it, I despaired. But I was with you, Lucas told me. Don't you remember? I disturbed your assailants and fought them off, he claimed. I thought of his huge hands, lily-white, made for slow strangulation. Then what happened? I asked him. One of the men fell on the floor, he said. He slipped and banged his head. I wish I could have got a photo, he said. The blood on the white tiles, it was like Hitchcock. I got my hands around the other one's neck – it was like attempting to compress a tree trunk – but I felt my fingers meet behind his neck and at the moment that they touched he dropped to his knees and fell forward on the floor. Then I rushed to see if you were okay and you were conscious but you were delirious – you kept saying numbers, like you were doing sums under your breath – adding and subtracting numbers. The showers were still running – it was impossible to see three feet in front of you – and when I turned off all the taps and the steam started to disperse we were left with an empty shower room all except for smeared footprints on the tiles and a perfect crescent of blood. The assailants were gone, disappeared without a sound. Then we went to see Vanity, he told me. I have it all written down here.

Why did we go to see Vanity, man?

You asked me to take you there. You said you had just come out of the ocean – that you had made it to dry land and that you wanted to tell her that.

And you let me do that, man?

It was what you wanted to do, Lucas said. You were traumatised – I was willing to go along with whatever it was you wanted. I have it written down here – land ho, you kept saying, land ho.

I kept saying land ho, man?

You kept talking about these ships – these underwater clippers that were taking off – that were headed for the surface.

You were the one who told me about the ships, man, I said. Don't you remember? You said that you heard a sound, man – the sound of your own body, remember – you recorded your body at night and when we played it back you talked about seeing the ships – the submerged ships – all lit up from below.

I know that's what you said, Lucas admitted. That's what you told Vanity too. But I have no idea what you are talking about, he said. I never saw the ships, I never heard such music.

I had embarrassed myself in front of Vanity, humiliated myself in front of Lucas, lost an entire day out of my life and was possibly still a target for hitmen. I moved to Edinburgh and set up a yoga studio there. I never found out what happened to McManus. Vanity died, of course. I went to see Memorial Device once. They played at The Venue in Edinburgh while I was living there and I snuck in. The music they played was the same goddamn music. Ships rising up and passing through, the water full of sunlight and memory, the tricks that it plays. I couldn't stand to be around it for long, man. I saw

Patty on stage – he still looked like the kid in the sweet shop – and as I was leaving I saw Lucas look right at me – blankly – like the whole thing had taken place in another life altogether. I was glad of that, man. A forgetting is as good a resolution as any when you've been to the bottom of the ocean but anyway – my heart told me it was long past time to go.

23. An Inoculation Against Spirit-Devouring Life as Practised in the West Coast of Scotland: *Claire Lune nurses Remy's father and rides a horse along the beach in the past.*

You'll have to excuse me, pet_____ I have good days and I have bad days_____ hold on_____ but I really want to talk about this_____ important to me_____ no_____ hold on, hold on_____ okay _____ okay_____ where will we start? Okay bear with me, my love_____ okay, so_____ I got to know your friend Remy through looking after his father who had Parkinson's disease_____ I was hired privately by his ex-wife and tasks included helping to wash him_____ brush his teeth_____ dress him, feed him_____ and help him to the toilet as he was in a wheelchair. I also read to him as he was blind_____ I'm not blind, thankfully, it's not dark yet_____ and kept him company by talking to him and telling him stories. I also helped to encourage him to swallow as he had problems swallowing so I had techniques with a spoon which I carried out each day_____ help strengthen his swallowing_____ As his health deteriorated he went into hospital. I still kept visiting him on the request of his wife to read to him and keep him company. After hospital he went to live in a residential home in Grahamshill Street in Airdrie. And so I continued my work with him right up to his passing. Sorry, pet, would you mind just putting that on my forehead? Just there. That's right, pet, that's good. Sorry, pet_____ I was aware of all the rumours about him, of course. That he had his waterworks removed in a backstreet operation_____ that he was a poofter_____ that he had been dismissed from a college in Coatbridge for dalliances with young boys. I made no judgement_____ I made no judgement_____ I was there to provide succour, a balm for the wounded near the end of their life, not to measure right and wrong_____ hold on_____ oh sweetheart_____ I'm sorry_____ I apologise_____ _____ I never thought

217

I'd have a career as a carer____ that my life would be dedicated to this sort of thing____ little did I know____ To call it a career may be to elevate it to something it was not. I got occasional caring gigs and in between times I supported myself with part-time bar and restaurant work. And occasional freelance photography commissions. That was something I loved so much____ taking colour photographs____ I loved it so much____ Left school at sixteen with nothing but a C in woodwork____ Went to live in the south of Spain with no idea whatsoever. No clue, how delightful, no vision____ no vision except getting the heck out of here____ Met boys, met girls, worked in an ice cream parlour in Malaga and as a bar manager in a restaurant____ open-air restaurant called The Iron Gates____ what a place____ what a time. The owners were Bulgarian____ who no one knows have the best cuisine in the world, my heart____ which is where I first met Telos and Santiago, my two boys____ my two boys with curly hair and moustaches and floppy caps____ with shades on and smoking cigarettes and I told them____ I don't know why, to this day I don't know why____ I told them I was an archaeologist____ a mythologist____ a pagan to boot and they said, baby_____ exactly what they said____ baby you have big eyes and you look like you are Greek. I'm sorry____ can you just fix this pillow for me____ yes____ and if you can just hold me up for a minute____ okay, that's better____ I'm sorry, where were we? The Greek baby with the big eyes_____ that was me, that was really me____ yes, well, these young boys, these young men, really, these handsome young men, these wild artist types____ they were both members of a street performance group____ Inconcurring Colt, what a name____ Inconcurring Colt____ They said it was named after some small poetry magazine____ Hey doll___ Santiago said_____ that was how they talked, doll-face, baby____ sweet cheeks all the time – hey doll,

are you into symbolism? I'm into things meaning things, if that's
what you're getting at____ Symbolism goes way beyond that____
he said: *way beyond the long blank*____. I was falling in love with
him already____ the language and the eyes, the eyes that I was
instantly jealous of____ how can you be jealous of eyes____ Beyond
the long blank, that's a symbol. But a symbol isn't words____ that's
what he said____ a symbol is a sign outside of language that stands
for something____ the way of the gods, the inscrutable way of the
gods____ I'm sorry, pet, but could you just____ yes, just there, if you
could wipe it____ I'm sorry____ no, I know____ I know____ I've been
there____ believe me, honey____ He looked me up and down then____
Santiago, Santiago_____ I like to say his name, to form it with
my lips, though my lips are cracked and dry___ Santiago_____
he didn't say anything else____ I cleared their table and walked
away____ an exaggerated flick of my hips____ you know____ I saw
them come in regularly, late Friday night, the early hours of Sunday
morning, a Tuesday afternoon, a Wednesday, a Thursday, it could
be any time____ ordering bottle after bottle of wine and sitting
there, talking____ the girls on their arms, tragic models, suffering
beauties, I remember some of them so well____ though it was just a
furtive glimpse, a slow linger at the table____ My boys were never
less than charming or seductive even in the company of these young
sweethearts____ young sweet hearts____ my boys were so free and
so self-assured and so free so guilt-free____ That was a big thing
with me____ guilt____ all my life____ even now sometimes____
I need a shot of them or something____ an inoculation ____ an
inoculation against spirit-devouring life as practised in the west
coast of Scotland____ I saw a thing in the newspaper____ I read
every day in order to brush up on my Spanish____ about a street
performance Inconcurring Colt had____ they had instigated it____

and that had got them into a lot of hot water____ and that made them notorious____ I saw the picture of Santiago being led away by the two policemen, his arms behind his back, his head thrown in the air, he was screaming____ so handsome. It looked like a painting____ The action was based around a series of____ of break-ins. The troupe would go round the city looking for unoccupied holiday rentals and then they would target some suburban family home and using a convoy of vans and helpers____ they would transport all the contents of a single room of the house to an unoccupied apartment in downtown Malaga____ set it up exactly as it had been, only with everything round the other way____ as in the reflection in a mirror____ the reflection of a mirror____ sorry, angel ____ sorry____ ____ ____ sorry____ They post an invite____ then they post an invite through the door of the burgled home inviting the owners to a *private view* of their own living quarters, don't you see?

Things went well, people mostly responded positively to it____ believe it or not____ at least once it was explained to them that no harm had been done or anything lost or stolen, except for the odd couple that threatened to press charges____ get the police involved, but on the whole people were fascinated and moved____ and even repelled, you can imagine it, by entering the uncanny mirror____ the uncanny mirror of their own surroundings____ They would tiptoe around their own homes, regard them with something approaching awe for the first time____ just like it was God's eyeballs themselves that they were seeing it through____ God's bulging eyeballs popping out of his head ____ It went too far____ too far when they burgled some high-up government member's house____ his penthouse suite, and set it up in the middle of a huge abandoned warehouse on the front. Instead of contacting them himself the MP had gone to the authorities____ with the time and date of the private view_____ They were able to bust the troupe on camera and make a big deal about the possibility of secret documents being in the MP's flat____ it was a breach of national security as well as a criminal act____ blah, blah, blah____ blah, blah, blah, blah, blah____ blah, blah, blah____ Sorry, can you wipe me again, pet, I'm sorry___ sorry____ They got off scot-free in the end, only made them even more attractive, more attractive and more daring. That was the highpoint of their career. By the time I joined____ and I was invited to join by Santiago____ they had become more of a straight street theatre performance group, even down to doing one of those dreadful fire-breathing routines____ fire-breathing routines that the tourist towns are awash with___ Telos left, he said it was becoming bullshit, the Spanish word for bullshit, which escapes me now___ but he spat that word, he spat that word and he marched off____ That was so like him to do something like that____ to march off with a curse____ That was brave, I thought___ ____

Sorry____ let's stop for a second____ let's stop for a moment can we, baby____ ____ ____ ____ ____

Santiago got really into dance____ I want to say yes, he argued____ I'm sick of saying no, he said, of art that says no or against or refuse. And dance of course as we all know is the biggest yes going, the biggest yes out there____ they had these mass dance troupes, these spectacular dance troupes that would be choreographed across a whole area, sometimes a whole park or a whole city block, the length of a beach____ every move relating to the other so that spied from above in a plane or a small helicopter it would have looked probably like one of those kaleidoscopes with constantly shifting shapes, I think____ They had music, lots of cassette players, they would place them all around the event, playing the same tunes but of course out of synch so that the sound would seem stretched and endless____ stretched and endless with whole phrases drawn out____ whole phrases drawn out to the point that you could walk around the block____ you could walk around the block and feel as if you were walking inside this sexy moan____ this endless sexy moan____ It was so fun I became a dancer too____ Sometimes you got funny looks but it was okay, you know, it was okay. For a while we toured up and down the coast of France and Spain. I had a lover, my first full lover, a boy from Granada who everyone called The Rat, he was so tough that if he found a hole in you, no matter how small____ he would tear right through it____ but I was happy with him, at least at first. The love we had was so quiet____ peaceful and otherworldly____ so peaceful I didn't resent his daytime rodent persona thing____ Dance with a scowl on his face, like it was a showdown or an early-morning duel or something with some kind of real outcome or meaning. It was remarkable to experience____ trying to bore holes in anyone who looks at him and then there's this music, up close, next to him____ it could have been anything____ the grand design of the choreography there was The Rat dancing____ military vigour___ pop group____ pop music____ pop station____ Spent the nights in tents at campsites____ sleeping rough on the beach, the tall grass with the stars____ a big sand dune and camp in its hollow, in a semicircle____ a gypsy and one day we got horses, Santiago had acquired an eccentric benefactor and we got horses____ The rest of the trip we made our way along country roads____ and mountain passes____ suburban backstreets on horseback, on horseback from one tourist town to the next____ nights when we would camp in the sand dunes and plot our next performance____ Santiago would draw a basic outline across the scene of the crime____ Santiago____ that's what he called it___ the

222

scene of the crime___ fancy that___ a map and us offering ideas on positions, symbols to be evoked___ smell of horse's breath, the damp horses, salt sea air___ saliva and silver dew drops as I lay with my head in the lap of The Rat and watched Orion's Belt pass by so slowly___ The Rat became difficult as we knew he would and began to make his way through me too___ Maybe that's where it all started, maybe that's where all of this began___ Any sign of weakness or questioning, anything other than being a crazy maniac who never stops to ask because___ disappointed in you, he would say, disappointed if I complained of being cold on the beach at night___ disappointed if I ever suggested taking a room just for once___ disappointed in the pleasures of an en suite bathroom and me left feeling so guilty___ so terribly guilty about it all___ now of course I look back and he was right and I long to be back under the stars___ in his arms in the stars long ago___ but came back to Malaga___ a private care job, an elderly Swedish man who lived in Spain___ Visit him three times a day to make his breakfast, lunch and dinner. When he went to Sweden I would look after his house and take care of the upkeep until his return___ I did this for two years and on the third year he asked me to live with him in the same house___ He was getting frailer due to a heart attack which he took while in Sweden. I had the responsibility that Lars was taking the correct medication daily___ he was on a lot___ due to his heart condition. I stayed with Lars until he passed away___ ensured that he was buried in accordance with his wishes. I kept up my dancing career but the troupe drifted apart___ The Rat disappeared down some hole and soon I had lost all the friends that I ever had in Spain. I made the decision to move back home. I got off the train at Airdrie and prayed that everyone I had ever known___ in that place where I knew I would die, I just knew it___ was dead and buried already. I put a sign up in the library: Wanted: The Dead and The Dying. Well, not quite____ but I may as well have____ I may as well have done and soon enough I was employed as a carer by Remy's family. Remy's father___ his name was Clyde, Clyde Farr___ lived in one of those mysterious backstreets in Airdrie that are still lovely____ old retirees hidden behind high walls____ I turned up late for my first day on the job____ Oh don't ask don't ask me about me. The house was set in huge grounds and what would once have been gardens____ grand gardens____ opulent gardens was now a sea of red gravel with the house sat like a cube in the centre like Mecca____ There was an intercom system, Clyde was bedridden by this point, and when I rang the door it sprang open but no one spoke____ Bedroom, upstairs, I'm guessing, up a curving stone staircase. All the while I could make out the sound of laboured breathing_____ the sound of laboured breathing like this____ ____ ____ and there was something reassuring about it, something weird about it anyway and strange too____ I could make out the shape of a figure propped up on pillows in the bed. There was an antiseptic smell. I spied a used bedpan by the side of the bed____ the tools of the trade____ I'm your new carer, I said. How are you feeling today? How the f-u-c-k do you think I'm feeling? he said. That's what he said! Well, that was marvellous____ that was marvellous to me, said in this ridiculous high voice that almost didn't sound like it was made by a body. It sounded like a balloon being rubbed. Now, now, I said____ now, now, quickly taking charge___ what you need to do with these hard cases____ you'll get your blood pressure up if you continue on like that, I said, and I walked over to the bed and put my hand on his head_____ Can you put your hand on my head at this point, my angel? Would you mind terribly? The skin felt stretched and rubbery. Don't you think? Your skin feels rubbery, I said to him. I'm a rubber doll, he said. I'm a little rubber doll___ I'm a little rubber doll. I'm a space hopper____ You're not a space hopper, you're Clyde Farr and I'm your carer, Claire Lune. What do you know about caring for space hoppers, about inflating rubber dolls? Plenty, I said____ plenty. The spoon thing____ you want to know about the spoon thing____ I had a technique, a style. Clyde had trouble swallowing. If I swallow, everything ends in the bowels____ it's too much. I want my first bite, I want my first bite always. I would put some food on it____ I would put some food on the spoon____ hold open his jaw, I would feel it relax____ you can do it with me, my darling, if you like____ you can feel it relax____ there you go, there you go, feel that, that's the sign____ He never fought against it____ Then I would put the spoon in his mouth but deep enough____ go on, try it____ don't be afraid____ so that you almost begin to gag____ agghhh____ it's okay, that's alright, pet, you're doing it right, that's what's supposed to happen____ and as I deposited the food down his throat I would play with his uvula, tapping it with the silver of the spoon____ gah, gah, gah____ the handle goes against the top of the mouth____ then you tap____ gah, gah, gah____ there we go, he loved that, sometimes he would giggle like a young boy____ gargle like a young boy____ and he would smile and he would look up at me with his eyes like blank diamonds and his face would contort into an expression of sickly joy____ I thought this is what cavemen looked like____ what cavemen looked like without mirrors. Clyde had been abandoned, for shame____ for shame all day he lay in bed ranting, laughing, rolling around in agony. I would let him listen to his favourite programmes on TV which were *Crown Court* and *Miami Vice*____ On special occasion I would take him down in the lift____ been an old boys' school____ wheel him through the garden and sit together at the gate. Happy times with the wind behind us____ happy times with the wind behind us and the tall trees and out on the street____ returning home from work and school. Howdy, Clyde would say____ a puff of wind, a small leaf on his cheek. I've seen it all before, he would say____ peering out from his eyeless sockets there is nothing new under the sun____ but I've grown less fond of it, all the same____ cynical about birdsong____ my dear child they are little more today than the attempt to imitate car alarms____ and sirens and all sorts of____ monstrous machinery____ monstrous manmade machinery, he would say it like that___ Flatter yourself, go ahead flatter yourself that you are in communion with nature but nature has long fled the scene____ I have heard the last bird. Remy was the only member of the family who visited____ I wasn't big into my music back then___ but Clyde began asking for music____ real music as he lay writhing in bed____ Remy making tapes for his dying father was like singing a baby to sleep. At first he would play him these long pieces made up of just one sound, it was minimalism___ that's what they call it____ I later learned. I began to get into the music myself. I was involved with artists and musicians in Spain, after all____ then he told me he was in a group called Memorial Device. At first when I heard it____ to tell you the truth I had to brace myself against the sound. The singer looked like an oversized baby____ he had bare feet on stage____ his feet as well, pale and deathly____ his skin still pale from the womb it was like, his head translucent, his soft crown. His soft crown. Can you rub my head, pet, can you rub my crown, please, angel? Just this once, angel, I'm sorry___ I'm sorry____ I'm sorry. The one on the guitar looked more like a funeral director and they had a girl playing the bass guitar, a beautiful young girl. Mary Hanna was her name. Spending time with Remy and his blind father and attending concerts by Memorial Device my ears opened up____ now I can hear lots of things as music that I would never have been able to before____ ____ ____ Mary came to visit____ to visit Clyde____ quite a few times. She would visit with Remy and Remy and I would sit downstairs while she sat with Clyde upstairs ____ Barely heard them say a word together. Not a word. Once when I could see them through a crack in the door. Clyde was sat up in bed____ Mary was sat next to him, holding his hand. The two of them are staring into space right then. She was an artist, a sculptor____ She took Remy and I in a car and showed us some of her wonderful work where she made pieces in the wild____ left them there. Then Lucas, the singer, died, the singer who looked like an overgrown baby killed himself____ then Clyde, then Clyde had to go into hospital. When he came out they moved him into a nursing home and I continued with my duties____ continued with my duties until he passed away. Don't ask me what happened next. Please____ let's leave it there. I'm sorry____ I'm tired now___ you've been a love. I'm sorry. And besides____ besides I don't believe in twilight, sweetie.

24. Blood and Water Inside Me That Needs an Example: *Johnny McLaughlin is in Paris or is it Airdrie with Patty and Valentine years after it all went down.*

I lived with Patty and his girlfriend in Paris for a while (this was long after the end of Memorial Device, long after Lucas had died). I got a letter from Patty out of the blue. No one had heard from him in years (he had pulled off the definitive disappearing act). He wrote to my mum but she was dead too. My sister was living in my mum's old house (I could never stand to go back to Airdrie, too many memories) and she forwarded me the letter even though we hadn't spoken in years. Patty was inviting me to come and stay with him in Paris. They had a spare room, he said. They lived near Gare du Nord. Come on over, he said. It would be good to catch up. There was nothing to stop me (no commitments, no relationships, no successes). Patty had never struck me as the nostalgic type but perhaps our relationship ran deeper than I thought. A week later I took the train to London and the ferry from Dover (and the train from Calais). When I arrived he wasn't in so I walked around Paris for almost ten hours and wore a hole straight through my boots (which were the only pair I had). I walked from Rue Louis Blanc (which is where Patty's apartment was and where he was supposed to be) right down Boulevard de Strasbourg and Boulevard de Sébastopol (and then over the bridge by Notre-Dame) and I dropped into the bookshop (Shakespeare and Company) and asked the girl behind the till (who was cute but a little boyish for my tastes, perhaps) if they had a guide to literary Paris (you know) where Rimbaud was and where Verlaine died, but she said no, she didn't have anything like that except maybe about Hemingway, fuck that I thought, but I didn't say anything and instead I bought the complete works of Rimbaud (which I already owned but which I had always dreamed of buying in Paris) and I was going to buy a book by Kenneth Rexroth (some imaginary biography or something) but then I read on the jacket some comment about him thinking that sometimes even Poe and Melville were just trash and I couldn't stomach having it on my person. I asked the girl, who was a tomboy for sure, but still alluring, or maybe it was just because she worked in a bookshop (maybe she was unattractive and dull at home, out of context), either way I asked her if there was a place she could recommend where I could eat something good, something French (I was on a budget, but I had only just arrived and wanted to mark the occasion), and she told me that it was a really touristy area and that most of the restaurants were expensive (and poor quality) but then she mentioned one (and it had a name like The Burned Earwig, The Charred Twig, something like that) and she said it would be closed now, that they had strange hours, but that I should come back later and try it (that it was worth it). I couldn't tell, I thought she might have been asking me out for a date (maybe Paris was going to my head already), but I decided to come back and find her later and take her out to dinner (at The Blackened Rod or whatever it was). In the meantime I went to a bar and sat at a table outside on the pavement and had three drinks (one after the other). Next to me there was a Chinese man with a trim grey beard and a grey hat and across from him there was a fat woman who seemed mesmerised by him. At one point the woman pulled what looked like a Bible from her bag (only the cover was wrapped in cellophane and it was falling apart) and the Chinese man took it from her and kissed it and then read from it and she was mesmerised and afterwards he gave her a small laminated card (that had Jewish letters on it) and he seemed to be explaining what it meant to her and she was rapt and emotional (it was like she had been given the key to her own life) and when they

229

upped and left I wondered if I hadn't projected the whole thing on the inside of my skull or something (you know, like wish fulfilment or serendipity or something like that). Afterwards I made my way over to the Bibliothèque Nationale (by this point I was quite drunk, the beer was strong) and I climbed up the wooden steps towards the building (it was like scaling the pyramids) and I thought to myself I'm closer to the stars with every step and by the time I got to the top it was so warm (the sun was beating down) that I ended up just lying there and falling asleep, only for twenty minutes but still enough time to dream that I was attending a surrealist conference (I think William Burroughs might have been there) and that everyone was introducing themselves with strange titles, like First Hegemony of the Pussying Father, Procured Spirit of the Maelstrom, Mentis Notion of the Heaven Electric, Thought of the End Phrase, Prank of Pure Volition (I wrote them down on a piece of paper as soon as I woke up), Condition of the Non-Form, Meat of the Remains, Shield of Sublimity, one by one, standing up and announcing themselves and sitting back down again, sometimes with no face or sometimes with a beard or a hat, or a long robe or a bad suit, Suicider of the Four Thousand, Dungheap of the Living Flesh, Rememberer of the Undivided.

It's Paris, I told myself. I must be getting transmissions (no wonder people come here to write). There was an exhibition on at the Bibliothèque (something to do with geography and history and space) and I went inside and there was a series of photographs, I remember one clearly, of a mountaintop village (somewhere in France or maybe it was Switzerland) where a group of artists had met for a conference and the buildings seemed as if they were rising up from the clouds (which were beneath them) and there seemed no possible way in or out (although there were roads snaking around the buildings but tellingly no cars, although it might have been taken before cars were invented) and I wondered if the conference had been a dare (like a midnight assignation) and I imagined the artists making their way there any way they could (like walking along the spine of the mountains with this huge drop on either side or parachuting in) and I thought of my own journey to Paris, on a whim (after a promise). On the way back I stopped at a bar near Gare de Lyon (where there was a lot of betting going on, a lot of gambling) and I got into a conversation with the manager who asked me my name. I was starting to feel like a local. It takes me ten hours to get a feel for a place (then the city is basically mine). I walked back to the bookshop but the girl who had served me was gone (replaced by a stern older woman) so I went to the restaurant on my own where I had some kind of meat stew with turnips and potatoes and onions (some kind of French country dish), this is the real deal, I told myself, complete with a bone marrow in the middle of the bowl. It's now or never (I said to myself) and I sucked the marrow out of the bone, which was actually gross, it was like a kind of soft fleshy liquorice. What the hell (I was in Paris). Afterwards I walked along the Seine in the early evening where groups of friends and lovers were drinking wine and picnicking on coats spread out on the grass (as the sun was going down). I sat on the grass (a couple with bare feet were sleeping on a blanket right next to me) until nearly ten o'clock when I guessed my friend would probably be home by now (either that or I would be sleeping on the grass next to them for the night, which actually appealed to me, in a way) but even so I went to one more bar but looking at all the unattainable women drinking on the pavement (with beautiful heels on and nylons and with handbags overflowing with personal stuff and their own lives that had nothing to do with mine) made me melancholy for the first time and I felt old, somehow (or too young), and wanted to go home.

When I went back and knocked on Patty's door he buzzed me in without saying a word. The door (this great wooden door that looked like it once belonged to a castle with big metal studs in it) opened onto a cobblestoned tunnel that led to a square courtyard with plants in broken plant pots (and lit-up windows with washing hanging out to dry). I heard a voice from somewhere up above. Fourth floor, it said, and I followed a winding stone staircase (past old stained-glass windows that were cracked and had pieces missing) up to the landing which was covered in shoes, piles of dirty boots and training shoes (and even some high heels). It's like a fucking Holocaust memorial up here, I thought to myself (but I also thought that maybe I could borrow a pair to replace my own).

When he opened the door I barely recognised him. He had lost weight (a lot of weight) and somehow he seemed younger, not gaunt, just naturally skinny (like young people are). What's up, brother? he said. Things have changed, I said to myself (this is going to be interesting). We went inside and the flat was amazing (weird), piled high with obscure stuff. The hallway was set up like a dining room, with a dinner table right next to the front door and across from the toilet, which I thought was particularly weird, as the toilet had no door and the entrance was only covered with an old curtain (I'm in France, I told myself, anything goes). I spotted a portable record player in the corner of the hall balanced on top of a pile of old encyclopaedias (maybe that was to drown out the noise from the toilet) and around it there were a few choice LPs, Can, Philippe Doray, the Red Noise LP on Futura and the Rob Jo Star Band album (which I'd never heard of at the time but which became the soundtrack to my trip). But it proves he was still listening to music (even if all of it was old).

Everywhere there were old wooden boxes stacked on top of each other (that they used as bookcases). The living room was at the end of a long corridor (that had yellowing pages from old comic strips pasted onto the wall instead of wallpaper) (stuff like *Krazy Kat* and *Little Nemo in Slumberland*) and when I first walked in it was really dark and it took some time to make out what was going on (in the room). There was a pair of thick floor-length brown velvet curtains (that were pulled shut) and some candles burning (and some lamps) and on the couch there was the most beautiful woman I had ever seen, done up with dark hair and red lips and oversized glasses (her hair like a dark silent river, a river that was moving in complete silence, that's what it seemed like the first time I saw her) and her ears (don't even ask me about her ears), I can't even describe her ears, she had hair pulled back over one of them and it was like seeing the earth from space, the hollow earth (or seeing yourself as a foetus, in the womb of your mother), and she was smoking a cigarette, her arm at a perfect angle (taut, not without effort, but still somehow easy, relaxed), and she was so slim (barely budding) yet (still) she seemed sophisticated and mysterious and old. This relationship is ass-backwards, I said to myself. Her name was Valentine (how could it have been anything else?). This is Valentine, Patty said, my paramour (that's how he introduced her). I felt unsophisticated (and poor). Valentine stood up and offered me her cheek. I forgot that in France you are supposed to kiss both cheeks so I did it all over again and she laughed but when I looked into her eyes they were like marbles. Let's get something to eat, Patty said, grabbing his coat, and although I had already eaten I decided to go with the flow.

We went to a bar and restaurant a few blocks away (which seemed to be their local). The guy behind the bar shouted and waved when they walked in and Patty replied in French (which impressed me). We took a seat in a booth and Patty ordered us a bottle of wine (I would have preferred beer but once again, it was Paris). They both sat across from me. There was something awkward in the atmosphere. We hadn't mentioned our old lives at all (at one point I went to bring it up but Patty got Valentine in a neck hold and began mock wrestling her so I let it go).

Money was a problem, they said, they were totally skint (although on a day-to-day basis it really didn't seem to matter). He was working as a comic book artist (an illustrator was what he called it). They would rise about twelve or one in the afternoon (after having sex, loud sex, every morning) and Patty would appear in nothing but a towel with his newly skinny body sometimes with bites or bruises on it (it was like my old self come back to haunt me) and they would make an elaborate lunch (and drink a bottle of wine between them), always in the dark (which during the day was more like an eerie half-light in the apartment, like neither day nor light, this permanent limbo, it seemed, which was idyllic in a way), and then Patty would settle down to draw at his desk in front of the fire (they had a real coal fire that they stoked night and day) and he would draw all this fantasy stuff to commission (all this sword & sorcery crap) with women with heaving breasts chained to rocks and gladiators and alien assailants. Its good money, he told me, it's a piece of piss. Plus he would do pin-up art, cheesecake stuff, retro shit and sometimes Valentine would pose for him (so that you would walk into the living room and she would be there on the couch in nylons with a push-up basque and those red lips and those ears and her hair flowing down her back

234

like it was running straight out of Eden). I would walk into the room and I would feel like it was a set-up, like they were both in on it, like Valentine wanted me to see her there and Patty wanted to show her to me (why me, I asked myself).

I fell into a routine (I had the run of the house). In the mornings (before they were up) I would head over to a boulangerie on Rue du Faubourg Saint-Martin where I would order the same thing (a baguette with tomatoes and peppers and salmon that they would heat under the grill for me) and then I would sit on a bench in the sun (with the homeless and the beggars and the working stiffs) and watch the world go by. Every few days I would drop in to the bookshop (Shakespeare and Company) and look for my tomboy, my summer love, I called her (although by that point we had done little more than exchange tourist pleasantries). She was never in (or at least never working at the checkout) and I barely knew enough French to ask after her. I wanted my own Valentine (it was that obvious).

Our evenings were spent in small talk, in drunken reverie, or with Valentine cooking for the both of us, she was a great vegetarian cook (which wasn't my style, but still), she would prepare huge bowls of this or that (asparagus and pecorino and pine nuts and salad leaves) and have us help ourselves with wooden spoons and then she would present a perfect dessert (a crème brûlée or a perfectly toasted crumble) all in the dark, all in this perpetual twilight that we lived in (which made it extra-special in a way).

I started to become close to Valentine. She was half Japanese and half Swedish (which meant she was lithe and radiating and secretive and naive all at the same time). Sometimes when Patty was working towards a deadline we would take walks together through Paris, sit in parks (or at the edge of rivers) or wander around art galleries. I asked her why Patty had invited me to stay. He told me about you, she said. This was during an afternoon that we spent at a park near the Sacré-Coeur (one of our favourite haunts). He said you came from a part of his life that he didn't want to forget. He talks like I'm a figment of his imagination, I told her. That's how I feel, sometimes, she said, and she laughed. Still, the topic never came up between Patty and me. He had a way of looking at you that dictated the terms of the relationship and of the conversation, like a wall coming down or like barbed wire (then you were in no man's land).

The more time I spent around Patty and Valentine, the lonelier I became. Back home I had cherished my solitary lifestyle but there was something about Paris that made me want to become its confidant, its true lover (like back when I was a kid and fell for Glasgow and everyone in it).

One afternoon I went back to the bookshop (Shakespeare and Company) and there she was (finally) seated behind the till (my summer love). She was talking to some tourist about Gérard de Nerval, the poet (L'homme Pendu, she called him). I stood to one side and picked up a copy of *Satori in Paris* by Jack Kerouac and read a few pages (like an idiot backpacker). I felt bad, I read the pages and it meant nothing to me, it seemed trivial (impossible even). Things are definitely changing, I said to myself, this is a tragedy right here. I had to put the book back on the shelf. It felt like a death or a stroke (like a voice in my head had finally succumbed to nothing). I walked up to the counter. Remember me? I asked her. Ah, she said, the literary tourist, Le Dilettante. I'm no dilettante, I said,

I'm no phoney (I've lived it, I went to say, but lived what?). Right then I had the strangest feeling. The girl in the bookshop looked to me like a bird (like a girl with the head of a bird) and I felt like a feather (a feather with no weight whatsoever). It was like I saw the whole scenario from above. I saw the girl flap her wings (a single effortless movement that turned the bookshop inside out) and I felt that sudden lunging drop inside my body (like the velocity of her wings had caused my organs to spill out beneath me), dragged down by the force of gravity as we were lifted up into the air (it only lasted a few seconds but I'll never forget it). I felt completely empty (like a tomb). By the time we touched back down I knew I was capable of love, of being filled up, like I had never been before, with no heart or liver or hallucinated spleen to get in the way (that's the only way I can describe it) (I felt liberated). I held out my hand towards her and she wrote her name and her number in biro along my middle finger. Clementine, it said. I wanted to slide it into her mouth but the moment was gone and I turned and exited the shop without looking back (my heart beating elsewhere, far away and no longer my concern).

On the way back I got drunk (again) and when I got home I fell asleep in the bath (and had to be put to bed by Valentine). I woke in the night with my head throbbing and I had a terrible thought, that my organs were growing back again, that my body was filling up, and that soon (once again) there would be no place for love. I sat up straight in the bed. The moon was coming in through the skylight with clouds suspended around it like an old man with a beard. That's not me, I said. And I hope it's not my father. I got up to have a drink and I crossed the living room where Patty was still awake (working on some art commission) with a small lamp over his desk (that made him look like a lonely planet). I made it to the bathroom and I filled up the sink and dunked my head in the cold water. I need to wake up, I told myself, I'm filling up with stars and planets (and friends and family). Soon there will be no room to move. I walked back to the living room and Patty was standing next to the window smoking a cigarette, looking out over the city (with the dustbins in the street and solitary figures weaving this way and that).

It felt like the right time to confront him. I moved to the window. Why did you invite me here? I asked him. We barely know each other, really. He took a long draw on his cigarette and then he bent double in a coughing fit. He wiped his mouth on his arm and it left a thick streak of blood-speckled yellow phlegm. You're coughing up blood, I said to him. Bullshit, he said. It's dehydration. I've been avoiding water. My entire body is pickled, he said.

I felt like I was going crazy. (What was happening inside our bodies?) Is that why you asked me here, I said to him, so that my insides could die off one by one? He looked at me like he was concerned. What's going on with your body? he asked me. I told him a bird took away my feelings, removed every one of my organs like it was an operation. Where are they now? he asked me. In the tops of the trees, I told him, at the bottom of the ocean. Then I had a feeling like the dawn coming up (silent, without permission) and I woke up in bed with a view of chimneys and television aerials and churches and clothes hung out to dry (stretching off into infinity).

I got up the next morning and no one said anything (they were both up early). Valentine had an interview as a cashier at some fashion boutique so for once they had set the alarm and were both sitting

238

around the kitchen table and eating bagels and drinking coffee when I walked in (wearing nothing but a pair of pyjama bottoms). Nice tattoo, Valentine said (back then I had a tattoo of a nautical compass just above my heart to the left, a compass with sea monsters and tides and ships sailing all around it, I've since had it removed).

Patty acted like nothing had happened. I told them I had a date (a girl who worked in a bookshop). Valentine said I should ask her round for dinner. Patty looked right at me, I thought he was going to wink at me (I could almost see his face moving in that direction, if you know what I mean), but then he just stared some more and looked away. In the end Valentine never got the job and so they were more skint than ever but as I say you would never have known it because they kept on eating these pyramids of goat's cheese and drinking all this wine (and buying new plants and art supplies).

I called Clementine and invited her to the house. At first she kept talking in French on the phone and it was confusing (I wasn't even sure if it was her) but eventually she settled down and we made our plans. I had arrived in Paris with little more than the clothes on my back so on the night I asked Patty if I could borrow some of his outfits and Valentine helped dress me (we were about the same size so it was no problem). I chose a pair of boots from the pile at the top of the stairs (a pair of motorcycle boots with a metal eagle on the heel) and I put gel on my hair and I combed it and parted it on the side (the first parting it had seen in a lifetime).

It turned out that Clementine lived quite far away (somewhere in Clichy) so Patty offered to go pick her up (on his moped). I thought about her arms around his chest, the smell of her perfume on his neck, but I said okay regardless. Back home Valentine and I cracked open a first bottle of wine.

Clementine looked different on the night (still boyish but older and sadder and making an effort). She was wearing a loose paisley-pattern dress (it came halfway down her thighs) and she had a black woollen shawl over her shoulders and a small purse in her hand. This is formal European romance, I said to myself. This is a movie script. I took her hand and I kissed it and she bit her lip (which was a sign of something).

How was the ride? I asked Clementine. Hair-raising, she said. We sat around the table in the kitchen, where Valentine was preparing the meal (I can't remember now but which might have been stuffed something, stuffed peppers, something like that), but the point is it took ages for her to make it and so we all ended up getting prematurely drunk. Have you heard about Johnny's tattoo? Valentine asked Clementine. No, she said, should I have? If you want to get your bearings you might, Valentine said, and she burst out laughing. Tell me, Patty said, how do we go about avoiding all those sea monsters? Do you have the coordinates? And when should we set sail, exactly? It's a map, I said, it's fixed, it's not a guide, it's a fantasy. Then why have it? Patty asked me. I don't know, I said. There's blood and water inside me that needs an example, maybe. I like tattoos, Valentine said. I'm always asking Patty to have one. What would you have, Clementine asked, if you were going to get a tattoo? Patty thought for a second. I could never have a picture, he said, never a graphic or a sign. It would have to be a word. What would the word be? she asked him. Three letters, he said. How about 'but', Clementine said? That's my favourite English word, that sums it all up, to me. No, 'yet' is better, Valentine said. Better yet, Clementine said, what about 'bun'? Bun, Patty said, that's nonsense, that's rubbish. No, she said, a bun in the oven. Tell us, Valentine asked him, tell us what your word is! But Patty just sat there smiling (even in Paris, it was the same old story).

25. My Dream Bride Which Is Of Course My Mother But Not With a Vagina Please: *Dominic Hunter aka Dom aka Wee Be-Ro from Relate confesses to Ross Raymond that he loved Remy from the moment he saw him.*

From: <domboy12395@towerrecordings.co.uk>
To: <rossrrraymondo17@mountainofdoom.co.uk>
Subject: Re:
Date: Fri, 21 Feb 2014 22:39:12 +0100

My dearest Ross, how I worry about you! How is your chest and that nasty cold? I'm doing fine thank you, keeping well, as well as can be. Thank you for the lovely mail and for the flowers and the chocolates and the little extras, I absolutely adored the Abner Jay record you sent me, that's right up my street, you know how to spoil me and now I shall spoil you, aha, as in ruin your book by contributing my own two cents worth of material! I always prided myself with my photographic memory, I never forget a face, or a slight, or a bit of rough trade in the toilets at Heaven or down the back of Covent Garden for that matter. Unlucky for them. But lucky for you, my dearest Ross, or at least I do hope so, in this instance.

I will tackle your queries one by one in my own way but forgive me if they all tend to blur into one tremendous sigh. When I think about the past it's all I can do not to wilt like a tulip.

– Yes, I fell in love with Remy the moment I saw him, it's all out in the open now, the whole cat's cradle, the whole kitten caboodle, it's true, I admit it!
– It was at a New Year's party where the host, this awful tranny who went on to terrorise Airdrie, to literally *terrorise* the place, had

us all write down our resolutions on a piece of paper and pass them around the table to read, a game of four wishes if you like, and when darling Remy's came around he had written four goals for the new year, normal ones that anyone would write like stay in shape and get more done, but then he had this one about how he wished to 'cultivate more aberrant thrills'. What a style! What a manner! Tout Suite! Ooh La La! Etc. I pencilled in a quick number five that said marry me xxx and passed it to the next person without a word, sweet as a nut. Mum's the word! Of course when it came back around darling Remy saw it. But he had no idea who had written it. Who wants to marry me? he asked. Of course everyone denied it. Including me. Which made it all the more delicious!

– Back then he looked like a young Tim Buckley. A young Tim Buckley cherub floating on a musky cloud of pure calm. He was really so calm and collected. And then on stage he would release the beast. That's what I would always say to him. I would give him a pep talk before we would go on. It's time to release the beast! I would say. That would drive him crazy. I told him he should have been in stand-up, in drag, preferably. But he was uncompromising that way, alas and alack!

– I was more of a performance artist in those days. I would dress up like a clown or a mime and I would play this big fuck-off amplified single metal string instrument. I had built it with dustbin lids for resonance and a wooden brush for a neck and a piece of fence for a string. But I would play it like I was in a silent movie with really exaggerated gestures. Totally oblivious to the din I was making. I based my style on the scream queens of the silent era. No one cared except one person, darling Ronnie.

– Ronnie was my partner at the time I met Remy. Ronnie saw me do this performance at Zanzibar in Coatbridge. I was a regular at

Zanzibar in Coatbridge. It was an oasis. Quite literally. A refuge, a haven. I think it even had a neon oasis on the sign outside. Plus there was a back room nobody knew about, just the queens, the queens of the scene. During the performance I got so carried away with my own devilish approach to experimental cabaret that I almost severed an artery in my wrist while playing the damn thing! Ronnie was the only person there quick-witted enough to get me off stage. He wrapped the wound on the spot and drove me to hospital. He was a non-drinker even then bless him. He told me that was when he fell in love with me. Oh my! Sitting in casualty, dressed like a clown! A tea towel stemming a wrist wound! You can see his type right there! They say you fall in love with your mother. They say all sorts of things. So I fell in love with my mother. So maybe I did. Ronnie was a heartbreaker. A real tough-looking salt but inside such an inquisitive nature. Such a faithful heart. I have so much love for the sincere seekers of this world. And he brought that kind of intensity to every aspect of his life. That's why he was a non-drinker. He had to be present at every moment. He insisted on it. So that he could silently marvel at it. What a champ! He was my dream bride which is of course my mother but not with a vagina please.

– He wore vests. White vests. He smelled of the sex of long ago. A leather jacket, a pair of jeans. Classic. It all comes back to me right now and I can see him and taste him on my fingers. At night when I was ill, sweating with a fever or with palpitations (I was troubled with palpitations so much that Ronnie compared my heart to *a rose that flutters every time a single drop of dew falls on it*), he would sit sentinel outside the bedroom door. Not even beside the bed. As though he were a bodyguard for a celebrity. And he wouldn't sleep. It was the same at my performances. He would sit in the front row or stand just offstage. He believed in me. I could see it in his eyes. And what a cook. I would sit at the table and shake my head in disbelief. If it wasn't coq au vin it was something with beetroot. We began to resemble each other, the way that old couples do. We morphed into each other. I was the more talkative one I admit it. Ronnie's style was to sit next to you on the couch and hold your hand. And look into your eyes like you were the Buddha or Diana Dors. I could've told him anything. I did. I lectured him on art. I read him poetry. I drank with him while he sipped carrot juice. I introduced him to marijuana. Nothing could derail this great spirit. He would still be the one to carry me to bed at the end of the night. And then he would have breakfast waiting for me in the morning. As well as telling me about all of the mail that had arrived for me. Which was a little annoying. I have to admit it. That was one thing. He opened all of my personal mail for me. But it seemed part and parcel of this whole mother without a vagina thing.

– He would always suggest a remarkable new experience. He was brave that way. Let's kayak on the River Kelvin he would say. We did that once. It was a disaster. Let's go climb a mountain he would say. That was too much for me. I'm a city girl don't you know Ronnie I would say to him as I sank a bottle of wine halfway up the Cobbler ;)

– This is my good example of how sweet and untouched he was. One evening as we smoked marijuana – he had become quite partial to marijuana. I had pushed it on him, dear me! You're developing a vice! I said to him. You had better watch it boyo! We had a game we liked to play and it goes like this. You give a name to each moment. Instead of counting to 60 you pick out a personality. One per minute. One after the other. When I say personalities I mean atmospheres. Then you live inside them. You try to experience them. Ronnie taught me how to do it. For instance this moment right now, he said, this moment right now is definitely *Casino Royale*. Okay I said to Ronnie.

I can roll with this. It's a new minute, Ronnie said, now we welcome
The Odyssey! You've got it wrong, I told him. This whole minute
wasn't written by the Latins! It's simpler than that, I said. This is
'Borderline'. The next minute, 'Like a Virgin'. The next minute, 'Live
to Tell'. Ronnie was blown away when I came out with that. What the
fuck was that? he said. That was incredible. He was naive that way. I
fell even deeper in love.

– And what a scrotum. Forgive me but that's the only way there is
to describe it. A great scrotum. It wasn't this cock and balls. It was
a great animal scrotum. Like a rhino that had to have its way. That
had to be milked, regularly. Which of course was my pleasure ;)

– I'm afraid I'm not even going to go there. I'm sorry. I'm not even
going to dignify it. I never heard a peep out of Leigh Bowery and all
of a sudden there he is, wearing a motorcycle helmet with this clown
make-up. Hello!?

– I put an advert up in Airdrie Library. That's how we did things
back then. That's where all the real freaks hung out. It read:
*Desperately seeking local saints, secret deities, fantastic film stars
for possible Relate-tionship. Inexperience an advantage, style a no-
brainer, must have been present in his body for at least 18 years.
Duties include: overthrowing, brainstorming, seducing, romancing,
usurping and distilling.* Then I put my post office box number.
I signed it: *a man under sentence of death.* I was big into my
Dostoevsky. No one wrote. Not a single fucking saintly 18-year-old in
all of Airdrie!

– Then I went to the fateful New Year's party with Ronnie. I wrote
marry me to Remy. I don't know why. I had this perfect relationship
at home. All except for the opening of my personal mail thing, which
I could put up with. But here I am lusting after young crumpet.
Dreaming of being married off to some young hunk. The place we

were at had a balcony. A very small balcony. Remy and I and Ronnie
squeezed out there together to smoke a joint. I was in such a bind. I
just kept squeezing my thighs together. And reaching down for my
foot and pulling my leg up behind me. I was in contortions over this
guy. Save me, I thought. I just want the sun to come up and blind us
all and put an end to this madness. But then I got it in my stomach.
It was like my cock was a string that rang a bell in my solar plexus. A
wedding bell.

– Remy told me he played music. This young man. This beautiful
young starsailor. I wanted to cup his face in my hands and take a
long cold drink. He told me he was a musician. Now there were light
bulbs in my balls. I'm putting together a group! I burst. I'm looking
for secret deities! Wait a minute, he said. Did you put that advert
up in the library? Are you a man under sentence of death? Yes, I
said. Yes, that's me! I thought there weren't any of you left, he said.
Darling Ronnie interrupted him. He always had my best interests at
heart. Dom is a great artist, he said, a serious conceptualist. Who are
you, Remy asked him, his mother? That was cheeky. I'll end up as
your son-in-law if he has it his way, Remy said. Then he pointed at
me and he winked. He was ringing all the right bells.

– Ronnie started dressing in this inexplicable outgoing style. It
was new to him. I think he felt the competition. He looked like a
Puerto Rican street killer. He would wake up in the morning and
immediately roll out of bed. Then he would start doing push-ups
on the floor in nothing but a white vest. His big scrotum would be
schlonging off the floor. *Wap, wap, wap.* Really schlonging. And
he always worked out to the same song. 'Party Fears Two' by The
Associates. It sort of became our song. I think of the way it starts.
It gets under your skin. You kind of breathe it in. You get a sniff
of memory and it's knockout. Sexy enough to generate a feeling

247

of experience. But then maybe that's just me. Maybe that's just me getting all moment in time again. Who knows? But there *were* moments in time. And there were ideas that went along with them. And every time I hear it, it takes me back there. To my lovers. To my young lovers. Even though it was all a long time ago now. Can music preserve a moment in time? Can it Ross? Do you think it can keep alive all the ideas that went along with it? Can it keep it young forever? Why is the future so quick to snatch it all away? That last line's a quote by the way. From Sinew Singer, do you know him? He's a great hero of mine. I will send you his record if you don't know him. He really should be in your book. It's a song he had, 'Why Does the Future?' where he sings all of these questions. Not really to the future, but about the future. As if he is the future. But like he's still a mystery to himself. Now that the future has come, now that I'm living there on my own without a wife or a mother or a boyfriend to look after me, now I finally know what he means.

Darling Ross I hope this helps you out and that it really doesn't ruin your book despite what I said and remember how much I worry about you!

Dom x

<u>26. I Saw All These Dead Moons Circling a Star:</u> *Paprika Jones*
recalls the last days of Lucas Black.

Complete contentment, that's what it said, if you must know.

I've never told anyone that before.

Why?

Because it doesn't make sense.

Or because it makes perfect sense.

Or because it somehow implicates me, my part in his happiness, my
part in his death.

I don't know.

I had been on the scene for a few years.

As a young girl I had blown my own mind.

It was one sexual epiphany after another.

I had grown up in the sternest, most backwards, illiterate, repressed
motherfucking viper pit in the west of Scotland.

And that was just my family.

It was all guilt and suffering and penance in the name of daily life.

I had been brought up to believe that every indulgence was punishable, that every time I listened to my heart I would be beaten down, like there was some objective standard for living that traded suffering for peace, though not really peace, more like a holding off of punishment, like the more broken you appeared the less torture you were forced to endure, as if all that reality desired was your complete debasement and obedience and that a confession of guilt obviated the necessity of breaking you forever.

But when you feel that first cock pressing at the back of your throat or your fingers disappearing between the legs of some stranger, if you can really feel it, you realise that life doesn't have it in for you in the slightest.

But it takes a lot of cocks to hammer it into your head.

I remember hearing 'Venus in Furs' by The Velvet Underground and thinking oh my god this is like the soundtrack to the escape from my brain, you know, the storming of the citadel, the lowering of a rope down into the wilderness.

I immediately based my persona on this fantasy idea.

I became a seducer, a spy in the house of love. My entire life was dedicated to encounters.

I began to think of people not as individuals but as destinations, as map points across this inhospitable desert, like an oasis of flesh, a port of spit and smell, and sometimes I would breathe it in, you know, with my legs spread in the back seat of a car or in a nightclub or in some bushes next to a train station and it would smell so bad that I would say to myself give me my own rotting corpse over the death in life of a suburban marriage, stick a glass bottle up my ass before you slide a ring onto my finger.

I saw all these dead moons circling a star.

Fuck you, I said.

I'm the fucking star.

I fell in with the music scene.

The art scene was up itself.

The fashion scene was vacuous.

The book scene was going on behind closed doors.

You have to understand that when you're talking about a local scene you're talking about an international scene in microcosm. We had our own Syd Barrett and Brian Jones and Nico and Pete Perrett. The thing about the music scene was it fostered belief. It encouraged you to take the music and the lifestyle at its word. So there were all these people, living it, probably living it harder than their role models. After all, it isn't easy being Iggy Pop in a small town in the west of Scotland. It takes some kind of commitment. And there was something about the backdrop. Seeing Patty and

Maya with their matching floor-length coats and their wraparound shades outside the dole office in Airdrie town centre, or what was that guy, Street Hassle they called him, I can never remember his real name, I don't know if I ever knew it, with a cut-up T-shirt and his mum's fur coat on passed out on a bench next to the cenotaph in Coatdyke and with all of the cars honking as they went past. And then there was the indiscriminate drug use, the drinking, the staying up all night.

The first thing I wanted to do was to invert day and night.

So that immediately appealed to me.

I started going to house parties and having sex in the bathroom or on the coats in the bedroom.

Then I began picking up musicians.

The first musician I slept with, I guess he's a footnote now, but it was Starkey, Richard Starkey, who at that time had a project called The Beguiled which was something to do with how he had been a poet and then got a mental block and so refocused his attentions onto music.

I saw him play in Coatbridge and he played the guitar while wearing black leather gloves, he could barely hold down a chord, and it blew me away, this commitment to image, and the sound he got from the guitar, this muffled sound that felt like it was embalmed, and these lyrics that were all like, beat me, pound me, finish me off. We went back to his, he lived with his mother who had a council flat just down the road from Sunnyside station in Coatbridge, and he had a mattress on the floor, it was the first time I had seen that in real life, and he used his record player as an ashtray, it was covered in ashes and butts, I thought this was amazing, it was alive, it was an installation, and he put on the third Neu! album, *Neu! '75*, and it started to snow outside and the snow was all lit up orange from the street lights and I thought to myself, oh my god I'm falling in love in slow motion.

Of course there were clichés.

It was inevitable.

Some people became 'poets', other people became 'musicians', but the good thing about a local scene like Airdrie was that everyone was so originally weird as to prevent most of them from servicing any fixed notion of possibility. It was impossible to be possible. That was the byword of the whole scene.

I stopped smoking marijuana.

It was using up all of my imagination.

Drinking became boring.

But sex never let me down.

In the space of six months I fucked Ray Gordon, whose penis was barely three inches long but was sexy nonetheless, like small tits on a young girl.

Then Richard Warden, whose penis was more like nine inches.

Then Tom Beatrix, who was more like a seven.

Then two women, Samantha and Bridget, who between them were packing eighteen inches of dildo.

Then another Tom, Tom C, let's call him, whose penis I could barely get my fingers around.

Then Rodney, The Rod, ha ha, whose penis was perfectly sculpted and clean and shaved, an immaculate cock, I would call it, but who couldn't ejaculate unless there was some kind of pain involved, only you couldn't harm his cock, that was off limits, so you had to find ways around it, you know, like inserting things up his ass or squeezing his balls or one time taking a razor and slitting open his sac, wow, that was amazing, like taking a lemon and biting it open just to see what was inside.

The thing about Memorial Device was that you always had the feeling that it was their last gig ever, like they could fall apart at any moment.

Of course it was literal with Lucas – you know, did he remember a single damn thing, did he know where he was, what was the history, was it the first gig of his damn life?

Of course people accused them of exploitation.

He's mentally ill, they would say, he's disturbed, as if that somehow disallowed his entire experience, as if that meant he should curl up on the floor of a locked room and cry himself to sleep, which was actually what the gigs were like, sometimes, so they had their fun, these bastards, these useless cunts.

I remember one show in particular, it was at their rehearsal room, which to me looked liked their mum had decorated it, with tables and chairs and paintings and even a few potted plants dying away from the light and they came on stage and there was this moment, everyone felt it, where it was as if Lucas was wide awake, as if he was suddenly transported there, from out of nowhere, from out of no history, right in front of us, and it was electric, his eyes snapped open and he took the mic and he said something about standing at the edge, something about hello here I am, again and again, like he was in a cave and he was listening to his own echo, like if he kept repeating it, it would become something else, something that wasn't himself.

Still, it all came with a price, for me at least, a psychic price.

Escaping all of that programming and all of that baggage is no cakewalk.

When I was a kid I used to laugh at the idea of dark places.

You have to exorcise your dark places, they would say.

Give me a horror story, I would say in return. I'll exercise them that way.

I would seek out frights, sit up all night and spook myself.

I was really into horror movies.

I sought out madness, read poems about sea creatures in the deeps and islands being swept away by typhoons and Atlantis and UFOs.

But when the time came I was forced to come face to face with my own madness.

Doppelgängers stalking my mind dressed as storm troopers,

nightmares where I would dream that I had woken up in a different room entirely and that felt so real that I would question my own sanity, wondering if I had had a blackout the night before or if my partner and I had checked into a hotel room and I had simply forgotten about it and then the whole thing would reveal itself to me as a dream,

a dream of bedrooms with the curtains closed that I couldn't wake up from

and other nights I would be caught on trains and placed on suicide watch and swept deeper into dark tunnels by torrents of water and assaulted with gas canisters by children who were out of control and pursued by smiling toy phones and zombies who raised their hands up and brought them back down again.

I would have vivid dreams where I would fly between floating islands in the sky with castellated towns hidden amongst great rock formations and I would swoop down and look for sex.

I'm dreaming, I would tell myself, so find your dream lover, and I would fly low across the surface of the water and pass rows of multicoloured cottages ranged along the shore and I would find my partner, plain, simply naked, unappealing and unsure, quite ugly, frankly, and as I moved towards him the windows would come in and the walls would pass through each other and I would walk outside and there was the same storm trooper watching me from the distance, only this time with his hat in his hands and his face exposed to the sunlight for the first time, though still too far to see, and I would realise that if the dream continued any further that he would pursue me to the ends of the earth and so I would struggle to wake up, throwing my body, in my mind, from side to side and then sitting up straight in bed and screaming, this blood-curdling scream that must have terrified the neighbours.

It was easy how we got together.

Memorial Device played a show at this cafe in town, this pre-theatre deal with sandwiches and hot dogs and alcohol in the afternoon so that everybody was drunk by 4 p.m.

It was part of a literary festival and Memorial Device had got the gig because in the past they had accompanied Patrick Remora for a few readings and he had briefly become this big deal because Allen Ginsberg had come through town in 1973 and an interview had just been published where he recalled performing with local musicians in Glasgow and had mentioned enjoying the work of the Scottish poets of the time and so now it was anyone's game and Remora was being

257

touted as the next – well, if not the next Ian Hamilton Finlay then the next Basil Bunting, as there was an uncredited photograph doing the rounds of Remora drunk and asleep, barely a kid, in Ginsberg's lap, just like the photo of Ginsberg with his head in Bunting's lap from their reading at Morden Tower in Newcastle in 1965.

On the afternoon of the concert I went about it very deliberately.

I dressed to kill in black strappy heels and in a minidress and with a tiny handbag over my shoulder in which I had a copy of a book by Blaise Cendrars, that was strategic, as well as make-up and condoms and a hip flask and a cassette of Lou Reed's *The Bells*, which is the best album ever made if you ask me, although I also had a cassette of *Berlin* for disrupting parties and for bringing everyone down on the advice of Lester Bangs.

The show was good, though not as great as everyone made out.

I think everyone wanted to see them do something iconoclastic and disruptive in the face of these uptight literary fuds, so they were ready to read into whatever they did some kind of deliberate refusal of the circumstances.

I remember Remy was playing synth, it was one of the few times they had a synthesiser in the set-up, and I guess it was supposed to be kind of like Allen Ravenstine on the early Pere Ubu recordings but really it sounded kind of gay, you know, like he was dancing around behind this keyboard up on a stand and it might as well have been an ironing board, it was that camp, and he was going crazy, mock crazy in a way, banging his head and dancing all around, I don't think he

258

was ever forgiven for being in a synth-pop duo and here it was, the ghost of Relate, live on stage.

At this point let me say this, let me underline it.

We all live out our unhappiness on different scales.

Lucas, it seemed to me, had given up on the idea of cosmic suffering or epic injustice in favour of a tolerable though constantly present low-level misery, a moment-to-moment survival that snaked, like the handwriting in his journal, from left to right and back and forth, backwards and forwards in time, but that remained trapped on the page, always in the same dimension, a form of compressed life that made me think of a crab, trapped inside its shell, moving sideways but somehow never gaining ground, and once, near the end, I woke in the night and saw him in his shorts by the open window, a microphone in each hand, and I thought that's his claws, in the moment between sleeping and awakening I saw him raise his claws and lower two microphones out of the window like he was running fishing lines down to the bottom of the ocean and I sat up in bed and watched his silhouette, which by this point was more like a starfish, the sun rising slowly behind him like it was twenty thousand leagues away, and after an endless moment where I'm sure he knew I was watching him but where he never spoke or made a movement, not even a shiver in front of the open window in the cold of the morning, which seems miraculous now, barely plausible, I asked him what he was doing and without turning round he said he was recording the dawn chorus and I asked him what does it sound like and he opened his journal and he read me those words, *complete contentment*, his final words, it seems to me now and even then, even without any idea of what was coming next, of what would happen to us and who would remember us and the horror of the situation that would engulf us, like placing my head in an oven, like being trapped in a fridge on waste ground, with no one else around and no way of opening it from the inside, and the night before he had led me around the room on his big feet, his huge bare feet, he had taken his socks and shoes off and had me stand with my feet on top of his and held my hands while I leaned back and he had led me around the room like a marionette, lifting his legs in slow motion and placing me in strange positions, and we had danced to his favourite song, which was 'Space Hymn' by Lothar and the Hand People, he had transcribed the lyrics into his notebook, but this time he just mouthed the words, the song is like a meditation piece where you picture seeing the earth from outer space and they call it a starship of stone and they rhyme it with dying alone.

I'm sorry for crying.

It still gets to me.

But that was like his one concession to cosmic loneliness, if you like, and even then it was just a daft song by a bunch of hippies.

He had a scar across his forehead, as I'm sure you know, and more scars underneath his hair, from all of the surgery, and it was so sexy.

The canals of Mars, he called them.

I can see the face on Mars, I would say, and then I would kiss him.

But sometimes I would look into his eyes and I would see that all memory had gone and he would look at me blankly, but still kindly, as if he had woken up in bed with a bewildered stranger and had to move quickly to reassure her that everything was okay, a kindness that it occurred to me must have been deeper than memory or familiarity, a basic recognition that was at the heart of his personality, a capacity not so much to reflect, he didn't simply mirror, he wasn't seeing himself, I'm sure of that, that was the hardest thing for him to see in a way, I don't know if he ever really recognised himself, but he was capable of seeing in others that same kernel of fear, that nut of terror, that empty silhouette that we try to flesh out with language, that we try to define into existence, though we're as nebulous as stars, which brings me back to Lothar and the Hand People, but he could see that, and his journals were like these attempts to write himself into existence, that's how they seemed, the sentences would go this way and that, crab-like, in angles across the page or little clusters of text that were illegible to anyone but himself, names, hand-drawn maps, sketches, codes, acronyms, long lines of initials, stories, lyrics, parables, homilies, reconstructions, reminders, his problems had become the little things and the little things had engulfed the big things, like how to get to a friend's house, what time was rehearsal, where do I live, who are you, etc.

It was like a walking frame or a wheelchair, a crutch, which when you think about it is what most writing is, something to support the figure of the writer, so that he doesn't fall back into the primordial soup of everyone else, which is no one.

261

So that he can believe in himself he creates a fiction, he invents something that he can then say, here, at least, is an outline of my life, or rather an outline of my life as I would have it, only with Lucas it was an outline of his life as he received it, he was more of a scientist or a mystic than an author or inventor, trying to penetrate to the heart of the mystery of himself through scattered clues, things that would never tie up, like plotting the constellations, he had to come up with some kind of coherent shape out of all these disparate moments, separated by a huge gulf of silence, by empty space, by what might as well have been thousands of light years.

It's no exaggeration to say that he woke each morning anew, unsure of who he was and where he was, but somehow it's possible to become accustomed to even that, so that when he woke there would be that moment of confusion, which in turn would trigger a memory, a memory of being confused before, and so the confusion would become his underlying base state and the foundation of his day-to-day identity, you know, like I was confused yesterday, I am confused today, I will be confused tomorrow, what are those lines of Rilke's he always used to quote from his journal, 'We did not know his unheard-of head/with eyes like ripening fruit . . .', there were more like that, he was in love with Rilke, and every day when he had the chance or saw his name in the front of his journal he would read him again as if for the first time and he said it was like a past life, every time, and I think it was the same with music, he was a huge fan of free jazz, German free jazz specifically, stuff like Peter Brötzmann and Peter Kowald and Alex von Schlippenbach, music that was so in the moment that it was like music without a memory, music that insisted on pushing forwards regardless, and with their history, their German history, this form of amnesia, this idea that velocity and forgetfulness could take us safely into the future, well, it cast a spell on him.

That explains the big break in Memorial Device, the rupture, where they moved from doing songs into this freely improvised rock music where Lucas would just spontaneously come up with lyrics, of course there were always echoes of Rilke, whether he was consciously aware of it or not, who knows, and of course they began to record the shows and issue live recordings and Lucas would listen to them for hours, taking notes, listening to himself the way you would someone else, like if someone had played you a Bob Dylan album and told you that was you, that you had made that – not quite, but I think there was that degree of revelation for him in the music, because you could tell he was hypnotised, mesmerised by his own performance, he would look round at me and then back towards the speakers and then back to me again, all with this incredulous look on his face, like was this some kind of set-up, was somebody leading him on?

It got to the point that he was able to formulate it in very simple terms, like if I do X then Y will result, but without any feeling of movement between one letter and the next.

X happened then Y appeared.

That's when it occurred to me, aren't we all stranded in single moments?

Do we ever experience that between state, the movement between X and Y?

Are any of us any the less stranded?

Isn't every act, every moment, every setting in play an act of blind faith based on limited examples?

But I don't want to go too far down that road.

I can already feel the storm trooper rising to his feet and putting his hat on and walking towards me and it's at this point that I have to shake myself awake and sit up in bed and scream, though who knows in what bedroom and behind what closed curtains.

Appendix A: Memorial Device Discography

– *Ur/On* LP (self-released/no label/paste-on sleeves, hand-numbered edition of #120) 1983: 'two massive sidelong tracks in the brain-erasing style of Ash Ra Tempel/Ohr Records et al.' – *Friction* #2.

– *Adherence* 12" (self-released/no label/paste-on sleeves, hand-numbered edition of #220) 1984: 'still the definitive Memorial Device release and the one that best captures the hypnotic power of their live shows, a single track over two sides of vinyl that combines the celestial sound of interstellar shortwave with a two-chord jam that is so echo-damaged and distraught that it comes over like The Velvet Underground live from Atlantis or the Sun Ra Arkestra caught in the orbit of the planet Jupiter while vocalist Lucas Black drops single seemingly unrelated phrases like depth charges into the void.' – *Go Ahead and Drop the Bomb: Memorial Device Memorial Edition* 1987.

– *Certainty of a Sleepwalker* 7" (Peacocks Wildly Excited by the Wind PWEBTW-113) 1984: 'sounds like an autistic Joy Division recorded with a broken microphone at the bottom of a well and played back using a coat hanger for a needle.' – *Contrition* #8.

– *Inverted Calder Cross* cassette (Sufferage Tapes ST-68 C60) 1984: live recording from a private show in a garage in Caldercruix 3/3/84. 'Memorial Device live report: Memorial Device are a four-piece rock group that have been making waves in the Lanarkshire area for the past year or so, making industrial-strength waves, to be precise, as their model seems to be the more experimental Krautrock groups of the 1970s crossed with a strange aspect of their own and with a singer who has been compared to Ian Curtis. Tonight's show, however, underlines their garage band heritage, quite literally, as it took place in a garage on the outskirts of Caldercruix. The support act was an overweight uncomfortable-looking guy in a woolly hat making bleeping noises with a table covered in what looked like broken computer parts. It was boring and pretentious. How much longer will we put up with this sort of thing? The audience seemed to be in agreement. During the interval there was an overwhelming smell of petrol that made me nervous every time someone sparked one up. By the time Memorial Device came on stage you could barely see them for all of the smoke in the room. They played one chord for what seemed like an eternity and then their singer, who cast a huge shadow through the smoke, seemed to rise up from the ground like he had levitated up through a trapdoor and began to sing, though when I say sing it was more like a chant, a chant where the words seemed to evolve and seemed to keep growing. Like the first word came out of the last one and so on like a twisted flower. It's hard to explain but the effect was admittedly powerful. It was just one track but one endless track that left your head spinning and that made you lose track of time. The musicianship was basic but with a raw appeal. I was glad to be invited and while they may never make it to the London stage – or even the Glasgow basement – it was good going for Airdrie and shows that we can hold our heads up alongside other small towns in the area when it comes to the post-punk scene.' – Rupert Gower, *The Monk's Chunk: Your Fortnightly Guide to Arts & Music in the Monklands Area*, April 1984.

– *Give Us Sorrow / Give Us Rope* cassette (Sufferage Tapes ST-76 C90) 1984: massively crude live recording of a show from Kilmarnock 21/4/84. 'The singer sings about songs in a voice like a ventriloquist while the band do their best to avoid playing anything that could be construed as a song whatsoever then they rub sandpaper all over the tape and expect anyone to buy it?' – *Popcorn Petals* #2.

– *Pentecost* 2x7" (Primitive Painters PP-1-1-1) 1985: 'starts off mediocre but soon builds up into a frenzy of musical genius.' – Giles Gordon.

Unofficial Releases:

– *Inverted C*Brig* cassette (Nothing Songs NO-001 C120): live Mary Hanna-era recording from 1985.
– *Inverted C*Dyke* cassette (Nothing Songs NO-002 C120): live Mary Hanna-era recording from 1985.
– *Backwards B*hill* cassette (Nothing Songs NO-003 C120): live Mary Hanna-era recording from 1985.
– *Backwards B*well* cassette (Nothing Songs NO-004 C120): live Mary Hanna-era recording from 1985.

(1st pressing: 'Vanity' sleeves. 2nd pressing: generic black-on-white text)

Addendum:
Lucas Black – *The Morning of the Executioners* LP (G.G.G.G.S. #001 hand-numbered edition of #333) 1986: 'field recordings' sonically dicked with by Patty Pierce and Remy Farr. Posthumous release.

Appendix B: A Necessarily Incomplete Attempt to Map the Extent
of the Post-Punk Music Scene in Airdrie, Coatbridge and environs
1978–1986

– Absolute Refusal – Nein Nein Nein offshoot.

– The Beguiled – aka Richard Starkey: poetry, no wave, a black leather glove.

– Chinese Moon – showroom dummies.

– The Clarkston Parks – mod/freakbeat group from Petersburn.

– Cold Stars – amazing glam-punk hybrid w/a Coatbridge wasteland edge.

– Dark Bathroom – whatever.

– Disabled Adults – crude DIY.

– Dissipated – wretchedly crude DIY group with one legendarily rare single, 'Fanny Pad', due to the group using most of the run of two hundred copies as target practice for an air rifle.

– Fangboard – no one would take anything to do with them, that was a whole other scene completely.

– Freaky DK – local DJ who had a freak hit in 1978 with the punk spoof 'Yer Maw', which consisted of verses filled with lewd and rude questions and a chorus that answered them with 'Yer maw, yer maw! Yer maw, yer maw, yer maw!'

– Glass Sarcophagus – legendary industrial-noise duo led by porn star and future pop star Vanity and with John Bailey on guitar.

– Jung Team – industrial-strength dub-rock.

– Kazoo Icing Compass – drone-rock loner from Gartness. Disappeared after a single album of 'broken instrumentals'.

– Memorial Device – the greatest rock group of the modern age or at least of Airdrie – Patty Pierce, Lucas Black, Remy Farr and Richard Curtis – but even better when they had Mary Hanna in them.

– Meschersmith – commie punk-pop.

– The Monarchs of the Night Time – Airdrie's greatest garage band managed by legendary local promoter Fuckface The Eagle.

– Mount the Bitch – metal band from Caldercruix.

– Nein Nein Nein – conceptual, bloody-minded, minimalist.

– Occult Theocracy – Big Patty's 'bogus' psychedelic rock band that briefly featured Street Hassle on vocals.

– Porous – four-piece with two bassists and two drummers who generated the kind of low-end wall of sound that made the name kind of ironic.

– Rat Tattoo – teenage metal for radio hams.

– Relate – performance art synth-pop duo with two lovers who looked like Leigh Bowery, one of whom joined Memorial Device for no discernible reason that anyone could make out whatsoever.

– Sentimental Mercenaries – prog group from Airdrie.

– Slave Demographics – Big Patty's first band best known for their cover of The Godz' 'Permanent Green Light', which was even more primitive than the original.

– The Spazzers – wheelchair-bound quartet formed by lead vocalist Mick Jazzer and with guitarists Bubonic Craig and Bob Noxious and drummer Pig Ignorant. No known recordings, unfortunately.

– Steel Teeth – aka Robert Mulligan, who built his own electronics and flipped hamburgers in Mount Vernon.

– The Traveller in Black – cheesy new wave one-man synth bullshit.

– The Tunnel – heavy ritualists.

– Ultra Violet – post-punk group from Clarkston, singer hanged himself from a tree after running up debts on a stolen credit card.

– The Whinhall Starvers – punk group from Whinhall. One 7" single, 'Chasing the Breadvan'.

Appendix C: This Is Memorial Device

– Sri Abergavenny – author of The Precepts, proponent of 'brain death', killer of compassion, inventor of 'whirlpooling', etc.

– Andrea Anderson – contemporary landscape painter and briefly, once upon a time, Mary Hanna's lover.

– Ljubljana 'Lubby' Athol – one-time star-crossed lover (?) of Richard Curtis and now a well-known human rights lawyer.

– John Bailey – guitarist and the other half of Glass Sarcophagus.

– Akbar Balithi – chess partner to Bruce Cook.

– Beano – rough justice.

– Tom Beatrix – seven inches

– James Begley – drummer in Ultra Violet.

– Mary Bell – Mad Mary Bell, not the child-killer Mad Mary Bell, got kidnapped and didn't even care.

– Jared Bishop – DJ at legendary Glasgow night Joy of a Toy who never wore no underwear.

– Betty Black – Lucas Black's mother before she changed her name and disappeared into another life altogether. The thing about Betty Black was she was so tiny it was impossible to imagine Lucas coming out of her, which of course, we found out, that he never did, that really he was The Man from Atlantis. Another thing about Betty Black was that she was spacey and naive and really very sweet. I always remember hanging out with Lucas at home and there were three of us and she came in all pleased with herself and announced that she had got us 'a carry-out' that consisted of four beers. That was one and a bit beers each. That was her concept of a carry-out. I wrote to her years later, I found out she was living in Paris, she wrote back, once, but then I never heard from her again.

– Lucas Black – vocalist in Memorial Device, autonomic dreamer.

– Bridget _____ – nine inches

– Alan Brooks – late bassist with The Whinhall Starvers. I had arranged to meet Patty Pierce outside Benny's in Clarkston just along from the old barber's where he used to work and when I turned up he was eating a white pudding supper that he had balanced on top of a bin. Somebody threw something at him from a passing car, I saw it happen from a distance, but he didn't even flinch. Plus he had a book sticking out of his pocket, *Under the*

Volcano by Malcolm Lowry. We walked over to the park and sat in the grass, it must have been the summer, not long after Memorial Device had started, the first summer of the glory years, which would have been 1983, June, I'm guessing, I was always hopeless at labelling my tapes. Patty sat there on the grass, in the blazing sunshine, wearing a battered top hat and a trench coat. It was my second interview with Patty after my first inauspicious one where I had asked him something about the nature of love but even so I don't seem to have asked a single question beyond my genius opening gambit about what was the idea behind Memorial Device but luckily Patty just kept talking without any encouragement whatsoever. At one point Alan Brooks came over to him, he was trying to buy some hash. I remember he had this ridiculously high voice and he rolled up and he said, Cor I love it when the sun's out, it's the best! I still do that impersonation to this day.

– Tom C – (   )

– Manda Candy – porn star from St Andrews.

– Colin Cassidy – lead singer and guitarist for Petersburn mod group The Clarkston Parks. One of the Airdrie faces alongside Mad Mary Bell.

– Mr Chan – owner of a Chinese restaurant in Airdrie who was murdered in unexplained circumstances.

– Boaby Chan – astrologer and son of the owner of a Chinese restaurant in Airdrie who was murdered in unexplained circumstances.

– Stacey Clark – made-up name for a huge real-life pain in the ass.

– Bruce Cook – Buddhist, hippy, martial arts teacher, childhood friend of Big Patty, surrogate guru for Lucas Black, dated Vanity way back in the day.

– Dougie Cartwright – guitarist with Petersburn mod group The Clarkston Parks.

– Valentine Cloutier – Big Patty's summer love.

– Alan Cunningham – teenage occultist; 'drummer' with Chinese Moon; author of (currently unpublished) *A Critical History of 20th-Century Minimalism*; regular wearer of tracksuit bottoms pulled up to his nipples; current whereabouts unknown. Brother of Findlay.

– Findlay Cunningham – subscriber to *Newsweek* at the age of fourteen; 'vocalist' with Chinese Moon; regular wearer of tracksuit bottoms pulled up to his nipples; Boys' Brigade leader; charity worker; church leader. Brother of Alan.

– Margot Curtis – mean-spirited gorgeous battleaxe ex-wife of Richard Curtis who looked like Siouxsie Sioux back in the day, seriously.

– Richard Curtis – drummer in Memorial Device. Also played in Meschersmith. Every time I hear that song by Lou Reed, 'Legendary

Hearts', I think of him, wherever he is. Still, I hope he never reads this book, wherever he is.

– Ronnie Dare – Dominic Hunter's partner, the sainted Ronnie Dare, who looked like a Puerto Rican street killer.

– Michael Donnelly – gun for hire; lived in the McLaughlin family's 'secret annexe' while kitty-catting Johnny's dreams.

– The Doug – 'In 1984 when every cunt was going about with them Frankie Say Relax T-shirts I was going about with one I made myself that said We're All Frankies – We're All Lying in Hell. But no cunt got it. I was that far ahead of the curve. By the way.'

– Clyde Farr – Remy's father, author of 'Fate is Only Once'.

– Remy Farr – bassist/synthist in Memorial Device. Also one half of naff synth-pop duo Relate who supported Imagination at Zanzibar in Coatbridge, no joke.

– Bobby Foster – Patty's teenage partner in crime, a serious record nut and the only guy in Airdrie who ever had any cash, which meant everybody was forever tapping him.

– Goosey – bassist in Petersburn mod group The Clarkston Parks scalped by a biker in a fight and it was wigs from there on out which was lucky for the group 'cause previously he had tight curly hair like a snooker player and it ruined the look completely.

– Ray Gordon – three inches ☹

– Duncan Gracie – 'bassist' with Chinese Moon whose brother had the best collection of heavy metal LPs in Airdrie.

– Tam Gracie – best collection of heavy metal LPs in Airdrie.

– Colin Grant – vacant tosspot.

– Giles Gordon – the worst music writer on god's earth.

– Rupert Gower – clueless local journalist, a total square who consistently missed the boat and who one time Remy got up against the wall by his throat.

– Mr & Mrs Grey – early (agog) witnesses to Street Hassle busting moves.

– Mary Hanna – the legendary Mary Hanna; bassist for Memorial Device, member of Dark Bathroom, secret sculptor.

– Dominic Hunter – aka Dom aka Wee Be-Ro aka the other half of Relate.

– Randy Jewels – porn star from Dunoon.

– Alan Jones – drummer with Petersburn mod group The Clarkston Parks. No relation to Paprika.

– Paprika Jones – girlfriend of Lucas Black.

– Scott Kennedy – aka Sore Arse, notorious Airdrie drug dealer.

– David Kilpatrick – 'guitarist' with Chinese Moon, currently working as an electrician in Airdrie.

– Lars Kreiger – died in the metaphorical arms of Claire Lune.

– Monica Lawson – one-time Memorial Device archivist; succeeded Miriam McLuskie who was 'mental'; took some of the most iconoclastic shots of the band and went on to become an established New Age author with her philosophy of 'walking cures'.

– Claire Lune – performance artist, photographer, cared for Remy's father as he lay there dying, passed away from cancer herself at the age of forty-nine. Donated her body to science. Hopefully they can make some sense of it all.

– Spike McIver – Mary Hanna's pal, Street Hassle's teenage assailant.

– Maya McCormack – played in Dark Bathroom with Mary Hanna; also in The Ladybugs; Street Hassle's first girlfriend; her dad was the head guy in the post office and by all accounts a good guy to work for but a total sectarian asshole besides; later dated Patty Pierce, what a run.

– Scott McKenzie – Scott McKenzie, what to say about Scott McKenzie? He was the kind of guy who would sit in on a Saturday night with a two-litre bottle of cider and a copy of *Motor Mart* like it was the highlight of the week. He had no ambitions whatsoever. He was Airdrie's reigning snooker champ; he got to the Lanarkshire finals but then packed it in because he was 'tired of the uniform', whatever that means. His mum worked at the checkout in Safeway in Airdrie and was always apologising for him. He didn't care. Really he was a dark horse. He was smart and weird. There was a rumour that he slept with Mary Hanna and that they had a secret casual on/off relationship for years. Who knows? Neither of them are giving anything away. When I approached him for the book he said he was only interested in talking about how he met Mary because it had 'nothing to do with music'. I told him it was a musical history that I was putting together but then he just stopped picking up the phone. Okay, I said to him, okay, I was forced to write to him, in a letter that I hand-delivered to his mum's house where he still lives to this day, I give in, tell us how you met Mary Hanna. His mum apologised for him not coming to the door himself. He's on the *Motor Mart*, she said, I'm sorry. Anyway, he eventually gave us his piece with the stipulation that it couldn't be edited or changed in any way or he would pull it altogether but when I got back to him and said that I loved it and could he write some more please he went back to ignoring me all over again.

– Johnny McLaughlin – co-author; still crazy after all these years.

– Miriam McLuskie – on/off unofficial tour manager/publicist for Memorial Device, Big Patty's 'secret sidekick', daughter of the late guitarist and vocalist Mack McLuskie whose blues band, Big Mack and the Pack, were a draw in the Lanarkshire area in the 1970s.

– Adam McManus – ex-IRA ex-SAS ex-Special Ops ex-agent provocateur who the fuck will ever know the truth kung fu guru.

– Drew 'Tusky' McPherson – crap friend and coward long since sentenced to a lifetime job in a bank with no parole for his sins, what a dick.

– Valerie Morris – childhood sweetheart of Remy Farr.

– Robert Mulligan – instrument inventor from Greengairs who released cassettes under the name Steel Teeth on his own Sufferage Tapes imprint and worked in a hamburger-processing plant in Mount Vernon.

– David Nesbitt – gardener who employed Big Patty and Johnny McLaughlin and who knew nothing about music at all and who came to it like an alien from another planet.

– Teddy Ohm – Edward Thom; biker, pusher, rare record dealer, groover, supplier of historical weaponry to the movie industry and post-apocalyptic plotter.

– Clementine Pape – Johnny McLaughlin's summer love.

– Sidney Parker – real-life record industry asswipe.

– Yvonne Parker – sister of real-life record industry asswipe.

– Samantha Paytress – violinist and DIY-stockings seductress.

– Patty Pierce – guitarist in Memorial Device; also played in Slave Demographics, Occult Theocracy and Cold Stars.

– Assif Rajar – teen booze connection at the minimart.

– The Rat – Claire Lune's summer love who found a hole in her heart and went right through it.

– Rodney The Rod – baws like peeled lemons.

– Ross Raymond – me.

– Patrick Remora – poet who had a duo with Big Patty that has been likened to the early Patti Smith/Lenny Kaye duos, also backed by Memorial Device on several occasions. The next Basil Bunting, they said, but beyond falling asleep drunk in Allen Ginsberg's lap that was as far as he got.

– Samantha _____ – nine inches

– Santiago – gypsy, bohemian, cultural provocateur and founder of Spanish performance troupe Inconcurring Colt.

– Mr Scotia – calligrapher, astronomer, local historian, collector of maps, inveterate sniffer of bouquets.

– Sinew Singer – Airdrie's answer, Airdrie's retort, to Elvis and Iggy and everything.

– Simon Sparkles – made-up name for a huge real-life record industry asswipe.

– Peter Solly – aka The Traveller in Black; minimal electronics from Plains with 'scientific eyes'.

– Richard Starkey – had a solo project called The Beguiled where he dressed up like a cross between Von LMO and Sean Bonniwell of The Music Machine and read his poetry over automating cyborg drum machines and repeating atonal guitar chords. Paprika Jones's introduction to the music world. A footnote now.

– Jemima Stewart – friend of the sister of real-life record industry asswipe Sidney Parker, ex-stripper, current veterinary surgeon.

– Rod Stilvert – notorious Glaswegian porn entrepreneur; founder of Imaginorg Films and Gamma Productions.

– Street Hassle – notorious Airdrie punk often seen 'in the winter, in the snow, walking in the gutter with nothing but a cut-off T-shirt and a can of beer in his hand' or 'with a cut-up T-shirt and his mum's fur coat on passed out on a bench next to the cenotaph in Coatdyke and with all of the cars honking as they went past'. Played in Rat Tattoo, Occult Theocracy and Ultra Violet.

– Telos – member of Spanish performance troupe Inconcurring Colt who walked off with a curse when they 'sold out'.

– Megan Trayner – member of The Ladybugs alongside Maya McCormack.

– Ruth Turner – conceptual artist and founder of Gartlea Gallery of Geomancy and Geographic Speculation (G.G.G.G.S.) who presented Lucas Black's final recording, *The Morning of the Executioners*.

– Vanity – porn star, future pop star and one half of Glass Sarcophagus. Briefly dated Lucas Black.

– Richard Warden – nine inches

– Regina Yarr – hot mess and proof that Remy Farr wasn't gay or at least bi.

Appendix D: A Navigational Aid

277

fanzine, 1, 4, 13, 33, 70, 151, 173
'Fate is Only Once', 61
father(s), drunk but loving, 70
favourite record of all time (cards on the table), 153
feather boas (as lava), 10, 73
feelings (carefree) (post-alcohol), 24
feelings (cheap), 14
feelings (shop-soiled), 14
feet, big white, 104
feet, enormous, 103, 168, 199, 202, 205, 260
feet, like flippers, 103
Feldman, Morton, 84
feline women, sex with (kidneys talking), 200
fellow hobbyists, 114, 116
Fenric Wolves, The, 174
feral child, 112
Ferris wheel, 145
fifteen (minutes), 37
fifty (per cent), 22
fifty-nine, 165
figure of the writer, the, 261
final recording, the, 111
Finlay, Ian Hamilton, 258
Finsbury Park, London, 195
Fire Engines, The, 28
fireflies (in Airdrie), 26
First Hegemony of the Pussying Father, 230
first morning on earth, resemblance to, 18, 111
first summer after high school, the, 22
fish hooks, 91
fish out of water, 106
fishers of men, 165
five (-foot-high black hole), 195
five (foot one), 196
five (hours), 164
five (pounds), 146, 150
Five Keys, The, 94
flashbacks, 211
flat(s), abandoned, 55
flat(s), grim, 66
flat(s), modern, 66, 177
'Flood Water Blues', 102
Fluxus, 34
flyers, wad of, 102

Flying V (guitar), 71
foetus, 252
fog, 90, 104, 108, 192
foibles, zero, 98
footnote (now), 252
footprints, enormous, 86
'For the Good Times', 47
forehead (regal), 168
forever, 36, 38, 43, 62, 65, 69, 72, 74, 186, 248, 250
formal European romance, 240
Forrest Street, Airdrie, 24, 127, 157, 177
forty-five (degrees), 118, 190
forty-five (minutes), 36, 155
foul bread and beer (presiding demons of the east), 145
fountain in Kelvingrove Park (fucked for years), 207
fourteen (years old), 66, 181
Frankenstein, 74
freakbeat, 172
freaks, 72, 246
freckly complexion, 134
free jazz, 93, 191, 262
free jazz (German), 262
free vegetables, 14
French new wave movies, 195
fried breakfast (stale), 137
Fripp & Eno, 125
frog, leaping mechanical, 116
frog face, 136
frog torturers, 120
from out of no history, 255
fuck knows, 181
fuck off, you geek, 41
fuck off, you loser, 187
Fucked in no way, 57
fucking Atlas come to smother the world, 75
fucking barbarians, 101
fucking black box, 19
fucking cannibals, 102
fucking choirboys, 15
fucking concrete house with four windows, 16
fucking decapitate me, man, 212
fucking Dion and the Belmonts, 16
fucking Holocaust memorial, 232
fucking inflatable nightmare, 17

fucking instant hamburgers, 159
fucking job like a jail sentence, 17
fucking *National Lampoon*, 126
fucking skint, 188
fucking slugs, 102
fucking social experiment, 188
fucking Space Invader, 105
fucking think about it, 102
fucking top hat, 193
fucking Watts Towers, 110
fucking white leather trousers, 193
Fun House, 5, 9
funeral pace, 108
furnishings, drab, 110
Futura, 232
future, chosen representative of, 53

gah, gah, gah . . ., 225
Gala Day, 86, 87
Gallic tongue, 123
game of moments, 245
Gamma Productions, 54
Gang of Four, 195
gangsters (*see also:* toughs; hoods), 81
gaps in continuity, 102
garden, back, 59, 157, 158, 188
garden, rock, 47
gardening, 47, 91, 92
gardens, overgrown, 66
Gare de Lyon, Paris, France, 231
Gare du Nord, Paris, France, 228
garrotte, 212
Gartlea, Airdrie, 109, 110, 113
Gartlea Gallery of Geomancy and
    Geographic Speculation (G.G.G.G.S.),
    110
garlic, romantic and sophisticated, 198
Gartness, Airdrie, 55, 144
gay magazine, 61
gay speculation, 27, 31, 35, 154, 155, 156,
    258
gays, subterranean, 61
Gaza Strip, the, 129
GBH, 144
genitals = beasts of burden with heavy
    eyes, 201
genitals = circus animals, 201
genitals = elephants, 201
genius, as accidental, 16

genius, as plain fucking wrong, 16
genocidal conflict (phantom), 170
George Square, Glasgow, 27, 29, 191
German history, 262
ghost(s), come back to the scene of their
    own murder, 59
ghost galleon, 213
ghost movie, 108
ghost story, 192, 197
ghoul, would-be, 108
Gibson, Mel, 151
giggling (over a sandwich), 138
gin, 122
Ginsberg, Allen, 45, 257, 258
girlfriend, bitchy, 41
girls, walking past, 95
giro, 188
Giuffre, Jimmy, 85
Give Us Sorrow / Give Us Rope, 137
glacier water (as blue as), 104
Glasgow, 2, 5, 7, 24, 28, 29, 45, 54, 67, 84,
    111, 130, 137, 138, 144, 149, 157, 162,
    164, 172, 173, 174, 184, 189, 191, 199,
    203, 204, 206, 207, 236, 257
Glasgow Green, 51, 149
Glasgow Technical College, 23
Glasgow University, 164
Glasgow University Union, 164
glass bottle (up the ass), 251
glutinous, 103
go-go dress (short black-and-white), 189
'God Moves On the Water', 103
godforsaken hellhole, 111
gods, the inscrutable way of, 219
Gogol, Nikolai, 46, 127
'Goin' Down to the River', 103
going nowhere, 140
Golden Dawn, 84
Gor (books), 68
Gorgon (in a snooker club), 175
Gothic fantasies, 108
grace, definition of, 143
grace, suspended, 182
Grahamshill Avenue, Airdrie, 92, 158
Grahamshill Street, Airdrie, 217
Granada, Spain, 222
Grant, Kenneth, 108
grass (*see also:* marijuana), 152, 155

283

life as a series of internal disturbances, 41
lifestyle, the, 77, 251
lighter fluid, 181
'Like a Virgin', 246
Like Flies On Sherbert, 6
lingerie (*see also:* stockings; nylons; tights), 44, 58, 69, 194
lips, immaculate and blood-red, 124
lips, perfectly made up, 43
lipstick, 54, 121, 194
lip-syncers, bunch of, 82
Listen, Glasgow, 84
literary fuds, 258
literary Paris (you know), 228
Little Nemo in Slumberland, 233
'Little Rain', 103
Live 1969, 155
live-action painting, 158
'Live to Tell', 246
Loaded, 135
local legend, 177
locks to die for, 169
logbook, the, 11
London, 1, 48, 85, 132, 137, 142, 195, 228
'Lonely Planet Boy', 13
longing, 34
Lorca, 85
Los Angeles, 60
Lothar and the Hand People, 260, 261
loud, 57, 184, 234
love, 2, 5, 18, 30, 39, 43, 44, 46, 49, 50, 51, 56, 72, 77, 78, 87, 88, 105, 106, 124, 127, 133, 143, 162, 164, 167, 168, 217, 218, 219, 222, 224, 225, 227, 231, 235, 236, 237, 242, 244, 246, 248, 250, 253, 257, 262
love, lack of, 106
love, on the fly, 43
'Love in Vain' (misremembered), 100
love song, the greatest that has ever been written, 106
Lovecraft, H. P., 4
Lowry, Malcolm, 193
Lucky Star, Forrest Street, Airdrie, The, 127
lunatic, 11, 65
Lundtoftbjerg Compromise, The, 200

lynxes (prowling in the light of the moon), 200

M8, the, 129
McCormack, Mr, check this out ya prick!!!, 190
McDowell, Mississippi Fred, 103
McGuinn, Roger, 173
macabre, 6, 17, 110
Machine Gun Etiquette, 172
'Mack the Knife', 93
mad dictator (in a science-fiction novel), 119
mad stuff, 38, 106
magic, career in, 141
magic, the most efficacious, 142
magician, practising, 67, 98
maggots, 59, 112
magic squares, 104
Malaga, Spain, 218, 220, 223
Man from Atlantis, The, 168
man-pleaser, 49
Manchester, 1, 45
mannequins (*see also:* dummies; dolls), 70, 73, 74, 75
mansion, amazing, gloomy, 198
Mantle, The, 76
mantra, 56
marijuana (*see also:* grass), 154, 245, 253
marooned, 209
Mars (bar), 119
Mars (planet), 35, 166, 180, 260, 261
Mars, behind Mars (planet), 130
Mars, canals of (planet), 260
Mars, dead (planet), 180
Mars, face on (planet), 261
Mars, tornado on the surface of (planet), 35
masking tape, 58
Master and Margarita, The, 127
Mastermind, 42
masturbation (*see also:* chug; tossed off), 22, 24, 44, 69, 186
masturbation (on acid), 69
mattress on the floor, 164, 253
maudlin, 109
Maybe, 112
meatballs, 89
medicinal (so-called), 97
Meditations, 56

poet, tragic, 38
pointless shit, 158
Polaroid(s), 51, 211
police, showing up, 31
ponce, 193
poofter, 217
poor bugger, some, 79
Pop, Iggy, 9, 16, 32, 34, 101, 251
Pop Group, The, 4
pop star, 16, 59
porn mag, 157
porn mag, awesome sales technique, Queen Street station, Glasgow (what a pro) (check it out), 157
porn mag, soiled, 157
porn movies, 51
porn movies, catching your own reflection in, 51
porn stars, Scottish, 54
porno mags, 69, 159
porno mags, soaked and disposed of in plastic bag, 69
porno mags, stash of, 69
posers, 7, 126
possibility, 18, 65, 253
Post Office Tower, London, The, 135
postman, 187
Pot Noodle (best hangover cure known to man), 101
pot of ink, 90
Prank of Pure Volition, 230
Precepts, The, 169
precipice, 94, 150
pregnant (with every idea in the world), 79
prehistoric fact, 109
prelude, a, 75
presentiment, question of definition, 75
Presley, Elvis, 15, 16
prevalent, 141
Prior, Maddy, 84
prison cell, 62, 94
'Private Dancer', 50
private-press shit (weirdo), 151
private view, 220
procession, 51
Procured Spirit of the Maelstrom, 230
promo stickers, 84, 85
prophecies, 86

prophetic carvings, 109
Protector, The, 200
Protestant(s), 46, 188
Protestants, worse, 46
proximity, 116
pseudo-historical significance, 179
psychedelic, 5, 7, 56, 151, 155
psychedelic avatar, 151
psychedelics, 68
psychic price, 255
pubic hair, curled, 86
Pubic Triangle, Edinburgh, 197
publishing royalties, myth of, 33
Puerto Rican street killer, 247
pulpy French garbage, 108
punch, how to take one, 42
Punch & Judy, 87
punk, 14, 18, 19, 51, 99, 134, 158, 182, 184
punk, deliver us from, 182
punk, importance of, 182
puppet, 95, 175, 205
pure bikers' bar, 99
pure freezing rivers, 106
pure like a witch, 101
pure outrageous, 99
pure writhing, 106
puritans, 58
Pushkin, Alexander Sergeyevich, 127
pussy, completely bald, 128
pussy, newly shaved, 44
puzzling interaction, 64
PVC dresses, skintight, 194
pyjamas, hand-painted, 17
pyramids, the, 109, 141, 230, 239

Quant, Mary, 173
Queen, 34
Queen Street station, Glasgow, 157
queens of the scene, the, 244
quick zero, 112
quote, from a philosophical text about love god knows, 5

Rabe, Folke, 11
Radio Free Hebron, 139
Radio Scotland, 6
rain, a little pishing, 103
Ramones, The, 5, 67
rare shit, 151

scratchy shit (basically), 195
scrawny stick of dynamite, 94
scream queens (of the silent era), 243
screwdriver, 175, 176
scrotum, no other word for it, 246
Scrotum Poles, 28
sea creatures in the deeps, 256
seance, 101, 179
Second World War, the, 154, 200
secret annexe, 90
secret byways, the, 201
secret deities, 246, 247
secret kung fu cell, 208
secret sidekick, 97, 98
seducer, 250
Seine, Paris, France, the, 231
sentiment, a curse on it, 144
sentiment, worth fighting for after all, 48
serious conceptualist, 247
seven (brain operations), 11
seven (inches), 254
seven (per cent ABV), 101
seventeen (stitches), 145
seventy-four (years old), 177
sex, as procreation, 45
sex, in nightclubs, 56
sex, non-penetrative, 173
sex, on stage, 56
sex, on the edge of golf courses while
    playing truant in the summer, 24
sex, under railway bridges, 24
Sex Pistols, The, 172
sexist, 104
sexual epiphany, 249
sexy words, 51
shadow, lack of, 62, 63
Shakespeare, William, 18, 148, 205
Shakespeare and Company, Paris,
    France, 228, 235, 236
Shangri-Las, The, 139
Sharrock, Linda, 84
Sharrock, Sonny, 84
Shepp, Archie, 84
sherbet dip, 198
Shettleston, Glasgow (East End), 67, 70,
    71, 199
Shettleston, Glasgow, department store
    in, 67, 72

Shettleston Library, Wellshot Road,
    Glasgow, 199
Shield of Sublimity, 230
ship, going into the night, 110
ships, great ships, scuppered, illuminated
    in the dark, 209
ships, swaying in the tide, 209
shipwreck, rocking back and forth on the
    bottom of the ocean, 209
shoe shop on Dumbarton Road, Partick,
    Glasgow, 162
shoplifting, 19
shortbread, wet, 119
shorts, repellent, 20
Shotts, 174
sickly joy, 225
sideboard, 110, 122
silence, at night, 106, 140
silent gallery, that, 113
Silly Sisters, 84
silver belt, thin, 51
silver leggings, 183
Sinatra, Frank fucking, 15
singing, 7, 14, 15, 16, 57, 105, 106, 136,
    166, 174, 226
singing about nothing, 106
singing about plants growing up, 14, 105
singing about singing, 105
singing about the weather, 105
single malt, 159
Sioux, Siouxsie, 36
Sirius, the dog star, possible presence of, 26
Sisters of Mercy, The, 23
Situationist-style cartoons (crap ones), 15
skeleton crew, 213
Skidz, 82
skinned beetroot, like a, 177
skint, totally, 234
skip(s), 41, 66, 110
skirmish, 138
skirt, stuck out at a forty-five-degree
    angle (wow), 190
skirts, up to here, 55
skull and bones, laughing, now, 113
slacks, nice pair of (*see also:* trousers), 63
Slamannan, 154
sleeper train (Glasgow to London), 132
sleeping, naked in the snow, 29